Grandpa's New Year's Relocation

Also by Catherine Dilts

Survive or Die

The Rock Shop Mysteries:

Stone Cold Dead

Stone Cold Case

Stone Cold Blooded

The Rose Creek Mysteries:

The Body in the Cattails

The Body in the Cornfield

The Body in the Hayloft

Children's books by Merida Bass

The Apple of My Eye (written and illustrated by Merida Bass)

The Jelly Monster (by C.S. Gieck, illustrated by Merida Bass)

YA by Catherine Dilts and Merida Bass, writing as Ann Belice

The Tapestry Tales:

Frayed Dreams

Broken Strands

Grandpa's New Year's Relocation

The Ninja Grandparent Placement Mysteries
Book One

Catherine Dilts * Merida Bass

Cover art and illustrations by Merida Bass

Author photo by Winston Foto at https://www.winstonfoto.com

Paperback ISBN 978-1-967578-13-9
E-book ISBN 978-1-967578-16-0
LCCN 2025923853

First Edition: December 2025

Published by Top Hat Cat Publishing LLC

https://merida-creates.com/

Printed in the United States of America

10 9 8 7 6 5 4 3 2 1

Top Hat Cat

Publishing LLC

To Deborah Aumiller, whose solemn warnings to avoid the shadows resulted in the creation of this work.

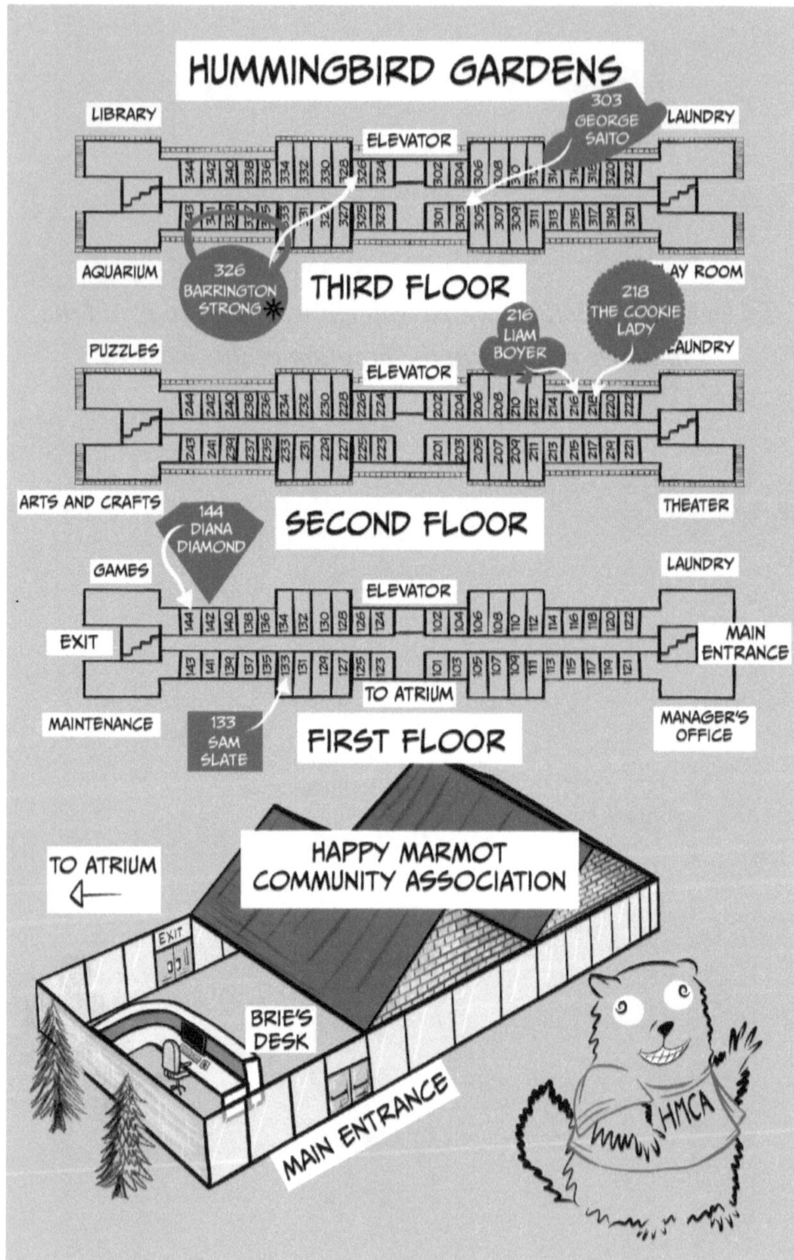

HUMMINGBIRD GARDENS
LIBRARY
LAUNDRY
303 GEORGE SAITO
ELEVATOR
344 342 340 338 336 334 332 330 328 326 324 322 320 318 316 314 312 310 308 306 304 302
343 341 339 337 335 333 331 329 327 325 323 321 319 317 315 313 311 309 307 305 303 301
AQUARIUM
326 BARRINGTON STRONG
THIRD FLOOR
PLAY ROOM
218 THE COOKIE LADY
216 LIAM BOYER
PUZZLES
LAUNDRY
ELEVATOR
244 242 240 238 236 234 232 230 228 226 224 222 220 218 216 214 212 210 208 206 204 202
243 241 239 237 235 233 231 229 227 225 223 221 219 217 215 213 211 209 207 205 203 201
ARTS AND CRAFTS
THEATER
144 DIANA DIAMOND
SECOND FLOOR
GAMES
LAUNDRY
ELEVATOR
144 142 140 138 136 134 132 130 128 126 124 122 120 118 116 114 112 110 108 106 104 102
143 141 139 137 135 133 131 129 127 125 123 121 119 117 115 113 111 109 107 105 103 101
EXIT
MAIN ENTRANCE
TO ATRIUM
MAINTENANCE
133 SAM SLATE
FIRST FLOOR
MANAGER'S OFFICE
TO ATRIUM
HAPPY MARMOT COMMUNITY ASSOCIATION
EXIT
BRIE'S DESK
MAIN ENTRANCE
HMCA

LAYTON LAMBERT
CABINS
LOVEY DEARHEART
PARKING
HUMMINGBIRD GARDENS SENIOR APARMENTS
ATRIUM AND SHOPPING CENTER
THE CELERY MAIDEN
FRISKY SHAMROCK
HMCA
SERVICE ALLEY

1

❋ Barry ❋

"You must be new to Colorado Springs." Barry Strong attempted a seductive grin, hoping his dentures didn't choose that moment to slip. He allowed his lashes to fall low over his blue-gray eyes as he gazed down at the woman in his arms. "Because I certainly would have noticed someone as lovely as you."

The woman responded to Barry's pickup line with only the slightest of smiles, causing her thick, chalky makeup to crease at the edges of her mouth.

Lame, Barry. But he was out of practice. There had been no place for romance in his life for over a decade. Mavis had been the love of his life. Since her untimely passing, followed a few years later by his son and daughter-in-law's shocking accidental deaths, Barry's existence had been hollow.

Empty. Devoid of meaning. Bodybuilding and helping his irresponsible twenty-seven-year-old grandson Marty pay his bills were his two reasons for living. Rather than fall into his familiar state of despair, he focused on his dance partner.

Despite her stiff silver hair and careworn face, the woman glided with graceful ease across the polished hardwood basketball court of the Happy Marmot Community Association. A sentimental Harry Connick Jr. song swirled from the speakers in the HMCA's gym. New Year's Eve balloons and decor adorned the walls. Disco balls hung from the tall poles that were usually home to basketball nets.

Barry stepped wide and felt his well-toned shoulder muscles bunch up as he led his dance partner into a spot turn. She followed effortlessly. *She's not a bad dancer.*

No woman could ever replace Barry's beloved Mavis. Yet he couldn't deny the electricity he felt holding his dance partner in his arms. *Can an old man like me really find love again?*

She was a quiet lady. Barry had learned nothing about her personality. During the three dances they shared, he'd barely heard two words from her. Any chemistry between them was purely physical. *Am I that lonely?* He attempted more small talk.

"When did you become an HMCA member?" Barry asked. He was at the gym nearly every day. He would have noticed someone like her if she had been working out. Although she probably looked like a completely different person without all the makeup coating her face.

"I'm just here for the party." She spoke in an oddly mechanical voice that reminded Barry of shadowy witnesses on television crime shows. *Maybe she smokes cigarettes.*

Barry waited for more, but the woman returned to silence.

Rows of folding chairs circled the dance floor. Barry navigated his partner through people of all ages, tripping the light fantastic. From toddlers to the residents of the nearby Hummingbird Gardens Senior Apartments where Barry lived, people dressed in everything from sweats to formal attire spun around the room.

Barry had retrieved his one and only suit from the back of his closet for the festivities. It found more use at funerals these days, sadly. But tonight, Barry felt spiffy despite the advanced age of his seldom-worn suit. Dressing up for Barry usually meant putting on posing trunks for his bodybuilding competitions. He was pleased when he discovered his dress shoes still took a polish and his suit fit better than it had before he started lifting weights.

His partner had monopolized his time for the last three songs. Not that Barry minded. Her face might display the march of time, but she had a trim figure under the long blue dress. Perhaps a bit saggy here and there, from what he could tell. The dress was not revealing by any means. Gravity was unkind to most seniors. Did she have old lady chicken wing arms under her long flouncy sleeves? Were her glove-covered hands covered in age spots?

And what did any of that matter anyway? At age seventy, Barry knew he couldn't be picky about his female company. Few people of any age held themselves to the standards Barry applied to himself.

Maintaining his competitive edge as a bodybuilder required long hours in the HMCA weight room. Competitions gave him a focus beyond life in his lonely apartment.

It wasn't a bad life. One fulfilling aspect was having an incredible physique that amazed his doctor despite Barry's geriatric status. But lately, he couldn't deny the hole in his heart where human companionship belonged. Watching all the families dancing together filled him with longing.

"I wish I had a family," Barry muttered quietly.

That was unfair of me to say. His mooching grandson should be all the family Barry needed. But the young man had laughed at the idea of spending New Year's Eve at the kid-friendly HMCA party.

Barry was momentarily embarrassed he had spoken his heart's desire out loud, but his dance partner didn't react. Perhaps she was hard of hearing. He craved something beyond his camaraderie with other bodybuilders, or his budding friendship with Thorne Bramble.

Barry glanced around for the man and quickly found him. Thorne was wearing his usual private investigator uniform of a tan trench coat and brown fedora. He stood by one of the long tables that earlier in the evening had been laden with fruit punch and treats. Only crumbs and crumpled empty paper cups remained at this late hour. Not that Barry had partaken of the sugary refreshments. His diet and exercise regimen demanded consistency. But Thorne hovered at the dessert table, scraping frosting from the platter that had held a large sheet cake earlier in the night. He licked his fingers greedily.

The poor guy was a sugar fiend. *Don't worry buddy. I'll get you in shape, starting tomorrow.* Barry promised Thorne a celery juice and a personalized workout for Thorne's birthday, which just happened to be New Year's Day.

The digital clock high on the wall marched onward toward midnight. *The inevitability of the passage of time.* Barry wasn't getting any younger, and neither was the night.

"The party will be ending soon," he said.

"That doesn't mean we have to call it a night," the woman said in her strange voice.

Barry hesitated to invite the woman to his spartan room. Even though rent included an HMCA gym membership, the Hummingbird Gardens Senior Apartments were expensive. Between that and his needy grandson constantly tapping him for money, Barry had little leftover for apartment decor.

Barry waited patiently, hoping the mysterious elderly woman would suggest they go to her place, wherever that was. She may not live in the Gardens. *I don't know anything about this woman. What's her name? Her age? Her birth sign?* He had been married since his early twenties and had never engaged in nameless one-night stands like some of his bachelor friends. *Can I really follow through?*

Even at the age of seventy, he attracted female interest, at least among the senior set. Being bald was not a disadvantage these days, when polished pates had been made sexy by follically-challenged movie stars. Despite the opportunities, Barry had yet to pursue female companionship further than a coffee date, theater play, or occasional dinner. Mavis had passed away far too young, in her late fifties, leaving Barry rudderless.

Too many years adrift in a sea of sorrow had left him feeling loneliness was preferable to grief. *Why try to love again? Especially at this advanced age?*

Barry realized they had danced their way toward one of the basketball court's open double doors. *Did I steer us this far? Maybe subconsciously?* Or was his dance partner leading?

The woman sure didn't talk much. Barry couldn't endure the continued silence.

"Are you leaving?" he asked. When she stood still, he added, "Are *we* leaving?"

She grasped his hand and tugged him through the doorway and down the hall. Her grip was firm and her steps confident. The *EXIT* sign glowed red above a side door leading to the parking lot.

This is apparently going to happen, whether I consent or not. A tremor of panic filled Barry. What if this dame wasn't pursuing romance? What if she wanted Barry's remarkably healthy kidneys?

"Now hold on," Barry said. He attempted to dig the heels of his dress shoes into the linoleum squares of the hallway floor. His shoes screeched, leaving twin trails of black. *She's so strong!* "Wait. I don't even know your name."

Instead of replying, she dragged him outside, into the crisp night air. No one was in the parking lot. They were all still partying. Based on the raucous cheering and tooting of party horns in the gym, it was now January 1st. A familiar song began.

"Miss," Barry protested. "This is all happening too fast. We're missing Auld Lang Syne. Let's go back–"

A hood dropped over Barry's head, blotting out the feeble light offered by the parking lot lamppost high above. He felt himself being pulled off balance. Barry reached out blindly, trying to grapple with the nameless woman.

All his carefully crafted muscles were useless. She had the advantage of surprise. But Barry didn't give up. He ducked down into a lunge and sprinted low to the ground. He tugged at the hood as he ran, sightlessly, as fast as he could. The hood was tied on too tightly. Barry ripped into it with his fingers. It tore in two. Barry could see the doors to the HMCA ahead. Just a little further and–

A lithe female figure dressed in all black popped up directly in front of Barry, stopping him in his tracks. The person looked like–

A ninja? What the–?

Barry turned to sprint in the opposite direction. But the ninja blocked his path again. This time, Barry hustled backward, keeping his eyes locked on the silent, black-masked woman before him. In a flash, the ninja was no longer in front of him. Barry's back butted up against a solid form. Before Barry could make another move, he felt gloved fingers pinch his neck. Barry reached up to slap the hand away, but his muscles disengaged. His hand fell slack at his side as his brain flooded with a darkness deeper than that of the hood.

Before he lost consciousness, he heard the words, "Happy New Year, Barrington Strong." The ninja had the same distorted voice as his dance partner. "Welcome to the end of your old life."

And then there was silence.

2

❋ Thorne ❋

Thorne Bramble sat on a barstool. A position he was all too familiar with. He adjusted the fedora covering his rapidly graying brown hair and smoothed the lapels of his tan trench coat. To be a great private investigator, he had to look the part, first and foremost. He was acing that little detail. From beneath the brim of his hat, he scanned the busy juice bar, The Celery Maiden Healing Brews.

Trust no one. Chances were slim anything bad was afoot in the cheery space. Happy people were going about their post-holiday business. Maybe a few were seeking a juice mixture to heal their aching heads, victims of their self-inflicted partying the night before. Thorne was no longer among that crowd. *Two years sober and counting.*

A Happy New Year banner hung crookedly from the wall. Gold, green, and red balloons sagged, the helium that had kept them inflated since after Christmas slowly leaking out. A ceramic hippie Santa Claus wearing a tie-dyed shirt and sandals perched on the bar counter near Thorne, perhaps overlooked during the transition from one holiday to the next.

The jolly fat man. Thorne tugged self-consciously at his tan trench coat, unable to cover his own paunch. *I'm not that fat,* he reassured himself. *And I'm certainly not jolly.*

While he waited for service, Thorne studied the usual patrons seated at bistro tables, or on stools at the counter. Residents from the nearby Hummingbird Gardens Senior Apartments and members of the Happy Marmot Community Association, often popped in for a drink. The popular juice joint was even busier than usual with people starting their health-centric resolutions for the year.

But one regular was missing. If he wasn't in the gym pumping iron, Barry Strong could usually be found at the juice bar knocking back protein shakes with the ferocity of a bear on a salmon run. Thorne had already checked the HMCA weight room and found no Barry. The old guy had promised to buy Thorne a birthday celery juice to replace his usual hearty slice of triple-layer chocolate cake. Thorne had even purchased a small candle to float on his drink so he could still make a wish. *Where* is *he?*

The guy wasn't answering his phone. Thorne hadn't seen him since the HMCA party that ended late last night. Or was that early this morning? Barry spent the end of the evening dancing with a woman Thorne had never seen before. Barry looked like he had things well in hand when he left the party. Maybe Barry and the mystery woman were still having a party of their own? Thorne remembered his stab of jealousy as Barry left with her. She wore so much makeup that it was almost more of a mask. And she might have had on a wig. But the effect worked. She was still smoking hot.

Lucky guy. The old ladies, and some not-so-old, were always chasing after Barry despite his lack of hair. Thorne was twenty years younger than Barry. But even with his full mane, already going steel gray, he couldn't seem to attract the attention of women like old Barry. *He's probably having the time of his life.*

Thorne tried to be optimistic, but his gut was speaking to him. Something about this situation was wrong. The elderly woman set off his spidey senses. With the swirling disco lighting, Thorne hadn't gotten a good look at her face. Now he wished he'd been paying more attention. As a PI, it was Thorne's job to get to the bottom of this.

The new year, ripe with possibilities, had begun. It was a new year for Thorne, too, in a very personal way. He was a New Year's baby, although at fifty years old, there wasn't much that was babyish about him.

Except for his chubby gut. Thorne tugged his tan trench coat a little tighter around his burgeoning belly. It was no use. Thorne's weight-lifting buddy, Barry, was supposed to be helping him reach a point where he could actually fasten the buttons again. They were only decorations at this point. Like most people, Thorne's New Year's resolutions included getting back into shape. *Was I ever in shape?* Either way, he needed serious help from Barry Strong.

The seventy-year-old was an amazing guy. Barry still competed in bodybuilding competitions. He'd promised to get Thorne set up with a weight-pumping routine focusing on whipping his dad bod into shape.

"Hi Thorne." Jade Grassey, the young hippie guy who ran the juice bar with his family, walked up to Thorne at the counter, carrying a menu. Every drink was infused with mineral water from a healing spring. "The usual? Or do you want to try something new?"

"Actually, I'm looking for Barry." Thorne searched Jade's dark brown face for clues. "Has he been in today?"

"The bald bodybuilder guy?" Jade asked.

Thorne nodded. Barry was bald as a cue ball.

"Not yet." Jade's green eyes peeked from under his tight, wild locks of black hair. He smiled in a peaceful hippie-like way. Like the world was perpetually groovy. He didn't look like he was hiding any secrets about Barry. "So . . . are you gonna order?"

"I'll probably come back later," Thorne said, standing to leave. "But do me a favor. If you see Barry, give me a call."

Thorne left his official-looking PI business card behind.

Barry stood me up.

Instead of a workout and a birthday juice, Thorne was left on his own. Not that being alone was such an unusual condition.

Instead of worrying fruitlessly about his senior friend, Thorne focused on investigating this disappearance. He made a very good living in his chosen career. Well, maybe an adequate living.

Face it, my PI business is hanging by a thread. What Thorne needed were clients, not another pro bono job.

This was personal, though. Old people were known to wander off. Get lost. Fall down. Recent snowfall in Colorado Springs created a dangerous world for all seniors, even ones in good shape like Barry. What if he went for an early morning run on an icy trail? Thorne's out-of-condition heart raced at the thought of Barry lying in a ditch, shivering.

Where are you Barry?

Thorne decided to make the rounds of the HMCA again, just in case Barry had dragged in late after his night of partying and romance.

Thorne stepped out of The Celery Maiden into the atrium joining the complex of buildings. At one end was the stately red and white stone of Hummingbird Gardens. The far side of the atrium butted up against the red brick of the HMCA. Between the two was a row of small local businesses like the juice bar. Outside the Colorado skies were thick with gloomy clouds threatening another bout of snow. Under the two-story high greenhouse-like atrium roof, potted flowers and tropical trees flourished.

"Cookie?"

A lady with her gray hair in a tight bun held out a tray. Thorne could never remember her name, but she always handed out free cookies.

"I'm on a diet," he said reluctantly.

"These are special," the elderly woman said. "They're my

New Year's resolution recipe. You can ensure the success of your resolutions by eating a cookie."

Thorne needed all the help he could get. Especially when the person who was supposed to be helping him with resolution numero uno had ghosted him.

"I shouldn't . . ." Thorne began. "Does one cookie cover all my resolutions, or do I need one for each?"

"My cookies are effective," the cookie lady said, "but they aren't magic. You need one cookie per resolution."

"In that case." Thorne plucked three off the tray. The white frosted cookies were decorated with Happy New Year in cursive purple letters and a generous quantity of gold sprinkles.

He bit into one. The crisp outer cookie gave way to a deliciously sweet filling. The flavor was complex, and the texture reminded him of homemade jam.

"What flavor are these?" Thorne asked.

"Rum raisin."

Thorne stopped chewing, hesitating. "Rum?"

"I used a little bit of rum extract. It's similar to vanilla flavoring. Whatever alcohol is in it cooks out," she explained.

Thorne relaxed. A few cookies wouldn't derail his two-year journey away from alcoholism.

She added, "I also tossed in fresh orange zest and a touch of cardamom."

"That explains the flavor. Wow." Thorne was impressed.

He visualized each of the changes he wanted to make this year as he savored the delicious cookies. *Get in shape.* His next resolution was even trickier than working out. *Be a better father to Brie.* He and his twenty-five-year-old daughter had a rocky relationship. Even though he had been physically present, living in the same house for the first twenty-one years of Brie's life, Thorne was never present in the ways that mattered. Repairing the damage of being an emotionally absent father might take an actual magic cookie, but it was worth a try with the available resources. He ate the second cookie with a hopeful heart.

For his final resolution, *keeping my house clean*, he expected the cookie to taste bitter. Thorne hated cleaning. The blame for his sloppy townhouse rested on his shoulders alone. He had lived as a bachelor for the past four years since his divorce.

"When do I know if the cookies worked?" Thorne asked.

But the cookie lady had wandered further down the atrium, leaving Thorne alone. Just like his wife and daughter. Just like Barry.

Speaking of Barry.

Thorne resumed his trek to the gym after being sidetracked by sweets.

He entered the HMCA, glancing around to see if Brie was near the front desk. His daughter seemed to do a little bit of everything, from paperwork to class scheduling to fundraising.

Thorne walked past classrooms. Music blared out of one open door. He glanced inside and shuddered. He chided himself for being ageist, but the sight of elderly people performing burlesque-style dances was a little shocking.

Lovey Dearheart led the class, dressed in frothy pinks and swishing a red feather boa around. She kicked up one toned leg, then shook her shapely hips. Thorne couldn't disturb the elderly lady and ask about Barry while she was teaching a class.

"Like what you see?"

Thorne jumped, startled by the voice at his side. Ramona Grant was the senior property manager for Hummingbird Gardens. Senior as in top boss, not as in old. Ramona had a trim, shapely figure emphasized by her slacks and tailored jacket. Her light-brown complexion was mostly smooth except for a few fine lines at the corners of her deep brown eyes and mouth. Thorne guessed she was in her thirties.

"What are you doing here?" Thorne blurted out. "I mean, I know you work at Hummingbird Gardens, but this is the HMCA, and you're standing here watching me watch Lovey, but I'm not like *watching her* watching her if you know what I mean . . ."

Thorne stopped talking and grinned at Ramona. He hoped everything he said was making sense. He seemed to have trouble organizing his thoughts around her. But why? It wasn't as if he couldn't handle himself around a pretty girl. His ex-wife Eden was also an extremely beautiful woman. After a few more moments, Thorne realized he was still just grinning at Ramona. He broke the awkward silence when he remembered why he began talking in the first place.

"Let me start over. Good morning, Ramona."

Ramona smiled. "Good morning to you, too. I'm just doing my job, making sure the Hummingbird Gardens residents are happy and having a good time."

"Then maybe you can help me be happy," Thorne blurted out. *Why did I say that?* He fumbled with an explanation. "Er, um–"

"But you're too young to be a resident of Hummingbird Gardens," Ramona interrupted. "So I don't think I can help you with that just yet." She winked, making herself even more beautiful in the process.

"Only five more years and I can move in," Thorne said. The senior living apartments were for ages fifty-five and up, which hardly sounded senior to Thorne.

"You're fifty?" Ramona asked.

"Just turned today," Thorne said.

"Oh! Happy birthday! I'll be turning fifty in May. It's not a milestone I'm looking forward to, but it beats the alternative of having no more birthdays!" Ramona shrugged. Her face looked so youthful and carefree.

"Gadzooks!" Thorne exclaimed. "I can't believe we're basically the same age."

"Yeah. Wild," Ramona said. "But 'gadzooks'? We're not *that* old."

"I made a resolution last year to stop being such a potty mouth," Thorne explained. That along with his resolution to quit drinking two years ago, had stuck with him.

"That sounds like a good resolution," Ramona said. "What brings you to the HMCA? You're not dressed for a workout." Ramona glanced at Thorne's PI attire.

"Actually, a good private investigator can do everything in a trench coat and fedora. Even pump iron." Thorne flexed his bicep under his coat sleeve and pointed at his arm.

Ramona nodded politely.

Thorne continued. "I was supposed to meet Barry Strong this morning. He never showed."

"I heard he's on vacation," Ramona said.

"Oh really?" Thorne asked. "I wonder why he didn't tell me. Where did he go?"

"I don't know. Hummingbird Gardens is an active senior residence," Ramona said. "People are free to come and go as they please. I'm sure Mr. Strong is having a wonderful time."

Thorne remembered how happy Barry had seemed to be in the company of the mystery woman at the party last night. As Ramona walked away, he frowned and rested a hand on his cookie-filled stomach.

I trust my gut. And my gut tells me something is wrong.

3

✳ Brie ✳

Finally, a moment to myself. When the newest members of the HMCA left her desk area, Brie Bramble undid her too-tight puffball ponytail. She gave her scalp a break, massaging it for a few moments before smoothing the curls back up with a scrunchy again. Brie had yet to decode whatever it was that other mixed women did with their hair, but nothing worked for her. Instead of stylish soft curls, Brie's hair always turned into a frizzy mess when she left it down, and was a nightmare to brush out later.

With her hair back in place, Brie popped an earbud into her right ear, leaving her left open so she wouldn't miss anyone trying to get her attention. She pressed play on her phone and settled into the sweet sounds of her guilty pleasure.

"And you said the victims were all single women in their twenties?" one of the podcast cohosts, Cattie Filson, said.

"That's right," the other cohost, Heath Smith, replied. "The Gymnast Reaper lured ladies into the foam pit at the gymnasium where she worked. She had a secret compartment beneath the pit she could swim up through and . . ."

Avoid foam pits at gymnasiums. Brie tapped the words into her notes app on her smartphone. She added this tidbit to a long list of forbidden activities and places she would never go.

Thankfully, there was no foam pit at the Happy Marmot Community Association, so this particular threat should be easy to stay away from.

Brie spent every free moment listening to true crime podcasts like, "Not Done Yet" and, "Serial Killers, Glamour and Gore." When Brie wasn't at the HMCA working, she enjoyed watching classic Rom-Coms. Both of her pastimes were investments in her future. Learning about true crime kept her safe. Watching romance movies allowed her to experience the magic of true love without having to actually interact with other people. So far, her approach had yielded a comfortable, predictable life.

Even today's crush of busyness was expected. On New Year's Day it seemed like the entire city of Colorado Springs came in with their resolutions to get in shape. The HMCA had a lot to offer, including a weight room, swimming pool, all the usual treadmills and stair steppers, and classes for everything from dance, water aerobics, and yoga to first aid and arts and crafts. The file folder was bulging with paperwork for new members she needed to process into the computer system.

We might as well be in the stone age. Everywhere else on the planet has upgraded to tablets! She only had fifteen more minutes before another new member, a senior named George Saito, was coming in for a tour appointment.

Brie looked up from her work to see if the new guy had arrived early. Everyone in the lobby looked like they didn't need her help. Except . . . *Ugh. What's he want?* Brie's father, Thorne, headed straight for the front desk where Brie spent most of her workday. He was in full private investigator mode, dressed in a ridiculous costume of a tan trench coat, with a fedora tugged low over his forehead.

Brie wasn't mentally prepared to deal with him this morning.

There was nowhere to hide. Not without being painfully obvious. She only had one wall at her back, painted in a cheerful light gold color. The front desk was wide open to the public, situated in a spacious foyer that was framed on both ends by floor-to-ceiling windows. The high, curving, L-shaped counter surrounding her bright beech wood desk hit the perfect welcoming note. But sometimes, it was too welcoming.

Like when Brie had to deal with a cranky patron. *Or my Dad.*

Ignore him. He's probably just here to work out like everyone else. He needs to. Brie reminded herself that she'd had trouble squeezing into her yoga pants this morning. *Let's face it. So do I.*

Thorne hadn't been interested in her when she was a child. But for the past two years, he seemed to spend all of his spare moments right in the middle of her business. The man barely had a job, so he had a lot of free time.

"Hey, Cheesy Briesy." Thorne used her dreaded childhood nickname and grinned.

Brie tried to be patient with him. She removed her earbud and paused the podcast. "I don't have time to chat." She shuffled papers on her desk. "I'm working."

"This is important. Barry owes me a celery juice."

Brie set the papers down and glared at her father.

"Don't look like that," Thorne said. Then he added sheepishly, "I'm worried. He promised to treat me for my birthday, but he never showed up."

Brie grimaced. *His birthday. Duh!* He was a New Year's baby and often told people how he was only four hours too late to be *the* New Year's baby. If Brie told him "happy birthday" now, would it be obvious she had forgotten? He might have been a cruddy father, but he never forgot *her* birthday. Not even during the dark years when she had written him off entirely. She decided on nonchalance.

"Dad, we can talk about your birthday after I get off work," Brie said in a gentler tone, and gave him a brief smile.

Before her father could argue, a man wearing the uniform

of the Colorado Springs Police Department walked up.

"Excuse me, ma'am. May I speak to you for a moment?" he asked.

Brie's mouth fell open as she stared at the man. He stood taller than her father in his crisp black slacks and long-sleeved smokey blue shirt. A badge and insignia gleamed in the light pouring through the front windows, and a wide, gadget-covered service belt circled his narrow waist. His straight black hair was cropped short at the sides and artfully slicked over the top. His dark brown eyes had folds at the corners, indicating East Asian heritage. His smooth, square jaw was . . .

"Ma'am?" The policeman's voice was deep. It vibrated through her whole core.

"I'm sorry?" she asked weakly. The guy was too handsome for words. She caught herself staring again. His lips were moving, but she couldn't hear him.

"Cheesy Brie!" Her father waved a hand in front of her face. "Snap out of it!"

Brie shook herself. *Yikes!*

"Sorry about Brie," Thorne said. "I don't think she's high or anything like that."

"Dad!" Brie cried.

"So what's going on, officer?" Thorne removed his fedora and placed it over his chest. "Is there anything I can do to help?"

The policeman looked Thorne up and down, his lips quirking into a grin. *He's probably laughing inside at Dad's ridiculous outfit.*

"I'm not here on official business," the policeman said. "I'm just getting my grandfather signed up for the gym."

An old man leaning heavily on a robin's egg blue walker rolled up beside the policeman. "She's high."

"I am not!" Brie said a little too loudly. "I don't smoke. Anything."

"The classic denial of an addict," the old man said, elbowing the police officer in the ribs. "Aren't you going to arrest her?"

The policeman chuckled. "Well, even if she is stoned, there's not much I can do about it. I'm not on duty for another couple of hours. Just remember, Brie, recreational marijuana usage is prohibited in public spaces."

"But, I–" The old man cut Brie off.

"There's something clearly wrong with her. Are you going to be able to process my new HMCA membership, or do we need to talk to your manager?"

"Gotta go!" Thorne dashed away.

Coward. At least he can't do any more damage now.

"My manager's not here," Brie said, finally gathering her wits. Her manager rarely spent time at this branch of the HMCA. Along with the general public flooding the facility today, there were a few new tenants of the Hummingbird Gardens Senior Apartments who received gym memberships as part of a package deal with their rent. "I have your welcome packet. You must be the new Gardens resident." She flipped to a sheet in her folder. "George Saito?"

"Good. Now that's better. This is my grandson, Riggs. He'll be keeping an eye on you."

Riggs grinned. Brie nearly melted into incoherence again, but the glaring look from the old man snapped her back to reality.

Having Officer Saito keep an eye on me would be awesome. Her chances of becoming a victim on one of her podcasts decreased dramatically with a policeman around. *Too bad his grandfather is one of those grumpy old man types.* But after George Saito's accusations, Riggs would probably never speak to her again. Even without George around, why would he, anyway?

Romance only happens in movies.

4

✳ Barry ✳

That must've been an awesome night. Wish I could remember it. Barry Strong didn't normally have memory problems. But at age seventy, he supposed it was inevitable. His stubbled cheek was itchy. He tried to lift his hand to give it a scratch, but black restraint bands prevented all movement.

She must be a really strong lady to overpower a guy like me. Barry's suit was still on. *Odd.* Perhaps her intention hadn't been to take advantage of him. Barry felt a brief twinge of disappointment. *Where did she go?* She'd probably be back any minute now. *When is now? What time is it?*

From his vantage on the bed, the room didn't look like one of the typical layouts for a Hummingbird Gardens apartment. Barry didn't remember driving anywhere, but they must have.

Wherever they were, he liked this chick's style. The walls of the big room were covered in framed posters of bodybuilders. Light spilled from around the edges of two thick, slate gray curtains. *I was here all night.*

Barry tried to remember the woman he went home with from the HMCA New Year's Eve Party. She was one hot tomato. Although she had a strange voice. And there was something off about her hair. A wig? Lots of older gals supplemented their thinning hair. What was her name . . .

Barry's partner danced him out of the glittering gymnasium before the New Year's countdown began. And then what? Where did she take him?

Where is she, anyway? Barry's bathroom needs were going to turn this hot date into a hot mess if she didn't release him soon.

"Hey, babe!" Barry called out. "Ready for more fun?" Although he wasn't certain he'd even had any fun yet.

He was still foggy, but a few more details were coming back to him. A black hood covering his face. His attempt to escape. *A ninja?* Surely it was all a dream.

Barry tensed when he heard high-pitched voices and footsteps. He reached to turn up his hearing aids, but his hands were abruptly stopped by the restraints. The muffled words, "He's awake," and "Finally," just barely reached Barry's ears. *It wasn't just the two of us?* He was suddenly very relieved all of his clothes were still on. Barry held his breath as the doorknob jiggled. The door flew open.

"Grandpa!" Two small voices yelled and squealed. A boy and a girl burst into the room.

Grandpa? Barry was bewildered. *How did that happen? I only have one grandson, and he's a twenty-seven-year-old hopeless bachelor!* Marty was irresponsible, but he wasn't the kind of guy who would have surprise children show up out of the blue. *These can't be my great-grandchildren.* And even that wouldn't explain why Barry was strapped down.

"You're here! You're here! You're finally here!" The boy, a white kid who looked to be around eight years old, began unfastening one of the restraints. His straight brown hair was cut close to his scalp on the sides. The hair on top of his head was longer and flopped over his forehead. He wore a t-shirt with Popeye the Sailor Man holding a can of spinach, giving a thumbs up. What could Barry say? The kid had good taste.

"Wait, Scott! Remember what the ninja said?" The girl moved Scott's hand away.

"Oh, right! Sorry, Scarlett." The little boy put his hands behind his back.

Scarlett looked older than the boy. Maybe ten. She must be the boy's sister. They had the same brown eyes. Her hair was pulled back in a ponytail. Her t-shirt sported Mighty Mouse. Another good choice.

"I have to use the bathroom," Barry said. "Very badly."

Scarlett looked at Barry with a comically stern expression on her innocent young face and said, "If we untie you, do you promise not to try to escape?"

Barry nodded enthusiastically.

"That's good enough for me!" Scott exclaimed. He began undoing the restraints again. "I can't wait to show you everything. The ninja said you're gonna love your new house!"

My new house? Man, a whole lot more must have happened last night than I thought.

"Did you say, 'the ninja'?" Barry asked. His need to go to the bathroom was suddenly replaced by a need for answers. Free of the straps that held him down, he sat up and rubbed his wrists.

"Yep. The ninja's so cool," Scarlett said.

"And she's super strong!" Scott flexed his bicep. It was surprisingly large for such a little kid. Barry was momentarily impressed. "But she's not as strong and cool as you, Grandpa!"

The ninja is a she. Barry had a vague memory of his dance partner vanishing at the same time a woman dressed all in black appeared. *And why do these kids keep calling me Grandpa?*

"You can call me Barry," he said.

"Mom said that would be unrespectful," Scott said.

"You mean disrespectful," Scarlett explained. "We have to call you Grandpa. Just like we call our mom, Mom, and our dad, Dad."

Scott leaned close to Barry and whispered, "I know their real names."

This could be a clue to what had happened. "And what are they?" Barry whispered back.

"It's a secret."

Of course.

"This is all very interesting, but where is the bathroom?"

"I know where it is," Scott said with a big smile. "You get your very own bathroom, Grandpa."

Scott led Barry to a door that was only accessible from the bedroom. Barry gasped when Scott took him inside. It was nearly larger than his entire apartment. A bathtub big enough for three people sat in the middle of the polished tile floor. It must have had a hundred jets in it.

Glass walls surrounding a stand-up shower made up one corner. There was a bench in the shower, and on the wall, Barry noticed a control panel.

He walked over to it. "What's this for?" Barry asked.

"It's for the steam," Scott said. "It gets really hot."

"Steam?"

"It's a wet sauna," Scarlett explained. "And that wooden room over there is a dry sauna."

Barry had assumed the wood was just decorative, or perhaps formed a closet. "Wow," Barry whispered. A hot tub and two saunas?

"I don't like saunas," Scott said. "But I love the cold plunge!"

He walked over to a smaller bathtub with a lid on top. Scott lifted it and put a finger inside. He pulled it out and shivered. "I can stay in for five whole minutes! How long can you do it, Grandpa?"

"Ten minutes." Barry was well aware of the benefits of submerging one's body in fifty degrees Fahrenheit water.

"Wow. Not even Daddy goes that long!" Scarlett looked at Barry in awe.

The kids had called the huge space a bathroom, but it was really a luxury spa. Barry was startled to see his toiletries on the marble vanity counter. His hearing aid charger. The tablets for soaking his dentures. Instead of grounding him, the sight of his personal items in this strange place caused him even worse disorientation.

"I still need to, you know," Barry said.

"Oh yeah! Here's the potty!" Scott walked Barry to a small door.

"Thanks." Barry stepped inside. A light came on automatically, illuminating what could only be described as the throne room. The throne itself must have come directly from Japan. It had no tank on the back and looked more like a spaceship than a toilet. Even though Barry only had a number one kind of job to do, he felt it was his duty to sit on the magnificent device.

It's toasty! The seat was just slightly warmer than body temperature. His tight glutes and hamstrings melted like frosting onto the smooth white donut beneath him.

Maybe he had died after the New Year's Eve party. Because this sure seemed like heaven.

5

✳ Thorne ✳

Thorne was in no hurry to go home to his empty townhouse. There were no client appointments on his calendar. If he didn't get investigative work soon, he might be forced to return to the corporate world.

He had made a lot of money as Head of Regional Legacy Product Sales for Warehouse Amalgamated Appliance Apparatuses, but that gain meant nothing. The long hours at WAAA, away from his family, and the stress-induced drinking, caused him to lose it all.

He'd lost most of his friends when his lifestyle changed drastically after his divorce. The rest had ghosted him when he got fired for drinking on the job. Although real friends would have stood by Thorne. So maybe he'd never had any friends after all. He and Barry had been coworkers in what felt like a past life to Thorne. They were only acquaintances back then. They'd made a connection at the HMCA after Thorne found sobriety and began reclaiming his health.

That's why it hurt so badly that Barry had stiffed him. Promised him a birthday celery juice, then vanished. *That's just not like Barry.* Barry Strong wasn't the kind of man to deny another man celery juice without due cause. *Even if a woman's involved.* Thorne had to find the bodybuilder, or at least satisfy himself that the old guy was okay.

Rows of lockers lined a wall inside the weight room. They weren't as large as the ones in the men's and women's changing rooms. These lockers were a quick place to stash a pair of running shoes, wallets, and car keys. Thorne scanned the lockers near the HMCA weight room for Barry's. Inside, there might be a clue to Barry's disappearance.

The small personal storage spaces were stacked five high and were only a foot wide. On this wall, there were three dozen lockers. Barry's assigned locker was definitely among them, but Thorne hadn't paid attention to which specific number. He was sure he'd recognize it when he saw it. Thorne Bramble, PI, always trusted his gut feelings.

As he scanned the identical doors and the variety of lock colors and styles, Brie breezed up with the two men who had been at her desk moments earlier. It was obvious his daughter hadn't made a New Year's resolution to improve her wardrobe. She had on the same tired yoga pants and HMCA fleece jacket she wore almost every day. The smiling marmot logo on the back looked a little deranged with its bulging eyes and toothy grin. Thorne waved his hand at Brie. She could probably tell him which locker was Barry's, but she didn't even look his way.

"Your locker is number 23, Mr. Saito." Brie lifted the door handle and pulled the door open.

The old man rolled his bright blue walker closer and peered inside. "A person can't fit anything in a space that small!"

"Grandpa George," the annoyingly handsome police officer said, "you don't need room for anything but a jacket and your keys. Your apartment is just across the atrium from the gym. Miss Bramble, let's continue the tour. We can figure out the locker later."

Good. They left Thorne alone. At least one locker had been eliminated. Number 23 was definitely not Barry's.

"Which one is ours?" A woman in snug leggings and a hefty sports bra ran her hand along the locker doors.

"We each get our own," the man with her said. He was a little on the chunky side, too.

It's a good thing they're joining a gym. Thorne tried to ignore his own protruding tummy. He couldn't exercise without his pal Barry.

The couple located their assigned lockers and moved on.

This wasn't going to be easy with the throng of new HMCA members finding their lockers and trying out the nearby gym equipment. Luckily, Thorne was a master of stealth. But he needed to be quick. He wouldn't want that policeman to come back while he was cracking this safe.

He noted the lockers the couple used. *Three down. Out of three dozen. Focus, Thorne.* Barry left his lock on his door all the time. So any locker without a lock wasn't Barry's. Thorne also had a pretty good idea of where Barry usually stood when he placed his apartment key and other stuff inside.

It has to be in this column of lockers. Barry reached up, so it's on the top row.

Using his superior detecting skills, Thorne had narrowed Barry's potential locker down to two possibilities. Two lockers, side by side on the top row, had the same type of black, rectangular padlocks.

16? Or 21? Did one of these numbers mean something to Barry? Thorne gave up trying to figure it out. There was a 50/50 chance he'd be right. And Thorne liked those odds. *Go with your gut.*

Thorne pulled the paperclip from his pocket he'd pilfered from Brie's desk when no one was looking. He placed his house keys in the same hand as the paperclip to make it look like he had a key for the lock. *Now, to check if the coast is clear.* He pretended to take a selfie in front of the lockers and used his phone camera like a rearview mirror. He waited for a couple to pass. *And . . . now!*

Thorne shoved the paperclip into the padlock of locker 16. He had only been a PI for two years and had learned much of his craft from YouTube tutorials. The guy he'd watched picking locks made it look so easy.

A twist of the fingers. A flick of the wrist. Just feel around and wait for the click of success. Any second now.

For several minutes, Thorne wiggled and wrestled with the paperclip as his real keyset jangled below. People were starting to notice him. A few folks gathered around.

A sweaty old man with a handlebar mustache asked, "Mind if I try?"

Thorne laughed as he covered the paperclip with his free hand. "I should get a new lock. This one's always giving me trouble. I have to turn the key just so. You know what I mean?"

"Not really," the old man said.

"I don't need any help," Thorne snapped.

The old man left in a huff. Thorne pulled the paperclip and his keys away from the lock and put them back into his pocket. *So much for doing this quickly.* Thorne launched the lockpicking tutorial video on his smartphone and reviewed the steps.

"Hey," a deep, quiet voice said.

Thorne dropped his phone on the cement floor, cracking the screen.

"Oh, ugh! Hi." Thorne picked up his phone and closed the video. "Diana Diamond?"

The woman had appeared out of nowhere.

"Right." Diana narrowed her brown eyes at him, activating the few wrinkles on her face.

Did she see the video? Thorne knew Diana was well into her sixties, but her dark skin told no tales. Just like Thorne's ex-wife Eve, who was forty-eight, but could easily pass for much younger. Hopefully, Brie got those anti-aging genes from her mother. No one would be surprised to learn Thorne was fifty.

"Uh, can I help you?" Thorne asked.

"16." Diana tapped manicured nails against the locker door. They were painted the same color as her vivid purple tracksuit.

"16?" Thorne asked.

"My locker. You're standing in front of it."

"Um, of course." So much for Thorne's gut. *This time. Must have been those cookies.*

He stepped aside. Diana studied the scratches Thorne had just etched into her lock.

"Were you trying to get into my locker?" Her intense glare shook Thorne. For a quiet senior lady, she commanded respect. Maybe even a touch of fear.

"I, um, thought that was Barry Strong's locker."

"Why do you need to get into Barry's locker?" Diana asked.

Diana knew he and Barry were friends. She might believe he had a good reason for getting into Barry's locker. "I need to put something in it for him."

"What?" Diana asked.

"It's a surprise," Thorne said, hoping she'd buy it.

"Right," Diana said sarcastically. "Give me the paperclip."

"What paperclip?" Thorne asked.

Diana raised an eyebrow and held out her hand. Thorne placed the paperclip in her palm.

"Don't tell anyone I did this for you," Diana said as she went to work on the lock for number 21. "Here it is New Year's Day, and I'm already violating my resolution."

The lock clicked open.

"Oh, wow. Can you teach me–"

"No. It takes years of practice. It's mostly in the wrist, but you have to know what the inside of a lock feels like." Diana handed Thorne the paperclip.

"What was your New Year's resolution?" Thorne asked.

"To be good."

Diana walked off. *I wonder why?* She seemed like a nice enough lady, even if she could be a little intense. *And how many old ladies know how to pick a lock?*

Thorne took the open padlock off the locker and tugged on Barry's door. Inside was an extra pair of Barry's knee-length compression socks, a couple of protein bars, and a letter.

Thorne glanced around. He pulled a sheet from an envelope that had already been torn open.

The letter read:

Dear Barrington Strong,

The HMCA has been notified that you are two months past due on your rent for the Hummingbird Gardens Senior Apartments. As your gym membership is dependent on your continued residency in the Gardens, your HMCA status will be terminated unless we are notified that your rent has been brought up to date. Financial aid is available for the HMCA should you no longer reside in Hummingbird Gardens. Please contact customer service for assistance.

The letter was signed by Brie's manager, who was never around. *What a jerk!* Thorne wished he could talk to Brie about how insensitive the letter was worded, but then he might have to admit how he'd learned this information.

Barry had money troubles. How bad was it? Maybe Brie could offer some insights. But she was probably still busy with those new gym clients. Ramona, the property manager for Hummingbird Gardens, had to know Barry was behind on rent. She might have been the one to report him to the HMCA manager.

If I ramp up my charm, I'll get the answers I need.

6

✳ Barry ✳

Barry left the bathroom feeling light-headed and confused. Was this a dream?

He shook his head. He mimicked Scott and put his hand in the cold plunge.

Nope! I'm awake.

Barry pulled his hand out and flexed it a few times to melt the blood that had frozen in his fingertips. He wasn't dreaming, but nothing made sense. Along with the lingering cold in his hand, he felt a stabbing fear. Had he experienced an episode of senility? Wandered away from the party and gotten lost? Barry pressed a hand to his forehead as he exited the spa.

Scarlett slid off her perch on Barry's bed.

"Are you okay, Grandpa?" she asked.

"I don't know," Barry said, truthfully. He was certain the kids must be in grade school. And the schools were on winter break. If it was still January. "What day is it?" Barry asked.

"It's New Year's Day," Scarlett said.

But what year? His smartphone could clear up his confusion about the passage of time in an instant. He could even find out where he ended up with GPS. He checked his suit pockets for it. Not there. Of course.

"I need my phone," Barry said firmly.

"We have it. It's charging." Scott beamed at Barry.

"Don't worry about it," Scarlett said. "The ninja said you can think of this as a vacation from technology."

How is that supposed to be comforting to a kidnapping victim? His stomach grumbled. Barry wasn't sure whether it was from hunger or anxiety.

"If it's morning," he said, "it must be time for breakfast."

"You slept forever, Grandpa," Scarlett said. "It's halfway to lunchtime."

If Barry could get out of this luxurious suite, maybe he could figure out how he'd ended up here. *Wherever here is.* And find a way to escape.

"Come on!" Scott tugged on Barry's suit jacket sleeve, leading him toward the bedroom door.

"Wait! Grandpa's still in his party clothes," Scarlett said.

"I don't have anything else to wear." Barry looked down at his rumpled suit.

"We got you some new clothes." Scott reached into a drawer and pulled out high-tech neon-orange weight-lifting gloves, still in the package. "I picked these for you myself because they look just like mine. We can match!"

"Let's go, Scott. Grandpa needs his privacy."

The kids left him alone again.

When the door clicked closed, Barry dashed back to the bathroom and looked for an escape route. But of course, there were no windows or additional doors. No vent ducts large enough for a grown man to traverse. The room was sealed.

Since he couldn't get away, he might as well enjoy this incredible bathroom. He took a long, steamy shower.

They kidnapped me. Maybe they're monitoring my every move.

If there were hidden cameras filming his process, they weren't seeing much more than he displayed willingly at bodybuilding competitions. Although there were some parts of his body that weren't immune to the effects of gravity, the way his muscles were. Barry stuck his tongue out and waggled his personals toward each corner. If anyone was watching, they'd be suffering with that imagery for the rest of their lives.

Feeling refreshed, but not much more clear-minded, Barry decided to get dressed in the new clothes for practical reasons. Only James Bond could be ready for action wearing a tuxedo and dress shoes.

The dresser was stocked with so much more than gloves. A dozen workout suits filled three drawers. Others held posing trunks, athletic socks, compression hose, and polo shirts. He selected a designer track suit with fabric that was buttery soft, but still moisture-wicking. In the walk-in closet, he discovered dress slacks and jackets, a puffy winter coat, and enough shoes for an entire gymnasium full of fitness fans.

He slid his compression sock-coated foot into a running shoe. It fit perfectly. He picked up the other shoe and examined the interior. *Holy Toledo!* The shoes had brand-new custom orthotics installed. *When did they get molds of my feet?*

The bedroom window, seeping late-morning light around the gray curtains, beckoned Barry. He lifted the window covering, revealing a white rectangular device that was obviously an alarm. *To keep intruders out, or kidnapping victims in?*

What would be the consequences of attempted escape? The release of bitey guard dogs? An armed sentry with orders to shoot? A mine field? Barry sighed. He needed more information before fleeing.

He went to the bedroom door and tried the knob. *Not locked!* But his tiny prison guards were waiting outside.

"Grandpa!" The boy grabbed one hand, the girl his other.

"The name is Barry," he reminded them.

But the kids just giggled like he'd said a naughty word.

He allowed himself to be dragged out the door, down a hallway, and into a bright kitchen that looked every bit as impressive as Barry's bathroom. Every kitchen gadget imaginable sat artfully on the spacious marble countertops. The fridge was tastefully hidden behind white cabinet doors. There was a professional gas range. The pots and pans hanging from the ceiling looked like works of art. A grow-light-lit planter held a variety of kale and lettuce plants. Fresh herbs grew in pots all along the sill of the huge picture window.

Barry looked out the window for a clue to where he was. The only thing to be seen outside was a wall of pine trees.

But there were two somebodies in the kitchen who could finally give Barry some decent answers. *Adults!*

A healthy-looking man wearing a skintight gray Workout Shield brand hoody and black stretchy pants stood at the marble island.

"Good morning, Mr. Strong," the man said. His muscled bicep bulged as he dropped a scoop of creatine into a top-of-the-line blender. "Or should I call you Dad?"

Barry didn't know how to respond to that. *Should he?* The man's dark blond hair was thinning just like Barry's had in his younger years. Was this guy a child Barry never knew he had? Or had senility stolen the memory of his existence from Barry's mind? *Or am I just going crazy?*

"I'm Garrett Brauny," the man said.

If I were supposed to remember him, he wouldn't be introducing himself to me. Maybe Barry wasn't going crazy. The situation he was in was the insane part.

"I'm Buffy." Her name was completely appropriate. The buff woman added leafy greens to the blender. She wore a pink unitard over white leggings and sported a brown ponytail that matched Scarlett's. "I see you've met the children."

"Would you like a fresh egg in your protein shake?" Garrett asked. "Or do you prefer egg powder?"

He tapped the lid of one of the dozen tubs of supplements on the island. Then he pointed to a large basket full of eggs sitting unrefrigerated on the marble counter. Barry hadn't seen eggs stored that way since he was a child. They must have come straight from the chicken and not the grocery store. Probably organic, too.

"Do you keep chickens?" Barry asked. Lots of people in Colorado Springs did, if he was still in Colorado.

"Our neighbors are farmers," Scarlett said.

"Sometimes we walk to get eggs. It's only a couple of miles," Scott said.

So no one lives close enough to hear me scream.

"Fresh eggs, please," Barry said, as though it was perfectly normal to request what type of protein shake he wanted from his kidnappers. "Where am I?"

"You're in our home. Your home," Buffy said. "I'm so excited you're finally here! This is going to be wonderful." Her brown eyes glittered as she glanced to her husband and back to Barry, and added, "Dad."

"I can't believe I'm making a protein shake for my new father. This is surreal." Garrett gave Barry a million-watt smile.

Before Barry could ask more questions, Garrett ran the industrial-strength blender. When it stopped, Buffy poured the green-tinted protein shake into three bottles. She screwed on the lids.

"The kids already had breakfast," Garrett explained. "Grab a bottle, and we'll give you the tour."

Barry wanted answers, but he decided that playing along would allow him to assess his situation. Both parents and even the children appeared fit and strong. Barry could probably take on one or two of them, but not all four at once. A direct confrontation might prove unwise.

Buffy grabbed one handle of a double door, and Garrett the other. They pulled them open at the same time.

"Ta da!" Scott announced.

Barry stepped across the threshold into a wonderland. Every piece of equipment was state-of-the-art. A treadmill and stair stepper took care of cardio requirements, while free weights and weight machines lined one mirrored wall. Barry had seen less impressive weight rooms in professional settings.

"I've died and gone to bodybuilder heaven," he murmured. Turning to the parents, he spoke louder. "But I know I'm not in heaven. Transport to the pearly gates doesn't involve being bound to a bed." At least, Barry didn't think so, never having gone there himself. "I demand you explain to me now – where am I, and why?"

"Have you signed the contract?" Buffy asked.

"What contract?" Barry asked. "That sounds so impersonal."

"Adoptions involve legal paperwork, too," Garrett said. "But that's just to protect people during a very emotional decision."

"We want to adopt you," Buffy gushed. "Make you a permanent part of our family." A beautiful smile lit up her pretty face, and she bounced on the toes of her sneakers.

"The kids need a grandparent." Garrett beamed as he clasped his strong hands around Barry's shoulders. "Buffy and I need a father. We just can't go on without you. You're exactly who our little family has been missing."

Buffy must have been holding her breath during Garrett's short speech. She exhaled dramatically before saying, "We won't be complete without you."

Barry frowned. "Aren't government agencies typically involved in adoptions? And when did the process evolve to include the elderly? Not to mention . . . kidnapping!"

"We've signed a non-disclosure agreement," Garrett said. "We can't explain the details until you see the contract. It's in the office."

As they walked down a spacious hallway, Barry took a sip of the shake. It came from the same blender everyone else was drinking from, so he trusted it wasn't poisoned. It tasted incredible. Barry looked more closely at the contents of his cup and saw tiny black flecks in it. *Fresh vanilla beans.*

Garrett led the way as Barry and the rest of the family

followed. The home office was full of display cases dominated by trophies and ribbons, not books. Buffy untied a black ribbon from a roll of parchment that seemed oddly ancient, yet modern at the same time. She and Garrett unrolled it carefully.

"It's simple, really," Buffy said. "You sign here."

She poked a finger on the parchment, at a line under two that had already been signed by the parents. Then she dipped a long, shiny raven feather into a small, ornate pot of ink with a Yin and Yang symbol carved into the side. Buffy placed the pen in Barry's hand.

"There's a lemon clause," Garrett said. "Both parties have the right to cancel the ninja's contract any time during the one-week trial period."

"Parties." That was what had gotten Barry in trouble in the first place. Letting his head be turned by a lovely senior lady. He had to wonder whether she was involved in this kidnapping scheme. What was in it for the family? Was this an elaborate plot to steal his meager pension and Social Security earnings?

"I can't possibly sign a document without my lawyer's approval," Barry said, even though he had never in his life had a lawyer at his beck and call.

"Sign it!" Scott stomped his foot. "I don't want anyone else for my grandpa."

"You're the perfect one for us," Scarlett added.

Barry raised his hands in mock surrender. "I just need a little time. This is all a lot to take in so soon after waking."

"You can sign the paper after you wake up a little more," Scarlett said. "Then you'll be our forever grandpa."

"Now, Scarlett," Buffy said. "Your grandpa has one week to decide. And we need to make sure he's a good fit for us, too."

"One week is forever," Scott whined. "I don't need seven whole days. I already love our new grandpa." Scott hugged onto Barry's leg.

One week? Barry didn't plan to stick around long enough to invoke the lemon clause.

7

✳ Thorne ✳

Thorne walked into the atrium that connected to the senior apartment complex. The humid air and vegetation made the place feel like a tropical island in the dry Colorado Springs climate. Thorne hurried past meandering seniors and shoppers and entered Hummingbird Gardens. The manager's office was down the hallway. Thorne peeked through the open glass door.

Oh great. Not him again.

Ramona was dealing with the new guy, Mr. Saito. Brie must have deposited the cranky old man with Ramona after the gym tour.

Luckily his policeman grandson wasn't nearby. The uniformed dude who had been accompanying George Saito and Brie had probably gone to work. *I wonder if Brie thought he was cute.* Thorne chuckled. *Girls have the strangest taste in guys.* At twenty-five, Brie was such a late bloomer that Thorne suspected she wasn't interested in human companionship at all.

From what Thorne could see, George was busy being an old man, wasting Ramona's time with his old manisms. Thorne to the rescue.

"Ramona, a word, please," Thorne said, quirking his lips into a roguish grin.

"What are you smirking at?" George frowned up at Thorne

from his hunched position, gripping the handles of his rollator. With his fuzzy ring of white hair circling his bald head, and his thick mustache, he reminded Thorne of Shigechiyo Izumi, the one-time holder of the oldest man in the world title. But minus that guy's beard. "Can't you see she's busy?"

"I'm in the middle of an investigation," Thorne replied with authority. "I'm a private investigator."

"Well, well, aren't you a special one." George actually smiled. It was the first time Thorne had seen that happen. He looked a little less angry that way. "What's your name, son?"

"Thorne." Thorne stuck his hand out to shake George's. "Thorne Bramble."

"Thorne Bramble, PI." George released his hold on the rollator and took Thorne's hand. He squeezed it with surprising force. *Must be from gripping that rollator all the time.* George still had Thorne's hand in his when his smile turned from congenial to scary. "*Detective* George Saito. Nice to meet you. What are you investigating?"

Detective, eh? And so I meet my nemesis.

"Now, now, George," Ramona piped in. "I'm sure whatever Mr. Bramble is doing isn't worth coming out of retirement for."

Ouch. Thorne nearly clutched his heart.

Ramona continued speaking. "Thorne, I can answer a quick question. Then I need to attend to Mr. Saito."

"*Detective* Saito," the old man said.

Retired Detective Saito.

Thorne gathered his wits. "It's about Barry. There's a rumor going around that he hasn't been paying his rent on time." *And by rumor, I mean a piece of mail in his personal locker that I probably wasn't supposed to see. But Ramona doesn't need to know that.* "How much does he owe?"

Before Ramona could reply, George interrupted. "Ms. Grant, you are under no obligation to answer any of his questions. PIs have no legal authority the way detectives do."

"Thank you, George. But I wasn't going to answer his

question, anyway." Ramona's words sent another blow to Thorne's heart. "I don't know where you got that rumor, but our residential records are confidential. We respect our patrons' privacy at Hummingbird Gardens."

"But he's my friend. He'd want me to know if he was having money troubles. Can't you just tell me?" Thorne blinked in a way he hoped was cute. He'd been told many times that his baby blue eyes were captivating. "Maybe I can help him out."

In reality, Thorne had his own money troubles. There probably wasn't much he could do to help.

"No, Thorne," Ramona said. "You'll just have to speak to him when he returns from vacation."

"But don't you see the problem with that?" Thorne exclaimed. "Why would he go on vacation if he's behind on his rent?"

"Have you considered that might be why he's behind on his rent, if this rumor were to be believed?" George asked. "Not every senior retains their cognizance with age. He may not be in his right mind. Perhaps he's out spending his Social Security while living his wildest dreams on a cruise around the world."

Thorne had not considered this very reasonable explanation. But it still didn't quite fit. "That kind of thing requires planning. Why didn't Barry ever mention it?"

"I've seen plenty of cases where senior men were taken in by younger women who sucked their finances dry," George said.

"A younger woman?" Thorne's heart skipped a beat.

"Oldest story ever told," George said.

Barry had not left the party last night alone. Although the woman didn't look young. Thorne thought she might have even been older than Barry with that weird wig and makeup.

"Ramona," Thorne said, "do you know who Barry was dancing with last night? Bad wig, cakey makeup, frumpy blue dress, but a great looking lady overall."

"That doesn't sound great," George grumbled.

"I don't remember anyone specific that fits that

description," Ramona said, tapping her chin. "You're sure it wasn't Lovey Dearheart? She wears a lot of makeup and owns some wigs."

"This lady was too frumpy to be her," Thorne said.

"What about the cookie lady?" Ramona asked. "All dolled up?"

"Definitely not," Thorne said. "She didn't have any cookies."

"Well, I can't say who that was then." Ramona shrugged. "I left the party early."

"You think this mystery woman spirited Barry away to spend his non-existent money?" Thorne wrung his hands.

Ramona shrugged. "Maybe."

This didn't sit right with his gut, either. Thorne tried out some fancy detective jargon. "That hypothesis does not fit Barry's personality profile. How could he just up and leave last night with no warning?"

George shook his head. "When you hear hoofbeats, don't go looking for zebras unless you happen to be in Africa."

"What's that supposed to mean?" Thorne asked.

"I think it means that you should probably look for a horse," Ramona said.

George nodded. "The obvious solution is usually the correct one."

In other words, look for the mystery woman? Would Barry really skip out on him for the affection of a stranger? Thorne frowned. "But–"

"Observe, Mr. PI," George said to Thorne, cutting him off. "So that you may take heed of your friend's financial ruin. Instead of bailing him out, perhaps you can learn from his mistake, that is, assuming there is any weight to your assertion. As the Japanese proverb says, 'One man's fault is another's lesson.'"

"Oh yeah? Well, I've got a proverb for you, too." Thorne said, "Don't count your chickens before they cross the road."

"That's not a proverb," George said.

"Fine! I've got a better one." Thorne reached into his trench coat pocket for his phone, flinching when his fingers brushed against the spiderwebbed cracks in the screen. *The phone is fine. It's just the screen.* Thorne had actually forgotten what a proverb was, if he had ever known. All he needed was the definition, and he could probably make one up on the spot. But before Thorne could type in a search, George interrupted him.

"You don't know any proverbs offhand?" George asked. "Most people don't. That's fine. Look one up. I can wait."

Thorne shoved his phone back into his pocket. "I was just checking the time!"

"Then what time is it?" George asked smugly.

Ramona, who had become a silent observer, looked at Thorne expectantly.

Thorne met her gaze and smiled. If he couldn't impress George, he could at least make himself look good for Ramona. He pulled his ace out of his sleeve. "Time for a song! That's way cooler than a proverb anyway."

"By all means," George waved Thorne on. "Sing me a tune."

Thorne cleared his throat. He had just the right song to shut George up and defend Barry's life decisions. And what woman didn't love a Frank Sinatra tune? He gazed at Ramona as he sang, "'Everybody needs some money sometimes. Everybody needs some cash somehow.'"

George raised his eyebrows. "Frank Sinatra? I don't think those are the right words–"

"Close! But not quite Sinatra. Don't you remember those old Western Union commercials?"

George and Ramona looked at each other. No doubt the perplexed looks on their faces were due to the awe Thorne's sultry baritone had inspired.

"'Something in my heart just told me, Barry's sometime. . . is now,'" Thorne sang his way out of the office.

Zing! Got him. And Thorne even got bonus points: he had swiped a fresh paperclip from Ramona's desk without the so-called detective even noticing. *Ha!*

Thorne only had more questions about Barry's money troubles after speaking with Ramona and George. Did Barry spend his rent money on an extravagant vacation? Or did he run away with the mystery woman last night? Who was she? Good questions were a great starting point.

Thorne made his way to someone who might hold some answers. And if she didn't have them, he'd try his luck again with the new paperclip.

8

✳ Brie ✳

Brie's earbuds streamed the conclusion of the true crime podcast as she browsed the rack of birthday cards in the Frisky Shamrock gift shop.

"The Gymnast Reaper is actually up for parole in September," Heath Smith said.

"You've got to be kidding," Catti Filson said. "Why?"

"Good behavior. She's in her late sixties, and she has expressed remorse about her career as a burglar and robber."

"Any tips for our listeners to avoid becoming victims of a devious criminal like this?" the cohost asked.

"Check locker rooms for cameras. Don't wear leotards in public. And keep your toenails long enough to scratch with."

"That's good advice for everyone. Your feet can be weapons if you–"

The podcast continued to play as Brie made notes on her phone. Then continued her search for a birthday card for her father.

One card was too sickeningly sweet. Another was a fart joke. *What happened to plain old birthday cards? A picture of a cake and balloons. And Happy Birthday inside. Simple.* She opened a few more.

A figure appeared at her side. Still tense from listening to the podcast, Brie suppressed a startled squeal.

"Good morning, Lassie! Can I help you find anything?" Liam Boyer asked in a mild Gaelic accent. The cheerful older man's fringe of white whiskers bristled around a wide smile. A plaid Irish tam covered his thinning hair.

"I'm looking for a birthday card," Brie said. "For my father." The shop offered mostly Irish-themed gifts, but there were some culturally neutral cards.

"We have a few more over here." Liam led her to a rack of birthday cards with animals on them. One had ugly cartoon giraffes wearing birthday hats, doing a kick line. Another had a baboon holding a balloon. It said, "Whether you have balloons or baboons, it's your birthday! Go ape!" A huge reptile chomping into a cake had the caption, "Cake you later, alligator." *These are the worst.*

Brie finally selected one. "I'll take this."

Liam rang up her purchase at a checkout counter covered with little snow globes. They looked like January in Colorado, except for the Nessie sea monsters, shamrocks, or leprechauns inside. Brie hadn't gotten her dad a present. Impulsively, she grabbed a Nessie snow globe.

"And this. I'm pretty sure Dad's part Irish." His white skin was pale enough to indicate Gaelic ancestry. Unless it was due to never getting outdoors in the sun. But his baby blue eyes were thoroughly genetic. *Too bad he didn't share those genes with me.* Brie's eyes were basic brown just like seventy-five percent of the rest of humanity.

"Nice," Liam said. "Technically, Nessie isn't an Irish citizen, residing in the Loch Ness in the Scottish Highlands. But she's still Celtic in nature. Are you doing anything special for your father's big day?"

"Actually, his birthday was yesterday," Brie admitted. "I'm a little late."

"Then perhaps you can make it up to him by bringing him to hear my band tonight," Liam said.

"Oh, you're in a band?"

"Plaid Melodies. We have a concert at the Singing Lamb Pub."

A concert might be fun, but an evening with her father sounded like purgatory. They just weren't close like that. Plus, there was no way she was taking her dad to a concert at a pub. He had only been sober for two years at most.

"This is too short of notice." Brie wasn't good at lying, but she thought that sounded like a reasonable excuse. "Maybe next time?"

"Of course!" Liam placed the snow globe in a cute little green bag covered with shiny silver shamrocks. "We play there often. I'm sure your father would consider it a real treat."

Brie smiled and nodded.

It had taken longer than she thought to pick out a card. Her break was already over. Brie rushed out of the Frisky Shamrock and through the warm, humid atrium to the side entrance to HMCA. People were already waiting for her. The Honeycombe family, with mom, dad, and two kids, was scheduled to finalize their membership today.

"I'm so sorry I'm late!" Brie rushed behind the reception desk.

Saffron Honeycombe shook her head, making her shoulder-length spiral curls bob. "You're not late. We're a little early."

"The kids are excited about their beginning gymnastics class." Bay Honeycombe's tight black curls were trimmed short, and made his brown, round face appear even more plump. A mustache dusted his upper lip.

Brie stifled a shudder at the word "gymnastics" before she handed the new family their membership cards and assigned them lockers. *Remember, Brie. We don't have a foam pit in our gym. The Gymnast Reaper won't come here when she gets out on parole.*

She had already given this family a tour yesterday before they committed to joining the HMCA. The Honeycombes headed for the locker rooms, clutching the straps of their new HMCA gym bags and chattering excitedly to each other. The entire family was a bit heavy and seemed enthusiastic about getting into shape.

January was a busy month, but sadly, attendance would drop off well before summer. People just couldn't seem to stick to their New Year's resolutions. That's why Brie didn't bother to make any.

Here comes trouble.

Her father marched up to the desk like he was on a mission. His tan trench coat wafted behind him like a cape. It seemed like he lived in the vintage coat. *Does he ever wash that thing?*

If Thorne was seeking yet another opportunity to humiliate her in front of the only cute guy to talk to her in months, he was out of luck. The policeman wasn't around today. And he hadn't even asked for Brie's number. *No one ever does.* But at least he left her his business card. As if she'd ever need to call the police. Nothing ever happened at the HMCA.

I'm ready for Dad this time.

"Hi, Dad." She thrust the pale green envelope and the gift bag across the desk. "Happy late birthday."

"Wow! Thanks!" Thorne grabbed them with greedy fingers. Like he was hungry for some acknowledgement of his existence by his only child. "Maybe we can do dinner tonight?"

"I have, uh, other plans," she fumbled. Brie hoped her brown cheeks hid the blush she felt as she thought of Liam's invitation to his band's pub appearance. Her 'other plans' involved rewatching the romantic movie "Moonstruck." The main characters were both neurodivergent, in Brie's opinion. So watching this movie was the perfect way to celebrate Mental Wellness Month. "Maybe another time."

"Okay," Thorne said quietly. "Another time."

Thorne peeped inside the gift bag. He pulled out the Nessie snow globe.

"Is that a lizard?" he asked.

"No, it's Nessie, the Loch Ness Sea monster."

"Wow, I love cryptids!"

He slid his thumb under the envelope flap and pulled out the card. The front cover showed a cartoon cat face, and the words, "Cats and dads are a lot alike." The message inside said, "Both can be found napping in recliners." It was stupid, but impersonal enough that Brie wasn't embarrassed giving it to a guy she barely knew.

Tears filled his eyes. "Wow. You remembered how much I love cats!"

He loves cats?

Thorne rushed around the desk before Brie could react and threw his arms around her for a bear hug.

She endured for a moment, then extracted herself. Maybe she should give him a chance. A person only had one dad. And it felt like she didn't have a mother anymore. Brie's mom Eden had flown off to India four years ago. She backpacked to Tibet, then found her true purpose in life in a yoga ashram.

She had to lose me to find herself. Brie tried not to focus on the hurt of it all.

The only upside was that Brie had become a permanent house sitter for Mom. She paid rent, which she'd kind of resented until she learned she could only afford a small apartment for what her mother charged. With Mom gone, Brie had the run of an entire house. *Not that I need that much space.* She only used her bedroom, bathroom, and kitchen while fighting the layer of dust that did battle with the rest of the spacious home.

"I have to get back to work, Dad." Brie patted a hand on a stack of papers.

"Oh. Yeah. Sorry." He began to leave, but turned back abruptly. "Hey, I did have a question for you. I was supposed to meet Barry Strong yesterday morning."

"You already told me. For celery juice." Brie gagged internally at the thought of the salty, watery, green vegetable fluid.

"I learned he's behind on his gym membership."

Brie squeezed her eyes shut. "How did you find that out?"

"My gut never lies," Thorne said. "Plus, a little birdie might have given me a hint. Maybe a birdie with a name that rhymes with cheese. You just confirmed my information, Cheesy Briesy."

Ugh! He's so annoying!

"We've never had problems before with Barry's membership," Brie said. "It's very important to him. He told me he had to help out his grandson, and his pension checks only stretch so far. He'll get caught up on his rent again."

"Odd, don't you think?" Thorne asked. "Money problems? Then poof! He disappears."

"We shouldn't assume Barry is actually missing. Ramona said he's on vacation."

"How would he go on vacation with no money?" Thorne asked.

"Yeah. That is weird," Brie said. "Some seniors get impulsive, though. Irresponsible. You know, with old age mental stuff?"

"Not Barry. He's even sharper than me!"

That's not saying much.

Thorne continued. "Barry is my buddy. He would have told me if he was going on vacation. And he never would have stood me up for a birthday celery juice. I'm worried."

Her dad's baby blues were rimmed with red as if he were about to tear up again.

Great. Now Brie was worried.

"And he didn't leave the New Year's Eve party alone," Thorne said. "He left with a woman."

"Good for Barry." Brie laughed, and then frowned. If a bald seventy-year-old bodybuilder could get a date, why couldn't she?

"Do you know who she was?" Thorne asked.

"Who?"

"The woman Barry left with," Thorne said.

"I only helped set up for the party," Brie said. She had spent all of the day New Year's Eve turning the gym into a dance floor. "I was home that night." She had fallen asleep long before the New Year.

"Do you have anyone who can corroborate your story?" Thorne asked.

"You're asking me for an alibi?" Brie blanched.

"Well, yeah. What if you're covering for her?"

"Why would I–" Brie took a deep breath. *Don't let him get under your skin. He's not worth it.* "Dad. I don't know who Barry left with. But I can ask around. Okay?"

"Okay. But trust no one." Thorne thumped a fist on the desk twice as though to drive his point home, then left.

No problem there. I already don't trust anyone.

She picked up the business card the cute police officer had given her. The official police department stamp in one corner gave the card authority. Brie shook her head. She was just using Barry as an excuse to call the guy.

Am I really that pathetic?

There had to be a logical explanation for Barry's disappearance. Her mind drifted to true crime. Had a woman like the Gymnast Reaper snatched Barry away? A Bodybuilder Burglar?

9

✳ Barry ✳

Barry had lost count of how many dumbbell shrugs he'd done. It was impossible to focus. His mind was roiling with questions. The family was making his resolve to escape difficult to keep top of mind.

"Seven days is a long time," Barry told his captors between sets. "I owe a friend a celery juice."

Thorne would send Barry to bodybuilder heaven if he didn't get that juice soon. Unless that's where Barry *had* ended up. What other folks dreaded – time in the gym – was pure bliss for a guy like Barry. The weight machines in this home gym were beyond state-of-the-art. Even the free weights were higher quality than anything Barry had encountered. His trapezius muscles ached delightfully.

"We have a juice press," Garrett said. "Should we make some celery juice for our post-workout electrolyte replacement, Dad?"

"I'm not your father," Barry grumbled. "Juice sounds nice, but what about my friend, Thorne? I hoped to share a glass with him yesterday morning."

"I like celery juice, Grandpa," Scarlett said. "We can both share."

"Please call me Barry."

The child's face fell like a dropped dumbbell.

Barry felt a brief stab of guilt, but he needed to nip this fantasy in the bud. "I had a son. He's gone now."

"I used to have a father," Garrett said, his voice nearly a whisper. "And a mother. I had hoped . . ." He stumbled into silence. With more firmness, he added, "I hoped to be your son."

"My parents are gone too," Buffy said. "All too soon, and too young. I need you, Barry. And the children's lives would be so much richer if they had a grandparent."

Barry focused hard to keep Garrett and Buffy's emotions from swaying his resolve. "But I already have a grandkid. Marty's a grownup, but he still needs me."

Or at least he needs my money. The boy was in his late twenties, but his gambling problem had made him as helpless as a small child. Thankfully, Marty had gone to counseling for his addiction, but he confided to Barry that he still owed a lot of money to some angry, dangerous people. And then there were those car payments for that ridiculous vehicle. But how was a young man supposed to make it in the world without a car? Despite being behind on his Hummingbird Gardens rent, Barry had agreed to give Marty another check today. *One last time. I hope it's not too late.*

"The ninja said Marty isn't very good for you." Scarlett picked up two fifteen-pound dumbbells and began doing triceps extensions.

"Scarlett, hush," Buffy said. "Sometimes families go through difficult times. I'm sure Marty will come around eventually."

How much do these people know about my personal life? Weird.

"In the meantime, Barry, treat this like a spa retreat." Garrett stood up from the weight machine he was using. "Phew! Thanks for the lifting tip you gave me. I don't think I've ever felt soreness in my serratus anterior muscles before." Garrett rubbed his fingers along the side of his chest. "Bulking these up could give me an edge at the competition."

Barry looked at the flier the family gave him. An all-ages New Year's Revolution Family Bodybuilding Competition was scheduled for the day after Barry's one-week trial period ended. It was clearly for people who were immune to the temptations of the holidays. Even Barry had trouble ignoring the cookie lady at Hummingbird Gardens at Christmastime. And poor Thorne never had a chance. Barry folded the flier and put it into the pocket of his brand-new workout pants.

"I really need your help if I'm gonna win a prize this year," little Scott said. He stood up from a squat and set down the barbell he had draped across his shoulders. Scott picked up the contract and held it in front of Barry. "Please sign it. You're awesome!" Scott threw his muscled kid arms around Barry and squeezed with surprising strength.

These cute kids were enough to make Barry believe in Stockholm syndrome. He could totally see how captives developed psychological bonds with their captors. He was falling in love with the whole family already. Barry stared at the contract. Surely it was a joke. There was something fishy about the whole situation.

If it's too good to be true, it probably is.

Barry looked down into Scott's face. The muscle-bound boy gave Barry a grin, revealing a couple of spaces where teeth were missing. His dimples reminded Barry of Marty's when he was this age. *Marty. My real grandson might be in trouble. I have to get out of here.*

"You all are pretty awesome," Barry told the family. And he meant it. He just had to get away long enough to help Marty out. Then he would return and explore this whole grandparent deal. Barry now knew more about the layout of the house, including the location of a normal-sized bathroom near the workout area. "I need to use the little boy's room. I remember where it is."

Before anyone could protest, Barry walked out of the home

gym. He glanced behind. Garrett followed closely.

"Sorry to be so formal, Dad," Garrett said solemnly. "It's just a precaution the ninja suggested."

"Who is this ninja person, anyway?" Barry asked.

Garrett laughed a little. "I honestly have no idea. One day, while we were shopping at a sporting goods store, Buffy and I were looking at pickleball paddles and talking about how sad it was that our kids didn't have any living grandparents. Then poof! The ninja appeared right in front of us, popping her head out of a barrel of pickleballs."

"That must have been terrifying!"

"Only for a moment." Garrett smiled to himself, apparently relishing the memory.

That was apparently the sum total of the information Garrett was going to offer. Perhaps it was all he knew.

On the way to the bathroom, Barry could see a glass patio door to the outside world directly ahead of him. A way out. Through the door, Barry saw a wall of evergreen trees interspersed with leafless cottonwoods and aspens. He remembered what the kids said about their farmer neighbors being a couple of miles away. *This house is in the woods. Maybe Black Forest?* That wealthy yet remote suburb of Colorado Springs was the perfect place to hide a kidnapping victim.

Thankfully, everyone let Barry use the bathroom by himself. If this went wrong, it might be the last time he got to "go" alone.

Barry closed the door and actually used the bathroom, because no man in his seventies should ever pass up the opportunity to do so. Then he devised his plan. He examined the bidet on the fancy toilet and looked for a way to use it for his escape. An extra pipe fed water into the sprayer. For a man as strong as himself, most connections were hand-tight. Barry strained only a little as he undid the fitting. Water began pooling up under the toilet immediately.

"Is everything okay in there?" Garrett asked from the other

side of the bathroom door.

"Um, I think so. Your toilet sure is high-tech."

Barry let the water level rise enough to signify an emergency. Then he washed his hands and opened the door, just as the water spread across the tiles like a growing lake.

"Oh no!" Garrett ran into the bathroom. "What happened?"

"I can't seem to turn it off," Barry said.

While Garrett frantically worked on the leak, Barry raced for the patio door. As he grasped the handle, he expected an alarm to sound, and sure enough, it blared as soon as he undid the latch.

Now or never.

Barry ran outside into the forest surrounding the big house.

"Grandpa's getting away!" Barry heard Scarlett yelling.

"We have to catch him!" Scott called out.

Barry heard running footsteps trample pine needles. A warm spell had melted most of the snow from the last storm. But underneath the trees were huge patches of un-melted snow where Barry's footprints would be clearly visible.

I won't leave any trail.

Barry climbed an old cottonwood tree, bare of leaves in winter. He balanced along a big branch and leapt, catching the branch of another tree. Hopefully, the surrounding evergreens hid him in the branches of the naked cottonwood trees.

When he successfully clambered into a third cottonwood, he stopped to listen. The voices were distant. Barry took out one of his hearing aids and increased the volume, just to be sure. He put it back in, and the voices sounded even further away. *They must have gone the wrong way.* But off in the distance beyond the property, Barry could hear lots of cars driving. Fast. He climbed down and followed the sound.

When the road came into view, he immediately recognized it.

Highway 24. This isn't Black Forest, but I'm still in Colorado. He saw a sign for The North Pole amusement park, boasting the "world's highest Ferris wheel." Not to be confused with tallest. He could see the normal-sized Ferris wheel that just happened to be perched on the side of a mountain. Barry remembered taking Marty there when he was little. Maybe if this all worked out, he could take Scott and Scarlett there someday, too.

But Marty comes first.

The North Pole was ten miles west of Colorado Springs. An easy hike if Barry wasn't in a rush. But escaping a kidnapping required haste. Barry jogged down to the highway and stuck his thumb out, unafraid of the dangers of hitchhiking.

Standing still, the January air seeped through his sweat-damp workout suit. Barry hoped he didn't have to wait long for a ride. Cars whizzed past, unwilling to take a chance on picking up an old man from the side of the highway. Vehicles sprayed through the slush of melting snow, dousing Barry with the gritty, dirty mush.

An old-looking box truck with rear dualies pulled over. The grizzled driver leaned across the seat and manually rolled the passenger window down. He had a crazed look in his eyes. "If you can beat me at arm wrestling, I'll give you a ride."

What luck!

"You're on."

The driver hopped out of the truck cab and trotted to the guardrail, his big belly quivering like a dish of gelatin. He shoved the sleeve of his T-shirt up, revealing snow-white skin contrasting with his sunburned arm. He rested his elbow on the top rail. Barry clenched and unclenched his hands, getting his blood going. Then he crouched opposite the burly man and rested his elbow on the railing.

The man clasped hands with Barry.

This might not be as easy as I thought. The large man had obviously done this many times. He leveraged his considerable bulk to his advantage. But Barry had toned muscles on his side.

He tried not to think about the family catching him mid-battle with the truck driver. The man grunted and strained.

"You're strong for a wiry old guy," the driver gasped.

"Never underestimate a senior citizen," Barry said through gritted teeth.

With one last straining effort, he slammed the driver's arm down. The man stood up straight, cradling his wrestling arm.

"Pretty good. I'm a man of my word. Hop in."

When he slid into the passenger's seat, Barry felt something poke him. He pulled the flier for the New Year's Revolution Family Bodybuilding Competition out of his pocket. Feelings swirled in Barry's chest. Feelings of . . . regret?

10

✳ Thorne ✳

Thorne told his daughter he was worried about Barry Strong. The truth was, he felt a creeping panic. Thorne didn't have many friends. Actually, he couldn't name anyone other than Barry.

The gym locker yesterday had been the first logical place to seek information about Barry's disappearance, and it had yielded gold. Using his private investigator skills, Thorne picked his next target: Apartment 326.

He peeked around the corner of the hallway in Hummingbird Gardens. The seniors had decorated their doors for the holidays. Last month, Santa Claus and wreaths, stockings and reindeer, sleigh bells and lots of red and green had been on display. This month, New Year's decorations were less exuberant. Maybe the elderly didn't celebrate the passage of time with the enthusiasm of younger folks. Thorne had to admit he understood. He'd wasted what should have been the most precious years of his life.

Passing doors with shiny cutouts of champagne glasses, top hats, and clocks with hands pointing to midnight, Thorne found Barry's apartment. Old Man Time was spotting for a muscled Baby New Year who was bench pressing a barbell with the Sun on one end, and the Moon on the other.

Thorne took his black leather gloves from his trench coat

pockets and slipped them on. He glanced up and down the hallway and gripped his new paperclip from Ramona's office. He steeled himself for another battle of man versus lock. If Diana Diamond hadn't helped out with Barry's gym locker, Thorne might have gotten arrested by George's grandson. *I'll just have to be a lot faster this time.*

First, he tapped on the door. Thorne didn't want to walk in on the old guy if he was entertaining that lady friend. There was no answer.

Thorne tried the knob. To his shock, it was unlocked. Hummingbird Gardens was a safe senior building, but he would have to remind Barry to pay more attention to security.

Stepping inside, Thorne saw why Barry might be lax about locking up. There was nothing worth stealing. No thief would risk jail for a few pieces of mismatched thrift store furniture.

On the walls hung photos of Barry's insanely muscled body clad in nothing but tiny posing trunks that left barely anything to the imagination. There were also photos of Barry fully clothed. Barry, with a full head of blond hair, in a wedding photo. Barry, holding a baby wrapped in a blue blanket. An older Barry holding another baby who must have been his grandson.

The rest of the decor consisted of a few dumbbells and exercise bands, a balance ball, and a surprising number of trophies. The trophies looked like they were made of solid gold. Thorne picked one up with his gloved hand. It weighed almost nothing. *It's probably just plastic coated in metallic paint.* The trophies weren't worth any money.

The bedroom door stood open, but Thorne approached it with dread. He hoped Barry's money troubles hadn't made him resort to taking his own life. Or had he passed away from natural causes in bed? Or worse, in the small bathroom? Only after Thorne had cleared both areas could he exhale a sigh of relief.

There was no evidence Barry had packed for a trip. One shabby suitcase sat in the bedroom closet. Barry's clothes were well-worn, except for his workout and competition clothes. But

Thorne realized he had seen every set of shorts, running slacks, tech shirts, and jackets in the gym over and over.

Barry is broke.

Hummingbird Gardens was one of the nicest senior living communities in Colorado Springs. Barry couldn't keep up with the rent. Thorne felt bad for his friend. And himself. Thorne was headed for golden years that were likely to be as rusty as Barry's, unless his PI business improved.

A flash of bright yellow caught Thorne's eye from the closet floor. He stooped to pick up the tiny scrap of fabric.

"Ahh!" Thorne dropped it.

Barry had informed Thorne he would need posing trunks if he got in good enough shape to be in bodybuilding competitions. Trunks hardly described this article. They were comparable to his ex-wife's thong underwear, but with a little more fabric in the front.

Thorne brushed his gloved fingers down his pant leg, hoping the yellow posing trunks hadn't been worn.

Thorne nosed around the rest of the sparsely furnished apartment, seeking clues. On the kitchen counter were store-brand protein shake mixes, bananas going brown, and an ancient blender.

Returning to the dining-living area, Thorne saw an old leatherbound checkbook. He opened it and scanned the register. At least eighty percent of the entries listed Marty Strong as the payee. *He gives an awful lot of money to his grandson.*

Then Thorne noticed a life insurance policy on the two-person dining table. Odd, for it to be sitting out, instead of being filed away in a drawer or somewhere more private.

Thorne felt a clutching in his chest, like his heart was constricting. Had Barry been bumped off for the insurance money? If that were true, the recipient wouldn't hide his body. Barry would have to be found for a person to file a claim.

Thorne turned pages in the policy with his gloved hands, looking for the beneficiary.

Martin Strong. Barry told Thorne that his grandson Marty was his only living relative.

On a plastic end table, Thorne found an address book. He was happy seniors didn't rely on their cell phones to contain their entire lives, like his daughter's generation. Thorne still owned an old-fashioned address book, but he hadn't updated it since he started using smartphones. He flipped through Barry's book until he found "Marty Strong."

Thorne took a photo of the contact info with his phone. Little shards of glass sprinkled onto the floor from the cracked screen, but it still functioned. Maybe after he got a paying PI gig, he could replace it.

Was Barry so broke he moved in with his grandson? It would be easy enough to go to Marty's house to find out.

I'm not buying that vacation story.

When it came to murder cases, the primary motivations were love or money. That mystery woman from the New Year's Eve party . . . From Thorne's observations, Barry wasn't the heartbreaker type. It seemed more likely this was all about money. Thorne hoped he was wrong. He glanced again at the life insurance policy.

One sole heir. Payout amount: $250,000.

11

✳ Brie ✳

Brie was going brain-dead, performing the monotonous task of updating the HMCA website with the new year's registration dates for spring classes and sports programs. She barely noticed the people entering the building and walking past her curving desk.

"Mowrow."

An enormous orange Persian cat in a harness, dragging a woman at the end of his leash, rubbed against Brie's leg. "Professor Fluffingston? What are you doing here?"

Brie leaned over to pet the cat.

"Wait!" Poppy Prince darted between Brie and the cat brandishing a bottle of hand sanitizer. "Your oily, germy hands will ruin the Professor's fur."

Ugh. Poppy. She worked as the assistant manager for Hummingbird Gardens. Ramona Grant was her boss. But because HMCA and Hummingbird were connected properties, Brie and Poppy spent a lot of time in each other's spaces. Brie dried out her oily, disease-laden hands with the harsh sanitizer. Only then did she place the cat in her lap and begin giving Professor Fluffingston a rub down. *So soft!*

"I thought Ramona told you not to bring your cat to work anymore," Brie said loudly over the Professor's rumbling purr.

"She did, but we're legal now. Professor Fluffingston is my officially certified service cat."

"Really?" Brie asked. "I thought Colorado laws were pretty strict about that sort of thing."

"I become a danger to myself and others without the Professor," Poppy said.

Brie couldn't question that, though she wondered how Poppy had gone about proving it to the state of Colorado.

"Do you need something?" Brie asked Poppy.

"I just came to get George Saito's new membership card for the HMCA. Have you printed it yet?"

"It's in his welcome packet. Here you go." Brie held the cat to her lap as she reached for a shiny blue and white folder with the Happy Marmot logo on it. The giant mountain rodent's toothy smile was more scary than cheerful. But a big donor to the HMCA had created the logo, so they were stuck with it. "I can't reach it."

"Got it." Poppy lifted the folder. "What's this card underneath for?"

Brie glanced at the official business card for Officer Riggs Saito.

"Oh, George's grandson left it in case we have trouble."

"Trouble with what?" Poppy said flippantly. "Nothing ever happens here."

"Trouble with George?" Brie suggested. The old man was a handful, from what she'd seen already. *And he's only been here two days.* "I was debating calling Officer Saito about Barry Strong."

Poppy grinned. "What's that old charmer up to?" she asked.

"Barry hasn't come to work out at all the last couple of days," Brie said. "That's not like him."

"I heard he's on vacation," Poppy said. "Even though he didn't mention anything about it when we were dancing on New Year's Eve."

"Oh?" Brie focused her attention on Poppy. Was she the

mystery woman her father had mentioned? Poppy was in her forties, which meant Barry was old enough to be her father. *Gross.* Brie wasn't close friends with Poppy. She was too embarrassed to come right out and ask her if she went home with Barry that night. Instead, she asked, "What did you and Barry talk about?"

"Cat kibble brands with the highest proportion of protein per gram," Poppy replied.

Brie knew Barry didn't have a cat. Was he so hard up for money that he'd been fueling his bodybuilding workouts by eating cat food? Brie shuddered.

"The man knows his protein sources," Poppy continued. "He's a very interesting gentleman. But I'd better get going. Come along, Professor."

The cat dug its claws into Brie's thighs to launch himself down from her lap. He trotted after his mistress. *More like his slave.* Fur that soft required hours of brushing each day.

Brie studied Poppy as she left. Brie's father must know who Poppy was, but maybe he didn't recognize her all dressed up for the party? He wasn't always the most observant person, despite his chosen career. Poppy might very well be the mystery woman Barry had been with before he disappeared. What if Barry's body was now the protein source in Professor Fluffingston's cat chow?

Brie picked up and held the police officer's business card. Should she call him and report Barry was missing? *Tell him I suspect Poppy of kibblizing his corpse?* Brie set the card down. *I'm letting my true-crime obsession color my thoughts.*

Maybe he blew all of his money on his vacation. The unpaid rent. Not telling her dad he'd be gone. Irresponsible, but nothing worth calling the cops for.

Brie turned her attention back to work, but she was interrupted almost as soon as she started.

"Excuse me," a male voice said. Brie looked up from her computer monitor to see a handsome guy standing in front of her desk. Well, almost handsome. He was a cute white guy in that average Joe kind of way. A little on the pudgy side. *As if I should judge someone for that.* He gave her a slick smile that suggested he thought he was cooler than he actually was, and put out his hand to shake hers. "Hi, my name is Marty."

"Brie. Nice to meet you," Brie replied, shaking Marty's soft hand. He held on uncomfortably long. Brie pulled away. "What can I do for you?"

"Lots of things," Marty said with a wink.

Brie looked behind her. What was he winking at? "Okay?"

"But for now, have you seen my grandfather, Barry Strong? He told me he's usually here at the HMCA, working out."

"You're Barry's grandson?" Brie asked. There was definitely a resemblance. It was like looking at a young Barry if Barry were out of shape and had thinning dark brown hair. "I haven't seen him since New Year's Eve."

Maybe he really is missing!

"I just checked the weight room and the men's locker room. He's not there. And he hasn't been answering his phone." Marty pulled his smartphone out of his pocket. It was the latest iPhone. Probably expensive. "His voicemail greeting is what weirds me out the most. Listen to this."

Marty punched a button. Brie listened as the call went to voicemail. Instead of Barry, a distorted recording of a female voice played.

"Barry is on vacation. He will not be available until January eighth. Have a nice day!"

Brie's father was actually right. Something was very wrong with Barry's disappearance.

"I wonder if the lady talking was the one he left with on New Year's Eve," Brie said.

"Grandpa never told me he had a girlfriend." Marty frowned.

"I don't know if they were in a relationship." If they weren't, the woman definitely shouldn't be recording new voicemail greetings for Barry. "I think we should call the police," Brie said. She pulled Rigg's card off the counter. But Marty placed his hand on her arm, stopping her.

"I . . . don't think we need to get the police involved. He's probably fine. I hope he's not avoiding me."

"Oh," Brie replied. *Why would Barry avoid his grandson?* "Have you checked his apartment?"

"Um, what number is that again?"

Marty doesn't know his grandfather's apartment number? If I had grandparents, I'd visit them all the time! Unless they were as grumpy as George Saito.

Risking being rude, Brie blurted out, "It doesn't sound like you're very close to your grandfather."

"We're close. Very. I feel really bad telling a stranger about this," Marty said solemnly. "But you and me won't be strangers for long." He winked again. Maybe he had an eye condition. "Grandpa owes me money. What's his apartment number?"

Brie did a quick check of Barry's HMCA folder for his address at Hummingbird Gardens. She hoped she was doing the right thing. There was definitely that family resemblance. But what if this guy wasn't his grandson? *What if he's a collector for the mob? The Colorado Springs mob? Is that a thing?* It definitely had been in Pueblo, Colorado.

"Uh, I need to see an ID before I can give out information about a patron."

Marty twisted his lips to one side in annoyance, but he extracted his wallet. He flashed his driver's license at her. Brie took note of his address and tried to memorize his birthdate. *Officer Saito might need this info later.*

"Apartment 326," Brie said. She wanted to gather more information about Marty, but people were queuing up behind him. They peeked around him, obviously wanting her attention. "I'd love to chat, but I'm really busy right now."

"Perhaps we could talk later." Marty's slick smile returned. "Over dinner?"

"Huh?" Brie asked.

"Like, a date," Marty said. "You know."

"A date," Brie said slowly. She didn't think Marty was her type, but did she even have one? No one had ever asked her on a date before. *Why not? What's wrong with me?* At age twenty-five, she was going to go on her first date with a guy she wasn't even interested in? *Just to see what it's like . . . No, Brie, you are not desperate! That's not why you're going to say yes. You just need to find out what's going on with Barry. You're working undercover. Like Dad.* "Yes. I'll go."

"Great. Do you work tomorrow?"

"Yeah."

"When's your next day off?"

"Thursday," Brie said. Having a weekday off was very convenient, and she didn't usually have anything to do on weekends anyway.

"Then I'll pick you up Wednesday evening. When do you get off work?"

Marty's concern for his grandfather flew right out the window. Thorne might credit his gut with suspecting something was off about Barry's disappearance. To Brie, all it required was open eyes and ears.

Something fishy was definitely going on, and Brie was going on a fishing trip. Hopefully, all the tips she had amassed from true crime podcasts in notes on her phone would be enough to keep her safe.

12

✳ Barry ✳

"My name's Barry, by the way. I'm sorry, I don't have any gas money," he told the truck driver. Barry had to be older than the guy by a decade.

"Frankie G. Nice to meet ya." The scruffy-bearded white man took one hand off the steering wheel and shook Barry's. "I don't need gas, but I hope you can entertain me. I'm bored to tears. Radio barely works on Highway 24. I've only got these cassette tapes, and I've already heard each like three times already."

Barry glanced through the relics. Marty Robbins: Gunfighter Ballads. Sons of the Pioneers with Roy Rogers: Tumbling Tumbleweeds. Gene Autry: Back in the Saddle Again. And two more from only a few decades ago.

"This is a nice collection," Barry said.

"Not really. I don't have much choice. These are the last five cassette tapes I've got that are still playable. I wore out the rest of them years ago. Cassettes are hard to find. And no way am I updating the stereo on this old truck. I'm only hauling ostrich feathers."

The cab of the truck was the lowest of low tech. Talk about old school. Barry didn't feel like such an antique next to this guy.

"Ostrich feathers?" Barry raised his eyebrows.

Frankie G. waved a hand toward the back of the box truck. "I've got about one-hundred pounds of them in the back."

"This truck seems rather large to carry such light cargo."

"The feathers take up a lot of space. There are about a thousand feathers per pound, and they won't sell if they're all bent up. Fancy boutiques in Denver buy 'em by the truckload. For what, God only knows. I'm on my way to the Mile-High City now. Me and the missus have got us a little ostrich farm this side of Gunnison."

"How'd you get into raising ostriches?"

"Good eatin'," Frankie G. said. "You'd probably guess they taste like chicken. But they don't. They're more like sweet lean beef than anything."

"That's . . . really something," Barry said, trying not to gag as he imagined Frankie G. gnawing on a giant beef-flavored drumstick. "Where did you get the birds?"

"Africa, of course!" The man laughed. "But that's not an interesting story."

Barry doubted that. But he didn't speak further on the subject.

Frankie G. sighed heavily. "I'm getting bored again."

He pulled the truck over to the shoulder of Highway 24. Traffic rushed by on the narrow, curving road. A sheer cliff wall towered above them on the left-hand side. On the right, a drop off fell away to a rushing stream.

"Why are we stopping here?" Barry asked.

"You gonna tell me about yourself, or am I gonna have to make room for a more interesting hitchhiker?"

Barry's heart pounded like he was running hundred-meter hurdles. The prospect of hitching for a ride again chilled him to his bones. Literally. His workout suit was damp from his previous dousing with snowmelt. He forced words out of his mouth as quickly as possible.

"I'm a seventy-year-old widower. I retired from quality

engineering at Warehouse Amalgamated Appliance Apparatuses three years ago."

"Boring." Frankie G. shook his head and pointed at the door.

"I'm a championship bodybuilder!"

"Now that's interesting." Frankie G. put the truck into gear with a grinding noise and pulled back onto the highway. "So what's it like taking steroids? They really shrink your you-know-whats?" The man nodded downward, eying Barry's lap.

Barry didn't take steroids, but would that make him less "interesting" to Frankie G.? Barry decided the best course of action would be to make up stuff to guarantee he got a ride all the way home.

"It's true. They've shrunk to the size of two hazelnuts," Barry lied.

Frankie G. burst into laughter. "You must be crazy to trade those for bigger muscles. Mind if I have a look?"

"Um, maybe when we're done driving," Barry said, hoping the man would forget about it by then. "But there's not much to see, if you know what I mean."

Barry made up a bunch of stories exaggerating popular bodybuilding stereotypes. "I'm on my way to Mexico to refill my supply of the hormones I inject every day. I've got a system for sneaking them over the border."

Frankie G. was eating it all up. The poor man had been bored out of his mind.

Or maybe he's just out of his mind.

The antique truck had at least one piece of modern tech resting in one side of a two-cup drink holder Frankie G. must have installed himself. His cellphone rattled back and forth with every curve in the road. The other cup holder struggled to contain a thirty-two-ounce convenience store beverage in an unnatural hue of orange, the melting ice sloshing and clinking.

Once they were inside the Colorado Springs city limits, Frankie G. seemed in better spirits.

"Could I make a call on your phone?" Barry asked. "I was unexpectedly detained out of town. My grandson must be worried sick about me by now."

"Lost your phone?" the driver asked. "Let me guess. You smashed it in a fit of roid rage."

"Yes," Barry said. "You guessed it. How embarrassing." He'd agree to almost anything to avoid giving the true answer. Being kidnapped by a ninja and held against his will by an entire family of bodybuilders sounded even crazier than being a professional ostrich feather delivery service.

"No problem. I've got minutes." Frankie G. unlocked his phone and handed it to Barry.

Barry was glad he had memorized important phone numbers. So many people completely lost touch if their phones were broken or lost. After three rings, Marty answered.

"Wh-who is this?" He sounded anxious, as though he'd been expecting an unwanted call.

"Your grandfather," Barry said. "I lost my phone, and a nice man let me use his."

"Where the heck are you?" That was the demanding, whiny tone Barry was used to.

"On my way home," Barry said.

"You'd better be!" Marty's voice was so loud, the driver glanced at Barry, one bushy eyebrow quirked high on his weathered, creased forehead. "I've been looking for you since New Year's Eve, but do you care? No! I need cash money. Now! Meanwhile, you're out partying with some slutty old lady."

"How do you know about that? You wouldn't even come to the party when I invited you."

"That's what you make all those muscles for, right?" Marty said in a nasty tone of voice. "To impress the ladies?"

Barry needed to end this uncomfortable exchange. "I'll see you when I get home," he said more calmly than he felt.

"If you don't get there soon, just come see me at the hospital," Marty said. "That's where I'll be after the loan shark takes both my legs as payment!"

Barry clicked off the call and placed the phone back in the cup holder.

"I couldn't help but overhear," the driver said.

"No doubt," Barry said. "My grandson can be . . . emotional."

"Are you giving him the money?"

Barry sighed. "If I don't–"

"If you don't, maybe he learns responsibility. I hate to butt in on family business, but it sounds like that kid needs some tough love."

"You're probably right." Barry knew the driver was absolutely right. He spoiled his grandson after his parents, Barry's son and daughter-in-law, passed away falling off a ski lift in Aspen six years ago when a bald eagle tragically mistook their fur hats for marmots. "Marty is all the family I have left."

"Then it's important you get him straightened out," Frankie G. said. "Before someone removes more than his legs. Like his head."

Was Barry doing the right thing, escaping the Brauny family to help his pampered grandson?

Better the devil you know than the one you don't.

Except the new family actually seemed to want Barry. Not for his money, but for *him.*

Frankie G. pushed a paper lunch bag across the seat. "Hungry? The wife makes me eat healthy, but maybe you can find something edible in there. There's no way I'm eating that rabbit food. I've got dinner plans to eat with a bona fide king." Frankie G. pulled a sheet of coupons for the Royal Hamburger King fast food joint from one of his pockets and showed them to Barry. "I'll make a pitstop in Castle Rock for a real meal."

Barry's stomach rumbled rebelliously at the mention of fast food. He hadn't finished his protein shake this morning, and it was getting close to dinner time. He opened the crumpled top of the paper sack and peered inside.

A bundle of celery with wide stalks took up most of the lunch bag. A travel packet of peanut butter and a baggy of baby carrots completed the feast.

"It looks wonderful," Barry said, "but I'll eat dinner when I get home."

Although, as he recalled, his refrigerator was nearly empty, and his pantry bare.

"I insist," the driver said. "It's just going in the trash if you don't eat it. I feel bad my wife wasted her precious time slicing it up for me."

Barry pulled out a celery stalk, dipped the narrow tip in peanut butter, and began nibbling. Before he had reached halfway down the stalk, the driver slowed.

"This looks like your stop."

The driver eased the boxy truck into the Hummingbird Gardens parking lot.

"Thanks, Frankie G.," Barry said. "You've been a real lifesaver."

Barry admired the stately old building, especially beautiful with the late afternoon shadows defining every hewn block of locally quarried limestone and sandstone. The historic 1892 structure had received new life and refurbishment when the abandoned building was repurposed for senior apartment homes.

"Maybe you *can* afford to throw money at your grandkid," the driver said, eyeing the elegant exterior and balconies. "This is a real nice place."

The truth was, helping out Marty put a serious pinch in his budget. Lately, the pinch had turned into a gouge.

Barry tried to open the door to exit the truck cab. The handle wouldn't budge.

"You thought I'd forget, didn't you?" Frankie G. grinned. "So about those hazelnuts you promised me . . . ." Frankie G. rubbed his hands together, then picked up his phone. "I'll need a pic for proof I seen 'em. Just for my wife, you know."

Barry did some quick thinking. *If this doesn't work, I'm in for a fight. I can take him, but it'll hurt.*

"Well, okay." Barry started to tug at his elastic waistband. "But aren't you gonna kiss me first?"

Now Frankie G. looked uncomfortable. "I'm not into dudes like that."

"Come on Frankie," Barry cooed. "I won't tell your wife. It's just a little kiss between manly men. Then I'll let you take as many pictures of my 'hazelnuts' as you want."

"Well, I, uh . . . Hoo!" Frankie G. leaned toward Barry.

Jiminy crickets! This backfired badly.

Just when Barry was about to resign himself to his fate, Frankie G. reached past Barry and tinkered with the door lock. He pulled the handle and set Barry free!

"I'll just have to take your word about your shrunken treasures. You have a nice day." Frankie G. practically pushed Barry out of the truck cab. "And you can keep the celery."

Barry held the stalk as the truck's tires squealed away.

That was a close one. Barry really didn't want his first kiss in years to come from someone with so many whiskers.

He headed for the rear entrance, walking past Thorne Bramble's white Ford Fusion. The guy was probably mad at Barry for not buying him a birthday celery juice. Barry noticed Thorne's windows were rolled down a few inches. It was January, and snow could happen at any time. For a PI, the guy seemed scatterbrained.

I'll get my car keys first. Then I'll hunt down Thorne.

Just as Barry grabbed the back entry door handle, a gloved hand clamped onto his shoulder. Barry spun around.

"You!" Barry stared at the ninja, trying to see beyond the mask to the identity of the person inside. It was hopeless. All he could tell was that the black-clad person had the curvy figure of a woman. "From the parking lot that night. The Braunys told me about you."

"The Braunys want you back." The sound of the strangely modulated voice sent a shiver up Barry's spine.

She sounds distorted. Just like my dance partner. "Who are you really?

"A wise ninja never reveals their identity. It is time to return to your new home."

"I have business to attend to here," Barry said. "Then I'll gladly return. I promise."

"Your word is worth nothing," the ninja said. "You violated the contract."

"I haven't signed the contract yet," Barry said. "And I don't like being treated like a prisoner."

He anticipated the grasping hand seconds before the ninja reached for him. Barry did a squat, evading the gloved hand. Then he scrambled to his feet and ran.

Some bodybuilders were all bulk and no grace. Barry prided himself on maintaining his agility and cardio fitness. He wove around parked vehicles. Escape didn't seem impossible. And yet, the ninja had already captured him once. Just in case, he nibbled the celery stalk into the shape of a ninja star, then wrapped it in the bodybuilder flier.

Racing around Thorne's late model sedan, he thrust the package through the gapped open window. Hopefully, Thorne would understand the message.

Barry bolted for the dim patch of woods growing behind the parking lot. He made it three steps onto the pine needle-padded soil when a silky black rope whipped around and circled his legs. He fell to the soft earth with a denture-jarring thud.

13

❋ Thorne ❋

Thorne eased out of Barry's apartment after a quick check of the hallway. Snooping around his buddy's place hadn't yielded anything solid.

Not true. He'd verified Barry hadn't packed for a trip. Unless he went to a nudist colony. And the insurance policy with only one beneficiary?

I need to investigate his grandson. Marty Strong.

It was the best lead Thorne had. Barry's apartment yielded no clues about the identity of the mystery woman. Perhaps the grandson's home held the solution to Barry's disappearance. As he trotted down the stairs, he heard the elevator ding. Someone was coming, and Thorne had barely escaped being detected. *Good job, old boy.* Thorne headed for the atrium.

A sea of humanity milled around the humid, plant-filled haven, busily going about their daily affairs. Each with their own story. Their own purpose. Full of mystery. Thorne eyed the senior citizens of Hummingbird Gardens with suspicion. Did Marty off his grandfather for the life insurance, or was one of Barry's neighbors mad enough to kill him? Motivation: old man jealousy of the attention Barry received New Year's Eve? Old woman romance gone wrong? Was he being held captive? Perhaps for a ransom he couldn't pay.

"Where are you, Barry?" Thorne muttered to himself as he walked.

"What did you say?" the cookie lady asked. She held a plate of warm, freshly baked peanut butter cookies. They made a small light brown mountain on the plate.

"Ah, nothing," Thorne said. He doubted she had anything to do with Barry's disappearance, but a good PI left no tree un-shook for information. "Has Barry Strong been around lately?"

"Oh, him." The cookie lady wrinkled her nose in disgust. "He acts as if my treats are poisonous. We don't get on well. I haven't seen him. Cookie?" She held her plate a little closer to Thorne's face. "I also tried my hand at making peanut brittle. Did you know that January twenty-sixth is National Peanut Brittle Day?" She moved the cookie mound aside to reveal golden slabs of brittle. "Give it a try."

"I'd better not," Thorne said regretfully. She had just mentioned poison after all. Did she dislike Barry enough to kill him and hide his body? But she was such a sweet old lady, and the treats looked worth dying for.

"Are you allergic?" The cookie lady looked concerned. "Or do you not like peanuts?" The woman looked ready to cry.

"No, nothing like that. I just swore off cookies after the ones you gave me yesterday. For the new year, you know." Thorne watched a tear spill down the woman's wrinkled cheek. "But I didn't swear off candy! Ha ha!"

Thorne removed his gloves and took a piece. Peanut brittle was always disappointing. It usually tasted like burnt peanuts and had the texture of a clay pot. He was sure that after a bite of this, he could restrain his appetite and get back to his resolution.

Thorne gave it a nibble. His teeth met very little resistance. The candy was only slightly more crunchy than a good flaky pie crust. Soft vanilla undertones married with the mildly salty nuggets of perfectly roasted peanuts.

"I hope it's okay. It mostly turned out." The cookie lady looked worried as she brushed the tear away.

Thorne nearly burst into tears himself. Tears of ecstasy. Composing himself, he replied, "Dear woman." *What's her name again? Does it even matter?* "This is the finest peanut brittle ever created by human hands."

The cookie lady looked pleased. "Would you like a little more?"

Thorne didn't want a little more. He wanted all of it. But he restrained himself to only four more slabs.

"Thank you," he said, and departed from her. He nibbled as he tried to remember what he was doing when she showed up.

Hunting for clues to Barry's disappearance.

Thorne exited the atrium. Chill air swirled inside his open trench coat. He really wished he could button it closed over his round tummy. The parking lot was dim. Sunset came so early this time of year.

Then he saw Barry's car. Thorne put the rest of the peanut brittle in one of his many trench coat pockets for later. If it got fuzz or dirt on it, he could just rinse off the candy when he got home. *Time to investigate.*

Thorne ducked slightly and walked with a little more shoulder and hip movement than usual, imitating a spy he'd seen in a movie, and slunk over to Barry's car. He pressed a palm against the hood. *Cold. Of course. It's January.*

Thorne checked the tailpipe for a clue to jump out at him. He wasn't really sure what to look for. But then he noticed the snow underneath Barry's car. It was on the south side of the parking lot, facing the sun. If Barry had moved it in the last few days, that snow would be gone. Wherever Barry went, he didn't drive himself there. Odd, but there could still be a logical explanation.

I've gotta track Marty Strong down. Thorne had a photo of Barry's address book to lead him to his first strong suspect. *Strong suspect, ha ha.* Hopefully, the old-fashioned address book was up to date.

When Thorne got to Chandos, his 2012 white Ford Fusion,

he noticed his windows were still cracked open from that morning. He had left a head of broccoli in the back seat a few days before when he did some healthy shopping in preparation for the new year. The rotten broccoli had manifested like a poltergeist inside his car. A physical presence that Thorne could feel. A scent he could bite into and taste. Even mouth breathing didn't help. So Thorne had let his car air out all day with the hope of exorcising the stench.

When he opened the door, the rotten scent slapped him in the face. *Maybe I need a priest.*

Thorne turned his head to suck in his last few breaths of fresh air before his drive home and prepared to sit behind the wheel. *What's this?*

Thorne unfolded the colorful piece of paper.

"New Year's Revolution," he read out loud. *A family bodybuilding competition . . . Barry?* The competition looked like it was for all ages, from children to old people. Something fell out of the flier and onto the asphalt of the parking lot. Thorne picked up a pale green piece of . . . celery? *Barry still owes me a celery juice.* This vegetable was bitten into an eight-pointed shape. It reminded Thorne of a ninja star.

Thorne slid into the driver's seat and rolled down all the windows. The afternoon was dark and cold, and getting chillier by the second. It was going to be a long ten-minute drive home. He had a lot to think about.

Bodybuilding and celery could only mean one thing: Barry had been here. And recently, too. The celery was still crisp. *Why is it shaped like a shuriken?*

Thorne had been delayed by his encounter with the cookie lady. He and Barry might have just missed each other. *Bummer. I hope I didn't trade my friend for this peanut brittle.*

14

❋ Brie ❋

Despite agreeing to a dinner date with Barry's grandson Marty in a few days, Brie couldn't stop her eyes from straying to Officer Saito's business card. She admired the white rectangle propped between her keyboard and computer monitor.

The official CSPD emblem stood out prominently on the card, like the crest of some great house from medieval fantasy times. Brie imagined Riggs Saito as a knight in form-fitting shining armor, the eagle-topped CSPD badge enlarged to actual shield size. It protected him as he wielded a video game-style sword bigger than his whole body . . .

Riggs. Another person cursed with an odd first name.

Brie actually didn't mind her own. Most people thought Brie was short for Brianna or something classy like that. *Nope. It was inspired by the gourmet cheese aisle.* She shared a name with the soft French cheese product encased in an edible, white, wax-like coating of mold. Only her father tormented her with his dumb "Cheesy Briesy" nickname. She had to blame both her parents, though. One of them came up with her name, but the other agreed to it. *Why do parents do that to their kids?*

She wondered whether Riggs was short for something. Rigenald, a typo of Reginald on his birth certificate? Riggle, like a wriggling worm? Even though she was busy, the idea nagged at her until she gave up and did some online research.

Her search yielded an odd result. *Riggs is often short for Rigge?* Rigge was apparently the Old English word for ridge. A ridge might be even worse than a cheese.

How do you even pronounce Rigge? The phonetic version was spelled "Rig-g." *Yikes. That doesn't help at all!* Brie tried to make sense of the pronunciation. Rig geh? Rig-uh? Rig jee? *No wonder he goes by Riggs.* That was assuming Riggs was even short for Rigge. His parents might have gone to the food aisle like Brie's parents and named him after rigatoni, the tube-shaped pasta.

All her thoughts about stuff with the "Riggs" sound in them reminded Brie she had Wrigley's Big Red chewing gum in her pocket. *Is Riggs short for Wrigley?* She reached into her pocket. Her hand came back with a coating of cat fur along with the pack of gum. She looked down at her lap. Professor Fluffingston had left Brie much to remember him by. Her tan yoga pants were now pumpkin spice colored. She popped a piece of gum into her mouth and chewed.

Brie didn't regret her lap time with the Professor. She would just have to bring a lint roller to work for future encounters, now that the cat was "official." As she brushed orange fur off her pants, Brie wondered how Poppy had come up with the name Professor Fluffingston. It was a mouthful. Poppy was kind of an unusual name, too.

"Poppies!" Brie tried to sound like the Wicked Witch in The Wizard of Oz. Was Poppy even her real name? If she was responsible for Barry's disappearance . . .

Brie's chewing gum felt odd in her mouth. She pulled it out. More cat fur. *Ugh.*

"Why the sour face?" Lovey Dearheart pressed a hand against the service counter above Brie's desk and struck a dramatic pose. She flicked her pink, white, and red feather boa over one shoulder, tossing her wavy silver hair in the process.

The pink toy poodle cradled in her left arm yipped loudly.

Brie startled and dropped the chewed cat fur gum on her lap. Panicked, she picked it up and stuck it back in her mouth. *Even more cat fur! Yuck!*

"Hush, Duchess," Lovey cooed at the dog. The poodle quieted and licked Lovey's fingers. "Should I come back later, dear?" Lovey asked.

"No!" Brie choked out, keeping her mouth open as she exclaimed the word. "Jus a secon'!" She grabbed a tissue from a box on her desk and finally got rid of the gum. She wiped her tongue with another tissue, making things equally bad when she replaced the fur with white paper dust.

Her mouth was ruined. She pulled the pack out of her pocket. "Would you like a stick of gum?" Brie offered the pack to Lovey.

Duchess strained to sniff at the packet. Lovey pulled her back. "A lady never chews gum," Lovey said disapprovingly.

Brie's mother used to say the same thing.

"It's as offensive as spitting." Lovey cupped a hand around her mouth, leaned in, and whispered, "Or passing gas in public. It would do you well to end both of those bad habits."

What is she suggesting? Do I smell bad?

"Oh, sorry." Brie felt like she'd been caught smoking on an airplane. Hoping to avoid further judgment of her life's choices, Brie reluctantly put the gum back in her pocket. But she wished her mouth still tasted like refreshing cinnamon instead of cat fur and tissue. "What can I help you with, Lovey?"

"I've forgotten completely," Lovey sounded exasperated. "You wiped off your lipstick!"

Lovey's own was perfect. Along with the rest of her makeup, silver hair, and pink satin minidress. For an old lady, she had amazingly shapely legs, balanced on three-inch heels with cream laces crisscrossing her calves. The dog was as stylish as Lovey, with a rhinestone-encrusted ribbon around her pink furry neck.

Brie tried to pat the dog's soft head, but Duchess's tongue

created a wet forcefield between Brie and her goal.

"I wasn't wearing lipstick." Brie only owned one tube. It was left over from when she had dressed up as a Monster High doll for Halloween one year. The lipstick was purple and probably wouldn't fly with most of the HMCA clients.

"Well, no wonder," Lovey sighed dramatically.

Before Brie could ask what she meant by that, Lovey continued.

"How do you expect to attract the attention of handsome young men unless you make some effort to enhance your natural beauty?"

"Beauty?" Brie asked. She had always considered herself mousey and plain. Maybe her clothing choices didn't help that image. Because she worked at a gym, she got to wear yoga pants and HMCA t-shirts every day. All of it was a size bigger than she needed for the sake of comfort. She wasn't thin like her mother and was uncomfortable showing off her curves. As for makeup, she could never compete in looks with Mom, and so she had never tried. Brie felt like she was just a brown, poofy-haired female version of her white father. Not that Thorne was bad looking. He was just so average. *Like me.*

"You are a lovely young woman. Didn't you notice how that new tenant, George's grandson, looked at you?" Lovey waved a hand. "Oh! That reminds me of why I'm really here. Ramona wants me to sign George up for my class to help him feel welcome. Can you update my roster?"

"Yeah. Of course." Brie tapped her keyboard. "But he has a rollator. Will that be okay in your dance class?"

"Darling! Yes!" Lovey laughed. "Haven't you ever seen chair dancing?"

"Maybe?" Brie said, a little worried. She had only seen exotic dancing in the movie version of the musical Gypsy, about the burlesque dancer Gypsy Rose Lee. *Isn't a chair dance the same as a lap dance?* Brie pictured balding George grinding against his rolling walker. Hopefully, that wasn't what Lovey meant. But her dance class was more like burlesque than anything.

Duchess loomed over Brie as she updated the roster, panting and wiggling in Lovey's arms. When Brie was done, Lovey said, "George's grandson." She raised her eyebrows. "That policeman. He's quite a looker."

Brie felt her cheeks grow warm.

Lovey leaned in and whispered to Brie over Duchess's head. "And I have a good reason to believe he's single."

Brie doubted that. Nice-looking young men with careers were never single. *Maybe he doesn't even like women.*

"What's him being single have to do with me?" Brie asked. "What if I'm in a relationship?"

Lovey smiled. "If you were, then I would know about it."

She was probably right. The last time Brie had her annual physical, Lovey knew Brie's cholesterol and blood sugar results before Brie herself had gotten them. When Brie asked how, Lovey's only response had been, "A woman knows."

"I'll keep an eye on Officer Saito for you." Lovey winked. "But I noticed you talking to another gentleman yesterday. Who was he? He wasn't as dashing as the policeman, but he was quite attentive."

Of course she noticed, even though Brie didn't know Lovey was even in the HMCA at the time.

"Marty. He's Barry Strong's grandson." Flustered by Lovey's implication that Brie was hopeless in the romance department, she blurted out, "He asked me out Wednesday night."

"How exciting!" Lovey squeezed her green eyes closed and pressed her folded hands to her considerable bosom peeking over the top of her minidress. "Love is in the air!"

"It's just dinner," Brie said, sorry she had mentioned the date. She considered it more of an opportunity to investigate Barry's disappearance than an opportunity for romance. *Barry* . . . "By the way. Have you seen Barry Strong lately?"

"I noticed him leave the dance Friday night. It was quite late. I couldn't understand why he and his dance partner left before midnight." Lovey winked. "But then again, perhaps romance couldn't wait. I haven't seen him since."

"Not since the New Year's Eve party?" Brie asked. *Just like everyone else.*

Lovey tapped a finger to her chin. "I haven't noticed him in the weight room. He's easy to spot." Lovey patted a hand on top of her head. It was a polite way to point out Barry's baldness. The man's head was somewhat reflective under the harsh gym lighting. "I do hope everything is all right. He's missed two training days. That's very odd for him."

"Did you recognize the woman he left with?" Brie held her breath.

"No, dear. With all the makeup she wore and that ridiculous wig, she could have been anyone. Even you!" Lovey giggled. "I might have a video with her in it." Lovey spent the next several minutes scrolling through every image in her phone, even though the party was only two nights ago. "Here she is."

Lovey's video had been taken in selfie mode. She and Duchess took up most of the frame, but Brie could make out Barry's bald head reflecting rainbow light like an organic disco ball. The woman in his arms was difficult to see, but that wig could be covering a head of red hair. She could be Poppy Prince. *Or anybody, really.* Maybe Brie would be able to make out some details if she watched the video on a bigger screen.

"Can you send this to me?" Brie would open the file on her home laptop later.

Lovey struggled with her phone until Brie was on the verge of taking the device and sending the video herself. But Lovey figured it out on her own.

"Please have him check in at the front desk if you get to talk to him, Lovey," Brie said.

"Of course." Lovey pressed one finger to her lips and studied Brie. "I do hope you have something to wear on your date."

"Um." Brie did a mental inventory of her closet. Sweats, yoga pants, HMCA t-shirts. She was allowed to wear tennis shoes to work. Otherwise, during her off hours she sported generic Crocs. *Do I own dress shoes anymore?*

She might have to raid her mother's walk-in closet. Mom left impractical clothes and shoes behind when she started her spiritual journey. *And that woman had a very impractical wardrobe.* Brie was certain she could borrow some shoes. But could she squeeze her more generous curves into any of her mother's clothing?

"I'm sure I can make something work." An alarm went off on Brie's phone. "Oh! It's time for me to go home." She began packing up her tote bag and turning off her desktop computer. Lovey was still standing there with Duchess when Brie stood to leave.

"Is there something else you need before I go?" Brie asked politely, although she was growing impatient with Lovey. Retired people had all the time in the world.

"You need my help," Lovey said. She set Duchess on the floor and grabbed Brie's arm.

"What are you doing?" Brie asked.

"This can't wait." Lovey tugged Brie out of the HMCA and into the atrium that connected to Hummingbird Gardens. The little dog ran in circles around the two women.

"Where are you taking me?" Brie asked.

"To Sam Slate's apartment," Lovey said. "For a makeover."

"What? My date isn't until Wednesday night."

"This is an emergency. We're going to need every available minute." Lovey pulled a cellphone from her cream satin pocketbook and began tapping numbers one-handed. She held the phone to her ear as she kept dragging Brie. "Sam? We have a situation here."

15

❋ Barry ❋

"Help." The single word pushed past Barry's lips in a whisper. The fall had knocked the wind out of him.

Barry watched helplessly as Thorne's sedan drove off. His escape attempt had ended in failure. That was not a familiar state. At least in the physical realm, Barry was accustomed to winning, taking the prize at nearly every bodybuilding competition he entered.

Perhaps his physical prowess was going the way of the rest of his life. Losing his wife. His son and daughter-in-law. Loss after painful loss.

The ninja zip-tied his wrists together behind his back and pulled a hood over his head before unwrapping the rope from his ankles. He had no choice but to let her steer him behind the half dozen cottages and through the woods.

The residents of the senior apartments treasured their seclusion in the midst of the city. The vast lawns and heavily treed natural groves surrounding the Hummingbird Gardens Senior Apartments, the HMCA, and the connecting atrium, were a selling point that was working against Barry now. Didn't anyone see him being kidnapped? Again?

Doubtful. Even if someone happened to be looking out their window at just the right moment, the thick, snow-dusted pine trees shielded him from view.

A vehicle door clicked open. The ninja shoved Barry inside and strapped a seat belt across his chest. The door slammed shut.

"My arms," Barry said. "This is hideously uncomfortable."

"I obviously can't trust you," the ninja grumbled in her oddly mechanical voice. "You ran away once. You'll remove that hood."

"I won't." Barry pulled against the zip ties, pinning his arms behind his back. "I–" He almost uttered the word "promise," but realized how ineffective that would be.

"The Braunys are good people who will make you happy," the ninja said from what sounded like the front seat of the car. "You can't go back to an unhealthy relationship with your grandson. Sign the contract to make your wish come true."

Barry remembered his muttered words on the dance floor. *I wish I had a family.* The ninja was right about one thing. Barry was in a state of bliss with the Braunys. Their kids were adorable.

They want *to be my grandkids.* They could be one big happy family if Barry signed the contract.

But what about Marty? He wouldn't be happy with two missing legs. Barry needed to bail out the boy this one last time. He was in counseling for his gambling addiction. Marty wouldn't need Barry's financial help again. Then Barry could become a permanent part of the Brauny family.

"New Year's Eve." Despite her disguised voice and the hood, Barry was certain now. "You heard my wish. You wore a disguise. You tricked me," Barry said from his seat in what he guessed was an SUV. "It's rich, you accusing me of being untrustworthy, after you put on that act. Toying with my affections. That wasn't makeup. It was a mask!"

"Barry, it was for the best," the ninja replied.

"Who are you?"

Silence.

Barry huffed. "And why'd you zip tie me and put this hood

over my head? I can't see a blooming thing!"

"I have to cover your face so I don't have to cover my own. Wise ninjas never drive cars with masks on. What would the police think?"

She's insane. If I can get my hands free, I can see her face, then bail out of this vehicle. Run for help. He struggled again, but the thick zip ties dug painfully into his wrists.

"Where are we going?" Barry asked.

"Home."

Well, that's better than a shallow grave, I suppose.

"I was trying to go there when you stopped me," Barry said. "My home."

"Do you mean your residence?" the ninja asked. "That drab apartment? It barely looks lived in. Can you really call it a home?"

That explains the hearing aid charger and denture cleaning tablets in my suite at the Brauny house. The ninja has been in my apartment! Somehow, that felt nearly as violating as being kidnapped.

"You're taking me back to the Braunys?"

"Correct. If they'll still have you."

"What are you getting out of this whole bit?" The Brauny family, by outward appearances, had plenty of resources. Perhaps there was good money to be made by snatching an old man out of his world. That might explain the ninja's motivation, but what were the Braunys after? Was it really as innocent as it seemed? "You can't just put people together and make them become a family! I already have a family. Marty's in troub–"

"Barry. Let go. Let him find his way back to you."

She sounded like that truck driver. Barry suspected the ninja was much younger than him, like Frankie G. Who were these youngsters to give him advice?

"I'm seventy years old, and you think you can tell me how to live my life?"

"Ninjas are wise beyond their years."

What a load of malarkey.

After a half-hour-long drive, the ninja stopped the vehicle. She pulled Barry out. He desperately wanted a glimpse of her face, but his hands were bound, the black hood still blinding Barry to the world around him. He heard birds chirping. The skittering sound of a squirrel or chipmunk racing about its business.

"Be careful," the ninja said. "We just have to walk a little way before I can release you."

She held his arm firmly as she escorted Barry across a soft carpet of snow-dampened pine needles. Each awkward step he took released more of the woodsy odor. They were at the Brauny family's house in the woods. Barry was sure of it.

They stopped. The ninja released her grip on his bicep. He heard the chime of a doorbell. The zip ties snapped free. Barry reached for his hood, but the ninja was already jerking it off his head. He spun around to look at her.

She had returned her ninja hood over her head and face, masking herself.

"Behave," she said as the door began to open. She tossed a small round ball at the ground. *Poof!* Smoke erupted from it. The ninja vanished in the cloud.

Barry tried to peer through the smoke to see her vehicle. A license plate. But she had parked it somewhere it wouldn't be visible. Plus, the pine trees' dusky shadows obscured everything.

The door opened, and a shaft of yellow light set the front steps aglow.

"It's Grandpa!" Scarlett exclaimed and threw her arms around Barry.

"Thank goodness the ninja found you," Buffy said, wringing her hands nervously. "Dad, I'm so glad you're all right. We were so worried we might have lost you!"

Scott came running. "Grandpa!" He joined Scarlett in the hug.

Garrett walked up and shook Barry's hand firmly. "I'm so

happy you're back." He didn't cry but his eyes looked awfully shiny. "We understand why you left. This is an unconventional situation. But if you just trust in the process–"

"Just five more days, Grandpa! Please!" Scott stared up into Barry's face.

"Then we'll be a forever family!" Scarlett exclaimed.

It was difficult for Barry to be mad at people who cared about him so much. Despite his concern about being a kidnapping victim, Barry couldn't suppress a smile.

He followed the family into the house. No one demanded an explanation. No scolding for running away. It was like he hadn't even been gone.

"We baked a cake for you," Scarlett beamed. "I decorated it myself."

"Oh, that's so thoughtful, Scarlett," Barry said with a pang of guilt. "But I don't consume sweets."

"Of course! We knew that, Grandpa." Scott said. "This cake is extra special. There's no sugar in it."

"It's my special carrot cake recipe," Buffy said with pride. "It's mostly carrots and eggs."

"My arm got a good workout grating the carrots for you, Dad," Garrett said.

"I helped make the icing!" Scott exclaimed. "I mixed up protein powder and water. It tastes *really* good."

"That . . . sounds wonderful." Barry felt tears coming to his eyes. A cake that he could eat without turning into a sugar addict like Thorne.

Barry sat down at the kitchen table. Garrett cut narrow slices of the small orange cake. White icing spelled out the words "WELCOME HOME GRANDPA!"

Barry took a forkful, and the family seemed to hold their breaths, waiting for his approval.

Barry tasted it and grinned from ear to ear. "This is the best darn cake I've had in decades," he said. It was the absolute truth. Barry hadn't eaten cake in decades.

"Please don't ever leave again." Scarlett hugged Barry one more time.

Here it comes. But not another word was said about his disappearance.

"I do really like it here." Barry set his fork down. "But I do already have my own life." He directed the words to the parents, but the children stared at him silently. "I hope you understand that. There are people I need to see." *Thorne must be frantic by now.* "You must allow me to see my old friends." He didn't mention his grandson.

Buffy placed a hand on Barry's shoulder. "Of course, you have a life outside our family. We all have different friends and activities."

The carrot cake beckoned. *Maybe one more slice.*

"Once we've completed the ninja's requirement of one week," Garrett said, "then you'll be free to set your own schedule."

Barry nearly choked on the carrot cake when he heard Garrett say the word "free." Could he tolerate captivity for five more days?

"I won't make any promises," Barry said, "because we never know what tomorrow will bring. But I do want to be part of this family."

Maybe not "grandpa," and maybe not on a full-time basis. But his words hit the right note.

The Braunys cheered and clapped their hands. Scarlett danced around the kitchen table.

"That's good enough for me," Scott said. "I'm just happy you're you."

"Well said, Scott," Buffy chimed in.

Everyone flitted around Barry, making sure he had everything he needed. He was so used to being the grown-up. Being the responsible one while his grandson frittered away his money on foolish pursuits like gambling and his impractical car. He wondered at his own sanity and clarity of mind that he'd been putting up with Marty's behavior for several years.

Now Barry was surrounded by beautiful people who only wanted to care for him and get bodybuilding advice. All they wanted was a father and a grandpa. *And all Marty wants is money.*

16

✳ Brie ✳

Sunday night, Brie uploaded Lovey's video to her laptop and spent hours trying to decipher the identity of Barry's mystery woman. Zooming in frame by frame, all she surmised was the same thing everyone else had told her: Barry's dance partner could have been anybody. The wigged woman wore so much makeup that the only thing Brie was certain of was that she was part of the homo sapiens species.

Brie tried to narrow down the woman's identity based on who appeared in the background of the video. Lovey danced with Duchess close to her face as she filmed in selfie mode. The cookie lady, whatever her name was, carried a tray of sweets around the gym. Several seniors were line dancing, but their backs were facing the camera. Brie couldn't account for Poppy. Or a hundred other HMCA patrons and Hummingbird Gardens tenants.

At work on Monday, Brie was exhausted from staying up so late. When it was quitting time, she wanted nothing more than to go home and turn in early. But she was too polite. It was a serious character flaw. Sam was busy Sunday night when Lovey dragged her away, so they agreed to meet Monday after work. Brie hoped the senior woman forgot about the scheme, but she showed up at the front desk right when Brie shut down her computer.

"Let's go, sweetie," Lovey said cheerfully.

Duchess the poodle yipped.

Lovey's bright pink pup led the way through the atrium to Hummingbird Gardens. She danced on her painted doggy toenails down the hall to Sam Slate's first-floor apartment.

Sam was the most bland person Brie had ever met. *So neutral.* She wasn't sure whether Sam was an old man or an old woman. *Is Sam short for Samuel or Samantha?*

Sometimes, senior citizens morphed into gender-neutral appearances. It was just an age thing. Certainly not in Lovey's case. She was a hyper-feminine senior lady. In Sam's case, the lack of specificity seemed like a deliberate choice. *Maybe I'll find out tonight.*

Lovey tapped on Sam's door, number 133. Unlike other seniors who decorated their entryways, Sam's was unadorned. Like Sam.

From Sam's short haircut and plain, thick-framed eyeglasses to their typical outfit of loose-fitting jeans, a white T-shirt with a long-sleeved denim shirt on top, there was no hint of who exactly Sam was. No earrings. No curves. No mustache or beard.

Duchess wiggled and yipped. The pompom puff at the tip of her tail wagged wildly. She was clearly delighted to visit her friend. Sam leaned down to pat the poodle on her pink head.

"Good evening," Sam said in a voice that was neither high-pitched nor low. Sam glanced at Brie, their lips puckering in distaste. "This is our canvas? Our Pygmalion?"

Lovey nodded solemnly. "Although we don't have to overcome a cockney accent like Henry Higgins dealt with."

Are they comparing me to Eliza Doolittle in "My Fair Lady"?

"Small favors," Sam muttered.

I'm not that bad. Am I?

The apartment was as bland as Sam. Very nicely decorated

and tidy, but done in soft earth tones with no pops of color. A gray loveseat and a couple of compact club chairs in muted sage tones surrounded a maple coffee table.

Lovey undid Duchess's leash and sat on a chair. The little dog paced in figure eights in front of Lovey's feet. Sam took the other chair, leaving Brie with only one seating choice. She eased onto the loveseat.

"Tsk tsk tsk." Sam rested their chin in one palm and stared at Brie for several awkward moments. Then they stood abruptly. "There's no time to waste. We have to get right to work."

Sam grabbed Brie's hand and dragged her to her feet, hustling toward a bedroom. Brie knew this floor plan. Most apartments were one-bedroom. Sam had a two-bedroom, although Sam was the only tenant.

When they threw open the door to the second bedroom, Brie gasped at the shock of color.

The entire room had been done over into a walk-in closet. No, more than that. It looked like the costuming department of a theater. On one wall was a long vanity table with a lighted mirror. Racks of shoes rose from floor to ceiling on either side of the violet table.

On the clothing racks filling the rest of the room were clothes – no, costumes – in a riot of colors and textures. Sequins glittered. Slinky fabrics clung to padded hangers.

"Wow," she whispered. "I never imagined . . ."

Sam patted the seat of the chair in front of the lighted mirror. "Here. Now."

Brie complied. Sam grasped her high pompom ponytail and sighed.

"Has this hair ever seen a professional?" Sam asked.

Brie cringed. "It's hard to find a hairdresser who knows how to work on mixed hair. My dad is white, my mom is black, and neither one knew what to do with my crazy hair."

"Find someone," Sam said. "Well, Lovey, what do you think?" Sam tugged a strand of one of Brie's curls, extending it to an amazing length.

"The girl has plenty of hair," Lovey said. "It could be worse. At least we have something to work with."

Sam unwound the hair tie from Brie's ponytail, not being gentle in the least.

"Ow!"

Duchess stood on her hind legs, whining as she patted a front paw on Brie's leg.

"All beauty requires a little discomfort," Sam said. "Do you want to be beautiful?" They didn't wait for an answer. "Of course you do. Let the magic begin."

Sam did most of the fairy godparent work on Brie's hair, with the assistance of oils, sprays, and all sorts of other goop.

Brie usually wore her hair pulled back, with her pompom of curls shoved into a ponytail. It was the easiest style to achieve. When she left it down, her hair had a tendency to knot up like a Rasta man's. But Sam managed to tame Brie's natural curls into a shape that framed her face and made her look classy.

"You are magic," Brie said.

"Yes, well. Now, Lovey, let's get started on that lovely face of hers."

Sam thinks I'm lovely?

The makeup station had every shade and variety of paints, powders, and creams imaginable.

"Did you work for a theater?" Brie asked. She knew Sam was retired, but their former career was not listed on their HMCA membership record. It was hard to tell how old Sam was, but they had to be at least fifty-five to live at Hummingbird Gardens.

"Tonight is about you," Sam said, sidestepping the question. "What do you think of this one?" Sam pointed out a brown rectangle on a makeup palette to Lovey.

"Too dark," Lovey said. "Try this one."

While Lovey assisted in the selection and application of foundation, blush, and more eye colors than Brie had ever seen, she chattered.

The spry sixty-eight-year-old was divorced twice and widowed once. The woman had lived a more interesting life than Brie. She knew things Brie might never learn.

"Treat each date like the first one," the senior lady said. "Even if you've gone out with the man a dozen times. Keep things fresh."

"This is my first date," Brie said.

"With Barry's grandson?" Sam asked.

"With anyone," Brie said. "I've never really been on a date before." Not anything that officially counted. Being formally asked out. Going somewhere special.

Brie watched the seniors glance at each other in the mirror. Was that a look of horror? Even the pink dog made a weird sound, half growl and half yip.

"Then you need all my first date advice." Lovey launched into a lecture. "Purse your lips whenever you aren't speaking to make yourself look kissable. Don't spend too much time talking about yourself. Always turn the conversation back to him. Men love to talk about themselves. Order a meal that isn't awkward to eat. No chicken wings! And get a box for half your meal. Men prefer women who don't eat too much."

Brie might be inexperienced, but she was pretty sure most of Lovey's advice was a few decades past its shelf life. However, the new look the two seniors gave Brie was on point. Eye makeup that looked natural, but added definition to Brie's boring brown eyes. Just the right shade of blush on the apples of her cheeks, setting her light brown skin aglow.

"What do you think?" Lovey asked. "Do we skip the false eyelashes?"

"Hers are long and thick," Sam said. "They need no enhancement."

People mostly thought Brie resembled her white dad, never seeing her likeness to her gorgeous mom. Tonight, for the first time in her life, she looked in the mirror and saw a lighter version of her mother staring back at her.

"You guys," Brie said, "I could just cry."

"Don't do that," Sam said. "You'll ruin all our hard work."

Brie struggled to blink back tears of happiness. She felt as beautiful as her own mother must feel every day.

"And now," Lovey said, "do you have anything in here suitable for a girl's first date?"

"I have something suitable for every occasion," Sam said.

Brie scanned the racks of glittery clothes. They looked like costumes a burlesque dancer would wear. She loved what they'd done to her hair, and the makeover was amazing. But dressing in sequins and feathers would be a step too far.

"I'm sure I have something in my closet at home–"

"I'm sure you don't," Sam said. "Lovey, what do you think of this?"

Sam pulled a pink satin bustier from the rack.

17

✳ Thorne ✳

After sunset Monday, Thorne drove to the location he'd found in Barry's address book. Thorne pressed on the brake pedal, slowing Chandos. The scent of rotten broccoli had finally dissipated thanks to some tricks he learned from the internet. Now the interior of the car smelled like coffee beans, dryer sheets, and apples. He had sprinkled a generous quantity of baking soda all over the back seat, too, for good measure. Thorne hoped he didn't get pulled over by the police, lest they assume the white powder was something else.

He parked his white, base model 2012 Ford Fusion under a bare-limbed ash tree across the street from Marty Strong's house. The house Thorne stopped in front of had several trucks in the driveway in various states of disrepair, and a couple that looked more drivable parked on the street. Thorne doubted anyone would notice one more vehicle.

Marty's small one-level ranch-style house was covered in cracked beige stucco. The front yard was messy with dead grass that looked like it hadn't been mowed the previous summer. It resembled a bad comb-over with hard-packed snow peeking from beneath the strands of overgrown grass.

The neighborhood was in an older part of Colorado Springs. The houses might have been built in the 1950s. The buildings looked a quarter of the size of the newer homes in town. From what Thorne could see of the neighborhood with the help of porchlights and streetlamps, Marty's neighbors had done a nice job of modernizing. Most of the homes looked neat and polished. Only a few dissenters like Marty and whoever lived in the house Thorne parked in front of neglected their properties.

From Thorne's vantage point inside his car, no lights were on in Marty's home, even though it was already dark outside. These old houses didn't have garages, and no one was parked in Marty's driveway. Barry had once told Thorne that Marty was a car dude. Thorne didn't see Barry's car or Marty's. By all appearances, no one was home.

But that didn't mean Barry wasn't inside. There could be lights on in the back of the house out of Thorne's line of sight. Unless Barry was taking a nap. He was an old man, after all, even if he had a ripped bod. Worst-case scenario, dead men didn't need the lights on. With no one else at home, this was the perfect opportunity to scan the property for bodies.

Time to get to work. Thorne pumped himself up to do some reconnaissance. Hopefully, all he needed to do was ring the doorbell and wait for Barry to wake up and answer the door. *Please be that simple.*

Before getting out of his car, Thorne hesitated. He reached inside his jacket pocket for a power-up in case things went awry. The peanut brittle was coated with lint and crumbs. Thorne dusted as much of the lint as he could off the piece before plopping it into his mouth. It didn't detract much from the flavor. It might have even complemented the texture. *That crunch! Sublime!*

Thorne was in a blissful state of sugar rush and ready for action when headlights reflected off his rearview mirror. He ducked down in the seat.

An orange and black sports car drove past and pulled into Marty Strong's driveway. It made Thorne think of Garfield the cat, although he was pretty sure that wasn't the effect Marty was going for. *Even though Garfield is almost as cool as that big orange cat that hangs around Hummingbird Gardens.*

Thorne pulled out a pair of binoculars and peeked from his hunched position in his well-worn car seat. He zoomed in as the driver exited the car. Marty's porchlight glinted off the beginnings of a bald spot. *Yep. That must be Barry's grandson. Male pattern baldness strikes again!*

Marty wasn't in shape like his grandfather, from what Thorne could tell in the dark. No passengers got out of the car. If Barry were in the vehicle, he would have to be low in his seat like Thorne. *Or he's folded up in the tiny trunk of the souped-up Gourami FSX.*

The celery star and bodybuilding flier told Thorne his pal Barry had been alive this afternoon. Thorne believed it in his gut.

Lights clicked on inside the house. Thorne pulled on his thin black leather gloves and eased out of his car, pushing the driver's door gently closed. He tucked his fedora snuggly onto his head and tugged his tan trench coat around him a little tighter. The stylish coat wasn't doing much against the freezing January cold. His breath came out in a frozen cloud.

Man up! Thorne mentally steeled himself against the frigid air while his body betrayed him by shivering violently. It was still worth it. He reasoned that the more he looked like a great PI, the better a private investigator he would be.

Teeth chattering, trotting across the street, he hurried to the side of the house. If he could just get a glimpse through a window, maybe he would spot Barry. Then he could confirm that everything was okay.

And I can hit him up for my birthday celery juice. Then again, celery juice cost money that Barry didn't have. But it didn't cost so much that Barry needed to go into hiding over it.

Thorne snuck around the house. Snow crunched under his feet and sprinkled into his dress shoes with every step. He went from window to window. Each one had blinds or curtains blocking the view inside. Thorne's ankles had rings of ice encircling them, and his face had gone numb by the time he reached the last window. One of the slats of the blinds was broken.

Hot diggity!

Thorne rubbed his gloved hands together, trying to bring some feeling back into them and wishing his fingers were "hot diggities" instead of frozen hand-sicles.

Marty was alone on his couch, playing a video game Thorne had never seen before. He had on a headset, and he looked like he was talking to someone. The cartoony avatar on his television screen was as ripped as Barry, but had Marty's face and hair. The character walked through a casino. He stopped at a roulette wheel that was manned by a gorgeous non-playing character. The NPC's mouth moved, and Marty's avatar made a bet on the number twenty-seven. The NPC spun the wheel. The ball landed on double zero.

Marty leaped to his feet and started screaming and tearing at his thinning hair.

"Sheesh. You'd think he was playing for real money," Thorne whispered. His teeth were chattering so hard now that he nearly bit his tongue off as he spoke.

Frostbite was becoming more and more of a threat. *I need to get out of here.* Thorne skulked back toward his car. He was almost there when a voice stopped him in his tracks.

"Hey," a man's voice said.

Thorne turned to see a huge bear of a man looming over him.

"You wanna buy a truck?" the man asked.

"Um, no?" Thorne was concerned that it was the wrong answer.

"No!?" The guy looked angry. "Well then, you can't park here. Where am I supposed to put *my* truck?"

Thorne looked at the half dozen trucks at the property.

"I'm, s-s-sorry," Thorne stammered, barely able to make the

words come out past his chattering teeth. "I-i-i-t won't ha-happen again."

"Right," the man said. "Just remember, Papa Bear is watching you."

Papa Bear made a gesture like he was drawing a knife across his throat. Thorne took the hint and escaped to his car.

A wasted night. Thorne drove home and logged his notes on his new case file: *Missing Person Barry Strong*. This case was getting real.

18

✳ Brie ✳

Brie used to like playing dress up with her mother's clothes when she was little. After middle school, she "outgrew" them. She wasn't taller than her mother. Brie's growth stayed concentrated in her round tummy that had its twin in her father. Except hers wasn't a beer gut.

As an adult, she didn't enjoy shopping. Nothing ever looked right, and everything was more expensive than Brie thought it should be. She liked going to discount department stores and buying one of each color of yoga pants, comfortable sports bras, multi-pack granny panties and athletic socks. Most of her oversized T-shirts and fleece jackets featuring the weird Happy Marmot logo were free. It was a perk of working at the HMCA.

But Sam Slate's dressing room was a wonderland. There were so many choices, Brie didn't know where to begin. She was pretty sure the pink bustier was not her style. *But . . . when in Rome.*

"Okay. I'll try it." Brie took the bustier and stepped into a fitting room that Sam had repurposed from their built-in closet. Brie had almost forgotten the space used to be a normal Hummingbird Gardens bedroom. The back wall and sides of the closet were lined with mirrors. A soft-looking padded bench sat on one side. Its curved legs looked like they were coated in gold filigree. Soft lighting from a small jeweled chandelier suspended from the ceiling illuminated the space. Even the ceiling was beautiful. Sam had lined it with pretty purple wallpaper in a paisley pattern. Brie inhaled deeply. The scent of lavender soothed her senses.

Brie set the pink bustier on the bench. She was about to close the privacy curtain when Lovey yelled, "Wait!"

Lovey staggered under a huge armload of clothes.

"You can't wear that with sweatpants!" Lovey dumped the load onto the bench on top of the pink bustier, burying it under a huge pile of feathers, lace, and leather.

"And you need shoes." Sam walked in with a small crate of heels, kicky boots, and sandals.

The toy poodle, Duchess, carried a stack of necklaces in her mouth and dropped them at Brie's feet. She yipped loudly.

"As Oscar de la Renta says, 'A woman makes an outfit her own with accessories,'" Lovey quoted.

Brie's eyes grew wide. There was a mountain of stuff to try on. And all for a date she was only going on because she was worried about a missing senior.

I'm only dressing up to go undercover.

"Where do I start?" Brie asked, feeling overwhelmed.

"From the top," Sam said. "But we can't do this without the proper ambiance."

Brie raised her eyebrows. The place couldn't be more perfect.

Sam pulled a leopard-printed Bluetooth speaker from out of nowhere and tapped their phone. "We'll play my girl-power mix."

Cyndi Lauper's "Girls Just Wanna Have Fun" blasted.

Brie danced the curtain closed and started playing dress up.

First, she tried on a white skirt that must have been made of ostrich feathers. She paired it with a white lacey crop top and white kitten heels. She draped a silver necklace with diamond rhinestones around her neck. Brie looked at her reflection and frowned. Her tummy poked out below the short crop top.

"This one doesn't look good. I'll try another," Brie said, starting to undress.

"Let us be the judge of that!" Lovey said.

That's exactly what I'm worried about. With her old-fashioned ideas, would Lovey body shame Brie? There was no body positivity movement for Lovey's generation.

"You have to show us," Lovey said. "Every outfit. Don't be embarrassed."

Duchess slid under the curtain and looked up imploringly at Brie. She wagged her puff of a tail.

"Everybody hates something about their body," Sam said. "Take some advice from RuPaul. To paraphrase, if you can't love yourself, how the heck you gonna love someone else?"

Wise advice from a famous drag queen? *Who knew?*

Brie stepped out hesitantly, sucking her gut in as much as she could.

Sam waved their hand flippantly. "Let it all out."

Brie exhaled. Her round tummy spilled free.

"Oh! You're so adorable, Brie!" Lovey clapped her hands.

"Thanks." Brie couldn't help smiling.

"Do you like it?" Sam asked.

"It's cute. But I don't think it's really my style," Brie said.

"What is your style, darling?" Lovey asked.

"I have no idea," Brie admitted.

"Well, we're going to find out tonight!" Lovey said.

"Another." Sam clapped their hands.

Brie returned to the dressing room. She tried on clothes that made her feel like everything from a princess to a dominatrix, and all the styles in between. Each time she left the room, she received a supportive round of applause from Lovey and Sam. Duchess yipped enthusiastically. But Brie just didn't feel sure about any of the clothes she tried. Could she really be any of these people?

I'm your Venus! I'm your fire . . . The girl-power mix was still going strong. Brie was down to one outfit. She strapped on the pink bustier and tugged a short, ruched, red skirt over her hips. The skirt almost came down to her knees, and the bustier flattered her stomach. The materials were surprisingly soft. *I like this.* But she wasn't sure she wanted to expose this much of her bosom.

Brie stepped into some red wedge heels with see-through bottoms. They were fairly low to the ground and comfortable to walk in. Brie brushed through the changing room curtain and spun in a circle for Sam and Lovey.

Lovey whistled. "Wow!"

Duchess yipped with approval.

"This is the one," Sam said. "But it's missing something." Sam produced a simple white satin blouse. "Wear it open over the bustier."

Brie slipped it on and looked in the mirror. "I love it!" she exclaimed.

"As you should!" Lovey said. "You look drop-dead gorgeous!"

Brie's excitement lowered a notch as she remembered the purpose of her date. *I hope dropping dead isn't on the agenda.*

19

❋ Thorne ❋

Tuesday was a wash. That often happened in the life of a PI. On Wednesday morning, Thorne got an early start. The HMCA gym would be crowded for several weeks with people determined to make good on their resolutions. He went through the motions of lifting barbells and using weight machines, hoping to tone his flabby abs.

His heart wasn't in it. Thorne even tried to imagine Barry yelling at him to try harder while he worked out. It just wasn't the same without Barry's shiny bald head bobbing with encouragement.

He hit the showers, even though he hadn't sweated much. *Time to get back on the case.*

First, Thorne went to Brie's desk.

"Hey, Cheesy Briesy!"

His daughter rolled her big brown eyes. Thorne just knew she really loved being teased. But there was something different about her today. Even though she was wearing the same sloppy clothes.

"Wow, Brie, you look more like your mother every day," he remarked.

"I'll take that as a compliment, even though you're divorced." Brie patted her hair.

Instead of the cute puffy ponytail she usually wore, her hair framed her face in soft waves. And was she wearing makeup?

"Just because we aren't married anymore doesn't mean your mother is any less beautiful to me," Thorne said. Eden really was the perfect woman. And he'd ruined everything.

"What do you want, Dad?" Brie plucked an earbud from her right ear and set it in its case. Her phone was screen-side up. Thorne made out the words "Serial Killers, Glamour and Gore" before Brie seemed to notice him looking and flipped her phone over.

My daughter has good taste.

"Can't I just pop by to say hi to my favorite kid?"

"Your only kid," Brie said. "Dad, I actually have a question for you."

"Shoot," Thorne made playful guns with his hands and pointed them at her.

"That's not funny." Brie frowned.

Yes, it is. Thorne attempted a sheepish look. "What's your question?" he asked out loud.

"Could the woman Barry left with have been Poppy Prince?"

"Who?"

"The cat lady!" Brie said.

"There are probably at least a dozen of those living at Hummingbird Gardens. Which one is Poppy?"

"She's not a resident. Poppy's kind of my co-worker. She shares an office with Ramona Grant," Brie explained.

"Really?" Thorne rubbed his chin stubble. He always kept his eyes on Ramona when he was in her office. Had he missed an entire other human being occupying the area? "She shares her office?"

"With Poppy! Red hair. Always has her Persian cat Professor Fluffingston with her . . ." Brie looked at Thorne rolling one hand expectantly.

Thorne shook his head. "Nope. Poppy doesn't ring a bell.

But that feline sounds familiar. Big, orange, squishy faced cat?" *I love cats!*

"What kind of a PI are you?" Brie huffed. "Poppy said she danced with Barry on New Year's Eve."

"Lots of women did. It was only the last one who he left with."

"Can you look into Poppy? Just in case?" Brie asked.

"Of course! I could use another lead on the mystery woman." Thorne sandpapered his fingertips in the process of making a note on his cracked phone. "I'd like to take you up on dinner tomorrow since you have Thursday off." When Brie looked confused, he added, "My birthday? Dinner?"

"Oh." Brie studied her fingernails. Thorne noticed she'd had a manicure. Her uneven nails were shaped and painted a pearly pink. "Actually, I have plans that night."

Thorne frowned. "Did that policeman ask you out?"

The last thing he needed was for his daughter to date a cop. That could put a crimp in his PI work. Some police officers didn't appreciate what they viewed as meddling civilians. Especially ones who made their living off of meddling.

"No, it wasn't Riggs."

This was bad. His kid was on a first-name basis with the cop already?

"Who, then?" Thorne asked. "I can run a background check on him."

"That's actually not a bad idea," Brie said, looking thoughtful. "You can do that?"

Thorne nodded. "Where did you meet this guy?"

"Here," Brie said. "At work. He was looking for his grandfather."

Thorne's gut spoke to him. Or was it yesterday's peanut brittle curdling in his stomach? "By any chance, is his grandfather Barry Strong?"

"Okay, Super Sleuth," Brie said. "You guessed it. I have a date with his grandson."

This could be the big break in my missing person's case.

"You're in luck. I already performed a background check on Marty Strong."

Brie raised her hands. "And . . ."

"He's got bad credit and he's way too into video games." Thorne didn't mention that the last bullet point wasn't on his background check.

"Has he ever been arrested?" Brie asked.

"No. Not yet. But that doesn't mean he isn't dangerous. Not having a criminal record could mean he just hasn't been caught yet."

"According to my true crime podcasts, you're right." Brie crinkled her nose. "But he seems normal enough in person. I still think I should go. It's been a couple of days since we made this date. Maybe now he knows where Barry is."

"You're planning to spy on him?" Thorne was delighted by the idea.

"I just wanted to go on my first date." Brie looked away quickly. She sounded defensive. "Is that so strange?"

"Your first date?" Thorne asked. "Ever?"

"Yeah," Brie whispered.

Thorne was beaming. Finally, a milestone in Brie's life he hadn't missed!

"May I take pictures? To preserve the memory," Thorne suggested. "I can come along and–"

"No!" Brie exclaimed. "You can't come with me on my first date! That's so weird!"

"Is it?" Thorne shrugged. *Maybe it's only weird if she knows I'm there.* "Did you know Marty is the sole beneficiary of Barry's life insurance policy?"

Brie shrugged. "That makes sense. He's Barry's only living relative according to our client records. But Marty doesn't have a life insurance policy on *me*." She crossed her arms over her HMCA sweatshirt. "I'll be safe. And I'd better not see you sneaking around during my date, Dad. That is so uncool."

"But what if–" Thorne started.

"Dad. Please. I'm working." Brie moved her mouse and began typing.

"Just don't let him pick you up from your place. You don't want him to know where you live." Thorne wasn't sure she had heard him. His precious only child was going on a date tomorrow night with a potential murderer.

Drastic times call for drastic measures. Thorne casually reached for Brie's coat. She didn't notice him. *So stealthy.*

He dropped a small GPS tracker into her inner coat pocket.

Then he headed where the next set of clues might be found– the office Ramona Grant apparently shared with someone named Poppy Prince.

Maybe I'll get to see that fluffy cat.

20

✳ Brie ✳

"Wow, Brie," Poppy Prince exclaimed. "You look amazing!"

Poppy is here? Great. Dad must have just missed her.

Brie frowned. *Like it's a huge shock I can look nice?* Brie had been embarrassed all day by people stopping at her desk to comment on her appearance. It felt intrusive. At least she only had a few more minutes until this workday ended.

I don't have the time to spend two hours on hair and makeup every day. They'll have to settle for ugly old me tomorrow.

"I'm just trying something a little different," Brie told Poppy, patting her hair. She looked closely at Poppy. Had Thorne learned anything about her since they last spoke? *He didn't even know she works here.* Brie decided to bite the bullet and see what information she could get from Poppy herself. "Did you go home with Barry on New Year's Eve?"

Poppy giggled. "I never kiss and tell. Unless it's about the Professor!" She picked up the cat and snuzzled his flat face.

The kissing or the telling part? Both?

Professor Fluffingston wriggled out of her arms and leapt down to the floor.

Brie tried a different track. Thorne had mentioned a life insurance policy. Marty was the beneficiary. "Do you know Marty Strong?"

"Isn't that Barry's grandson?" Poppy asked. "I've seen him around once or twice. Why are you asking me all this stuff?"

She's going to get suspicious. Tone it down, Brie. "I have a date with Marty tonight."

"Oh!" Poppy smirked. "That's why you're all dolled up."

"Yeah," Brie admitted reluctantly. "I don't really know Marty. Can you tell me anything about him?"

"No. Not really." Poppy shook her head. "Barry said he's into cars or something."

Poppy acted nonchalant, but was she lying? Hiding secrets? This would be so much easier if Brie could just come right out and ask Poppy if she kidnapped Barry, teamed up with Marty, and murdered the senior citizen for his insurance money.

Professor Fluffingston padded close to Brie's chair. "Merow!"

Brie was afraid the cat's orange fur would stick to her hair. Sam and Lovey had touched up her new 'do early this morning, coating it with oils and sprays. Glamor was definitely a temporary experiment. Brie held up a hand, warding off the fluffy orange cat. "Not today, Professor."

"Huh," Poppy snapped. "Now that you're all pretty, you're too hoity toidy for my kitty? Come along, Professor. We'll go where we're wanted."

The cat tilted his nose up and pranced away from Brie, his feathery tail waving like a flag.

That temper. Poppy could be the reason Barry was missing, but Brie had gotten nowhere with her interrogation. Hopefully, Thorne would be able to get to the bottom of that well of clues.

The newest members of the HMCA, the Honeycombe family, opened the double-entry doors, laughing and chatting as they entered the building. The Professor darted past their legs.

"Nooo!" Poppy screamed. "Someone stop the Professor! He'll freeze to death!"

With all that fur?

The round family dropped their gym bags and ran after the

cat. Poppy raced outside in a thin blouse and slacks.

From her desk, Brie could see the entire show. People chasing the cat off the cleared sidewalk and onto the snowy lawn, waving their arms. Professor Fluffingston trotted around two steps ahead like it was a game.

Their mistake was confronting the cat face on. Brie could see the only way to catch him would be to snatch him from behind while he was distracted. No one seemed to figure that out.

Brie pushed her hands against her desk and stood. "I guess it's up to me." She felt a little guilty anyway, because the Professor had only wanted pets from her. She had denied him a kitty massage, so he'd run away.

Brie hurried through the front doors. A blast of icy air slapped her in the face. She felt her hair blow sideways. *I should have grabbed a scarf.*

Brie joined the cat chase, quickly implementing her strategy. Leafless, snow-covered bushes formed a sheltered ring around the trunk of a blue spruce. Underneath, another cat crouched. Her golden eyes glowed in the shadows.

"Mew." The shorthaired calico cat rose and stretched her front legs. She raised her rump and tail in the air in a weirdly seductive move. "Mew."

Professor Fluffingston boldly moved toward the cat. *Great, even the cat has a love interest.*

"Keep away from that tramp!" Poppy screamed.

Brie hoped there wouldn't be a cat fight between Poppy and the bush cat. The Professor could not be stopped from entering the other cat's hiding place. While the young teen Honeycombe kids waved their hands at the cats, and the parents darted forward, Poppy ran in ineffective circles, shrieking, "My baby!"

With the Professor focused on his primary goal, Brie moved beneath the spruce's high branches and snuck up behind him.

I've got you now!

Before Brie got hold of the cat, a blast of wind battered the

HMCA grounds. The bough above Brie shook, and a load of snow dropped onto her head. Professor Fluffingston sprinted away from the falling snow. Brie ran after him. Her teeth chattered violently as she tried to brush ice from her hair with her bare fingers.

The cat was up to his tummy in snow, and it was slowing him down. Brie almost caught up. Just a little further. She leaped, chest first, like a football player trying to catch the winning touchdown. Her fingers just brushed the Professor's tail as she flopped onto her tummy. Now snow-coated and with no cat to show for her efforts, Brie struggled to get up. Her cold hands refused to obey her efforts to push herself to standing on the slick, ice-crusted grass. She was stuck.

A deep male voice crooned in front of Brie. "I've got him."

Brie looked up. Officer Riggs Saito, in full uniform, had Professor Fluffingston in his strong arms.

"Yay!" one of the teens yelled.

"Professor!" Poppy grabbed for the fluffy cat and scooped him away from Riggs. "Let's get you inside, where you'll be safe."

The Honeycombe family and Poppy all fussed over the snow-covered cat and dashed back to the doors of the HMCA. The calico cat darted inside behind them.

Riggs bent over Brie and extended a gloved hand. "Here," he said.

Brie's frozen hand melted into Riggs's. He pulled her to her feet. She toppled a little as she attempted to stand, falling against his body. He didn't budge, as stable as a tree trunk. His warm body and nearness made Brie forget how cold she had been just seconds before. He smelled clean, and spicy, and . . .

"Are you okay?" Riggs asked.

Brie whispered, "I'll never be the same."

"Do you think you're injured?" Concern creased his handsome face.

"Uh, no," Brie stammered. "Let's go inside."

Riggs led Brie indoors, where Poppy did triage on Professor Fluffingston's damp fur while the other cat circled the legs of the Honeycombe family. Poppy commandeered a padded club chair in the waiting area.

"Towels! I need towels!" She barked orders like a surgeon in an emergency room. "A blow dryer!"

Diana Diamond suddenly appeared in the lobby. "Oh! There you are, Ms. Payne, you little troublemaker." She scooped up the calico and left as quickly as she had arrived.

Riggs escorted Brie to her desk.

"We're lucky you were here. We may never have caught that cat," Brie said. "Thank you."

Riggs grinned. Dimples formed on his smooth cheeks. "I just came by to check on my grandpa before my shift starts."

"How is he adjusting?" Brie asked.

"Well, you know Grandpa George." Riggs sighed. "It's slow going. But he'll get there."

"He'll make a lot of friends in Lovey Dearheart's dance class," Brie said.

"I'm surprised he signed up for that!" Riggs said with a laugh. "But he used to take my grandmother dancing all the time, so I guess it makes sense."

Brie smiled at Riggs. He smiled back. And they just looked at each other for a few moments.

Riggs broke the comfortable silence. "Well, I guess I'd better go see him now. My shift starts in half an hour."

"Oh!" Brie said. "Have fun! Tell him hello for me."

She waved as Riggs departed. *Tell him hello for me? George can't stand me.*

Before she knew it, the time had come for Brie to get dressed for her date. She was thankful she hadn't risked wearing the clothes at work all day. The borrowed bustier, skirt, and blouse were in a dry-cleaning plastic bag, waiting for her workday to end so she could do a quick change. She still had the makeup Sam had insisted she keep with her at all times. Brie retrieved the heavy pouch full of every cosmetic known to humankind from under her desk. She took it and her clothes to the bathroom.

She'd probably have to touch up her makeup and adjust her hair a little. She shook the melting snow off her head and brushed it off her shoulders. *It can't be that bad.*

No. It was worse. Brie's reflection gave her a jump scare. She thought she and Riggs had just shared a moment. *No wonder he stared at me for so long.*

Between the wind and the snow, her hair was ruined, half hanging limp around her shoulders, the rest sticking up like a witch's broom. Brie grabbed a white gym towel and tried to rub her hair dry. Clumps of hair stood out from her scalp at bizarre angles. She tried smoothing it down. All that tamed curl came back with a vengeance, only now it was interspersed with stiff, straight strands.

Brie gave up, pulling the damp mess into her usual ponytail puff. It looked worse than ever, standing up like a weird combination of porcupine quills and bird feathers.

After she got the tangled, crazy mess pulled away from her face, she noticed her makeup. The snow had smeared the painstaking morning's effort into a clown's mask.

"It's okay," Brie muttered to herself. "I'll deal with it after I get dressed."

First, she stripped out of her snow-damp clothes and squeezed into the red, ruched skirt. Next, the bustier, covered by a white satin blouse. After a glance at her bosom, Brie buttoned the blouse up to her neck.

She stood at the sink and attempted to repair the damage the Colorado weather had inflicted on her face.

Not much time.

Brie attempted coating over the mess with foundation. That just made things worse. *I should have wiped off everything first and started over. But Marty will be here any minute.*

With toilet paper and coarse hand towels, Brie mopped at

her face. She rushed to reapply foundation, blush, lipstick, eyeshadow, and mascara. Why did women wear so many products? *Is this really necessary?*

Too late, she realized she'd switched the blush and eyeshadow. With her hair sticking out at crazy angles, Brie suspected she resembled a 1980s glam rocker. David Bowie?

"Oh no!"

Brie looked down at the satin blouse. She had dripped goopy foundation and eyeshadow dust all over the front.

"New plan." Brie stripped out of the blouse. "No, no, no." She was not going to wear just a bustier. That sent the entirely wrong message. "What to do? What to do?"

In near panic, Brie slung her feet into the wedge heels Lovey insisted she wear, and hobbled into the lobby. Her exposed cleavage caught the eye of a senior patron.

Hummingbird Gardens resident Layton Lambert untied his apron and held it in front of Brie's chest. Since the retired chef was a plump man, the apron was extra wide. The curtain of white shielded Brie entirely.

"Is that the kind of attire the kids wear these days?" Layton asked. "Lingerie used to be reserved for the bedroom."

"It's a bustier. It's like a fancy sports bra. Lots of women at the HMCA wear those," Brie reasoned. But she was already so embarrassed by his reaction, she grabbed a shirt out of the Turkey Tornado box leftover from the Thanksgiving 5K race the gym put on each year. "But it is a little chilly for this." She pulled the shirt on. "There. That's better."

"The view was lovely," Layton said, "but you have to watch the blood pressure of the residents here, if you know what I mean." Layton fanned a hand in front of his face, like he was overheated.

Brie was overheating herself. Her cheeks felt like an inferno. They might have actually turned her brown skin red. *Good grief!* The geezer was a handsome old dude, but he was old enough to be her grandfather.

Layton threw the apron over his arm and walked off.

Whew! It was almost time for Marty to arrive.

My first date. Brie fidgeted as she waited at her work desk. *I just made it.* She checked the time. Actually, she was a few minutes late. But Marty hadn't arrived yet. *Or did I miss him already?* There were no calls or texts from him on her phone. She kept checking the clock, and time kept marching on. Brie tried not to be impatient, but he was twenty minutes late now. *Where is he? Maybe he stopped to get me flowers!*

Brie tried without success to calm her racing heart.

Seriously, Brie? I'm not sure I even like Marty much. I don't know him at all. It was just so unusual for anyone to be interested in her that she felt she had to give him a chance. This might be her only shot at love.

All that love at first sight stuff is for movies and romance novels. Real relationships take time to develop.

Not according to Lovey. The flashy senior woman believed you knew the moment you set eyes on your true love. But should Brie take the advice of a woman who had two ex-husbands?

Unfortunately, Brie hadn't learned as much as she thought she had from the two senior citizens. About love, or about how to maintain her makeover.

All their attention had been wasted. Brie released a brief sob as she remembered how much she'd resembled her mother. Now she was a disaster.

Hopefully, Marty liked Brie for her personality.

The front doors opened. Brie cringed when she watched Marty walk in. He wasn't carrying a bouquet.

When he saw her, Marty emitted a squeak, like a mouse that had been stepped on.

He walked over to greet her and took both of her hands in his empty ones.

"Brie, you look–" Marty paused, looking her up and down. "Ready for dinner. *Gobble gobble!*"

Brie was surprised by the accuracy of his turkey noises. It

stung at first, but then she looked down at the shirt she was wearing. "Turkey Tornado 5K. Right!"

Marty didn't look much better than Brie. His worn-out polo shirt had stains that amplified his bulge of a tummy.

Brie picked up her purse and tugged her coat on.

"Have you ever ridden in a Gourami FSX?" Marty asked. Before Brie could respond, he began rattling off what sounded like the entire salesman's brochure for the car.

As she approached the sports car in the HMCA parking lot, Brie contemplated how she was going to sit that close to the ground without revealing everything underneath her too-tight skirt. Though her white cotton bloomers provided more full coverage than some of the shorts gym patrons wore.

Brie pretended to admire the orange and black car. "Isn't a gourami a kind of fish?"

"No. It's a tiger. Rowr!" Marty made claws with his hands.

Brie was certain she'd had a pet gourami in an aquarium as a child before her dad got involved in pet care. That ruined aquarium was still a sore point in their relationship.

"Rowr. Cool." Brie said as enthusiastically as she could make herself sound.

Just in case Brie ran into trouble, she checked her purse to be sure the pepper spray her dad gave her when she graduated high school was still there. It looked like a giant tube of pink lipstick from a distance.

She had watched several videos on how to use the spray and felt confident she could defend herself. Brie had reviewed all the notes she had gathered from her true crime podcasts. Before she got in the car with him, she needed to perform a safety check.

She pretended to admire the doors. "Wow! These are slick." She opened one and tried the locking mechanism. It functioned like a normal car. "The doors lock and unlock. Cool."

"Yeah. I think that's cool, too," Marty said.

She looked carefully around the car for ropes, zip ties, or weapons. She saw nothing dangerous or out of the ordinary. *But*

. . .

"What kind of trunk space does this 'tiger' have?" Brie asked.

Marty walked her to the back of the vehicle. She tugged her coat more tightly around herself as a gust of wind puffed across the parking lot.

"This baby's built for speed. The trunk is mainly for show."

Beneath the oversized spoiler was a handle. Marty lifted it, and a small hatch opened. There might have been room for one suitcase. Definitely not enough for Barry's dead body. *Or my own.* And the hatch was glass, so Marty couldn't hide anyone inside it anyway.

"Very nice," Brie said.

"Now let me show you where action is!" Marty grabbed her hand and dragged her to the front of the car. He lifted the hood to reveal what looked like every engine Brie had ever seen.

"Wow?" Brie didn't know what she was supposed to say. "That's impressive."

That must have been the right thing because Marty beamed. He proceeded to describe the amazing engineering involved in the mysterious contents beneath the hood. It didn't help her understand or appreciate what she was seeing. She was numb by the end of his recitation, and not just from the chilly breeze.

"Ready to go?" Marty asked.

"Um, sure," Brie said.

She kept her phone clutched tightly in her hand. She had programmed the policeman Riggs into her quick dial numbers. And her smart watch was set to automatically alert 911 if her heart stopped.

Okay, that's not the best plan, she admitted to herself.

Before climbing in, she glanced around to see if she had eluded her snoopy dad. But she only saw a couple of families in the HMCA parking lot. *Good.* Maybe he was finally exhibiting some trust that Brie could handle herself.

21

✳ Thorne ✳

Thorne's search for Poppy Prince yesterday had yielded no results. How could a redhead who traveled with a big orange Persian cat elude Thorne so thoroughly? It was a dead end he'd have to pursue later.

Priority number one was now tailing Martin "Marty" Strong. *Brie will thank me later.* Thorne could kill two birds with one stone: keeping track of his precious daughter and observing the behaviors of a potential murderer. If the guy would kill his own grandfather for the life insurance payout, what would he do to his date?

Thorne had been waiting inside his car, Chandos, behind a large dumpster for what felt like forever for Marty to arrive. He kept his mini-binocs glued to his face as he scanned the parking lot. The guy was at least twenty minutes late for his date with Brie when he finally arrived. *Disrespecting my daughter.*

At least Brie actually did follow Thorne's advice to not be picked up from her home.

Thorne watched as Marty helped a girl into the seat of his Garfield car.

Is that Brie?

Thorne switched from his mini-binocs to his full-sized pair for a better look. *What did she do to her hair?* The girl's wild, curly brown ponytail was arranged like an eighties pop star's, all spikey, rising high above her head. Her makeup had gone from subtly enhancing her natural beauty to glam rock. The Turkey Tornado T-shirt was a bold fashion choice, but at least it was modest. Thorne didn't approve of the crinkly red skirt. It looked like something his ex-wife Eden would wear. This mishmash of styles only showed that Brie didn't bow to the conventions of mainstream fashion. Thorne's heart swelled with pride. She was beautiful! And original.

Marty didn't hold the passenger door of his sports car open, like any true gentleman would. Brie was on her own, climbing into the low-slung car.

Marty revved his engine, and they were off! Thorne pushed his car's pedal as far as it would go to keep up. His base model Fusion was a stick shift, so he rode the transmission hard to get the most speed he could out of his 2.5-liter I4 engine.

"Come on, Chandos. You've got this," Thorne cooed to his car.

As the former Head of Regional Legacy Product Sales for WAAA, he never had time to learn how to work on cars, and could always afford to pay a licensed mechanic to do tune-ups. Now Thorne had no skills and no money, and Chandos was suffering. Maybe if he wasn't so behind on maintenance, he could have sustained faster speeds. His white polar bear of a car couldn't keep up with the tiger. He lost Brie within the first mile from the HMCA.

Plan B. Thorne pulled over and unlocked his cracked smartphone. The GPS tracker he'd stealthily slipped into the pocket of Brie's coat tracked her location. Thorne followed the signal at a speed more appropriate for a family-sized sedan. *Don't worry, Chandos. It's not your fault. That guy drives way too fast. And I promise I'll get you an oil change. Eventually.*

Marty took Brie to the newest brewery in town, Rocky's Mountain Brews. Lucky for Thorne, the place didn't require reservations. That irked him, though.

Does he think Brie isn't worth a nicer dining experience?

Thorne was already suspicious of the guy. Now he was developing a serious dislike of Marty. He waited for them to go inside and be seated. He watched through a large window until he could see them sit down. Thorne adjusted his fedora. Then he slipped on a pair of sunglasses. *Brie will never recognize me with these.* He stepped inside.

There seemed to be a hundred craft breweries in Colorado Springs. Many of them tried to be classy, family-friendly establishments that just happened to brew their own beer.

The interior was done up like an industrial garden. Tall ceilings with exposed silver ductwork were hung with potted ferns and vines. The walls were brick. But here and there, big shiny sheets of flashing posed as wallpaper behind shelves of exotic flowers in black flowerpots. Large stainless steel brewing kettles with fancy piping made a huge centerpiece in the middle of the restaurant. Bartenders tapped directly from barrels.

"Are you dining alone?" the host asked.

As usual. Thorne sighed heavily.

"Yes. I'd like to be seated there." He pointed to the booth adjacent to Brie and Marty's. He wouldn't be walking past their table. *Total stealth.*

He slid into the seat with his back to Brie. Thorne studied the menu. After eating nothing but peanut brittle for breakfast and lunch, his stomach was a mess.

Disguising his voice, he gave his order to the waitress. "I'll have the mac and cheese." His voice came out way too high and squeaky.

"The beer-battered mac and cheese bites are to die for."

"Just the Kraft kind will be fine." Thorne kept his voice squeaky for consistency's sake. "Mind if I order off the kids' menu? It's a dollar cheaper that way."

That was all Thorne could afford. He really needed a paying gig. Soon.

"I won't tell." The waitress winked. "Is that all? Our Yellow

Snowman pilsner won first place in a state contest."

Tempting. But Thorne couldn't risk two years of sobriety. "The kid's meal comes with a fountain drink, right?"

"Correct." The waitress began listing off sugary beverages in a variety of flavors and colors.

Thorne interrupted her when he heard her say what he wanted. "Oooo! Chocolate milk sounds good. But does it come in one of those little bottles?"

"Naturally."

"Can you pour it into a glass for me?" Thorne asked. "You know, make it look classy?"

"You bet. Mac and cheese and a chocky-miwk coming right up." The waitress rolled her eyes and left.

Now Thorne could focus on work. He unwrapped the paper napkin that was rolled around his silverware and listened.

"How did you like riding in my car?" Marty asked.

"It's fast," Brie said. "You do know the speed limit was only twenty-five miles an hour?"

"Rules are made to be broken," Marty said. "My . . . *car* . . . can't be held back."

Thorne crushed the paper napkin in his hand.

"You pay that much money for a vehicle," Marty said, "and it's a crime not to use all that horsepower. That's the nice thing about sailboats. There aren't any speed limits on the water."

Thorne had to look up that factoid. *Ha! Wrong!* Most bodies of water in Colorado enforced penalties for exceeding a mere forty miles per hour.

"Too bad it's winter," Marty continued. "We could go sailing on the Pueblo Reservoir."

Big whoopty-do. Anyone could go sailing on *that* reservoir. Wasn't Brie worth a trip to the French Riviera? This guy might be his buddy's grandson, but Marty did not deserve a rare jewel like Brie.

"What do you do for a living?" Brie asked.

"I'm an entrepreneur," Marty said.

"Neat," Brie said. "What's your business?"

"I manage portfolios."

Thorne was willing to bet the only portfolio Marty managed was Barry's. He should grab Brie and leave.

The waitress carried a tray to Brie's booth.

"Beer-battered steak and a baked potato with beer cheese sauce for the gentleman," she said. "Broccoli cheddar soup and Caesar salad for the lady."

Thorne put his phone in selfie mode and used it to peek over his shoulder at Marty. As much as Thorne wanted to rescue Brie from this jerk before it was too late, Thorne needed to take advantage of Marty being preoccupied with the slab of meat on his plate. The way the guy sawed into it, Thorne could easily imagine him dismembering Barry. The fractured view through his phone's spiderwebbed screen made the scene even more frightening.

Thorne fumbled his phone away as the waitress set his "chocky-miwk" on the table in front of him.

"Your meal will be out in a moment. Need a straw?" she asked.

"Actually, can you put this in a to-go cup?"

"Seriously?" The waitress didn't look happy as she picked up the glass she had just set down.

"And I'd like a box for my dinner, as well," Thorne said.

Thorne's gut told him the clues to Barry's disappearance weren't going to pop out and hit him in the face in this restaurant. But with Marty busy, this was Thorne's golden opportunity to get some real answers elsewhere.

22

✳ Barry ✳

Perfection? Heaven? Barry's last couple of days were blissful. With the Brauny children on winter break from grade school for a precious few more days, the entire family spent the morning in the incredible home gym. Barry and Garrett competed to see who could do the most triceps extensions while Buffy and the kids kept count. Both dropped their shaky arms at the same time and burst into laughter when they tied. Barry hadn't laughed that much in years.

The whole family hung on every word of advice Barry had to offer. Scarlett and Scott didn't have to be prodded or bribed to complete their workouts. They were joyous about pumping iron.

Unlike my grandson. The only fly in the ointment of an otherwise beautiful day was worrying about Marty. Barry had to resolve the nagging feeling his grandson was in dire danger before he could commit to this new family. Making sure Marty was safe was an almost sacred obligation. *I owe that much to my son and daughter-in-law, God rest their souls.*

If only I could get my hands on a phone. Like most people, the family kept their cell phones as close and secure as a bodily appendage. There was no landline.

Barry noticed Scarlett set her phone down. *A ten-year-old*

with their own cellphone. What is the world coming to? Barry felt even older than his seventy years. He was about to pilfer the device, but before he could act, he noticed Garrett watching him. Barry played off his sneaky move by grabbing his electrolyte water and taking a swig.

Midday, they watched the documentary *Generation Iron.* Not to entertain Barry, but because the family was genuinely that obsessed with bodybuilding. They munched on a snack of plain whole-fat Greek yogurt and organic apple slices.

After a dinner of grass-fed steak, oven-roasted sweet potatoes, and three-bean salad with avocados, the kids were bursting with energy. Barry was surprised when Garrett and Buffy suggested he take the kids out for an evening jog.

"You trust me not to bolt?" Barry asked.

"We know you would never leave the children in an unsafe situation in the woods," Garrett said. "Even if it is only the familiar forest surrounding our home."

"We've gotten to know you better, Dad." Buffy beamed.

But was trust really involved? Maybe Garrett had a tracking app on his daughter's phone. The man could have placed a GPS tracker in Barry's new clothes. It didn't matter. Barry was over trying to escape early. He could leave of his own free will in a few more days.

"Here," Buffy said. "Take an energy bar."

"I'm so full, Mom." Scarlett patted her tummy.

"Just in case," Garrett said.

"I'll carry the snacks," Barry offered. Buffy gave him three energy bars, which he slipped into the pockets of his fancy new running slacks.

Scarlett and Scott had a predetermined route through the neighborhood. Houses were spaced far apart on large, heavily treed lots. They ran on side trails parallel to the gravel streets. At times, Barry could hear traffic in the distance on Highway 24.

"Running is hard, but I like it," Scarlett said. She had a good handle on endurance running, pacing herself so that she could maintain a good clip while still being able to carry on a conversation. But she and Barry had both slowed down to a comfortable jog so Scott's shorter legs could keep up. "Does your friend, Thorne, like to run?"

Barry chuckled. "Maybe he would if cookies had legs and he had to chase them down before he ate them."

"He sounds really unhealthy," Scott said between breaths. "Having a dad bod causes heart disease."

"Where do you kids get this stuff?" Barry asked. Scott didn't sound like any eight-year-old Barry had met.

"The internet."

"I think you should help Thorne," Scarlett said. "After we're back in school and stuff. When you're not busy being our grandpa."

"I love being around your family–" Barry started.

"You mean *our* family," Scott said.

"You kids are my friends. But I'm not really your grandpa," Barry said.

"We never met our real grandma and grandpa," Scott said.

"*I* met one of them," Scarlett piped in. "But it doesn't count. Mom has a picture of me sitting on one of our grandma's laps. I was just a little baby, so I don't remember her. And I never had a grandpa before."

"What happened to all of your grandparents?" Barry asked. Losing one or two in childhood might be a normal part of the grand circle of life, but all four?

"Mom's mommy and daddy died early of stuff they wouldn't have gotten if they'd exercised more," Scott said.

"You can barely see me on Grandma Mimi's lap," Scarlett said. "Mom says she was a big lady. I think that means overweight, not like tall or something."

"And your father's parents?" Barry asked. He hopped over a branch that had fallen across their path. "They're not around either?"

"Dad barely talks about it," Scarlett said. "And when he

does, he gets all sad and stuff."

"Oh . . . yeah . . ." Scott said sadly. "They both died before we were even born."

Barry really wanted to ask more, but the kids made it sound like it was a traumatic story. He didn't want to upset them further.

But he needed to explain reality to these kids before things went too far.

"I'm not a replacement for those people. I have a life of my own," Barry said. "I have an apartment, a grown-up grandson, and a good friend who needs my help so his dad bod doesn't kill him."

The kids quieted. Barry could barely see their faces in the darkening evening, but he could feel their gloom. He felt bad, but he had to stay firm.

"It's getting too dark out here," Barry said. "Let's go back to the house."

The trio turned around and jogged their way back along the path toward the well-lit house.

"I'm not gonna make it," Scott complained. "Can you carry me?"

Barry knew he could easily, but the kid would learn nothing about endurance if he gave up now. He understood why Buffy had given him the three energy bars. It was just in case something like this happened. *She knows her children well.* Barry smiled. He pulled one of the bars out of his pocket and offered it to Scott.

"Oh yeah! I forgot you had these!" Scott tore open his energy bar. The foil wrapper crinkled loudly.

"I can't believe you're already hungry again," Scarlett said.

Scott bit into the bar, and Barry could smell the stevia-sweetened chocolate chips even in the pine-scented night air.

Scarlett must have smelled it, too. "We were going really fast," she said. "I'm out of energy now. May I have one?"

Barry handed her a bar. He had one left for himself, but he

decided to save it in his pants pocket for the growing kids. They could split it if one bar wasn't enough.

Still a good hundred yards away, the front door of the house beckoned. Now that they slowed to a walk, Barry felt the evening chill seeping through his running jacket. He looked forward to sitting in the sauna.

"We're almost back home, Grandpa," Scarlett said. "Don't you love it here?"

"I do. I'll stay these few days," Barry said. "And I'll visit. But not as your grandpa. As your friend."

After munching and smacking on a mouthful of energy bar, Scott spoke. "We don't want a friend. We want a grandpa. And that's you."

"Maybe the ninja lady can find you a different–" Barry started to say, but movement near the trash bins in front of the house stopped him in his tracks. He grabbed both of the kids' shoulders and pulled them close. "Do you see that?"

The kids exhaled clouds of breath into the chilly air like they'd sprinted a mile. They all stared at the black figure. It was *not* a ninja.

23

✳ Brie ✳

The man in the booth next to Marty and Brie's skooched across the vinyl seat and left, carrying a small take-out box and a to-go beverage. The collar of his long tan coat was turned up, and he wore a fedora pulled low. Brie couldn't see his face, but there was something familiar about the paunchy gut barely concealed by . . .

Dad's ratty old trench coat?

He was spying on Brie's date! But if that was true, why did he leave before she and Marty were halfway through their meal?

Brie tugged on her red skirt, self-conscious about how it kept riding up her thighs. She tried to ignore the feeling of being spied on and focused on her broccoli cheddar soup. Why did breweries insist on incorporating beer into all of their recipes? The alcohol was cooked out of it, but the gross taste of it remained. Did people really drink beer for the flavor? *Yuck.* Brie ate what she could of the broccoli and left most of the cheesy broth behind.

Her companion didn't make up for the lousy food. Marty seemed happy to do most of the talking, just as Lovey had predicted.

"Back in high school, believe it or not, I was kind of a loner," Marty said.

"Really?" Brie was surprised. *He seems too self-centered not to be a popular guy.*

"Yeah. People were always trying to hang out with me, but I brushed them off. A wild stallion cannot be shackled."

Right . . . Brie focused hard to keep from rolling her eyes. *Are shackles something you even put on a horse?*

"And high school girls threw themselves at me. You know? Like, where's your self-respect?"

Marty was in his late twenties. High school was at least ten years ago. Why was this all he had to talk about?

Marty stabbed a piece of steak with his fork and waved it in the air. "Women don't usually get me. They're not on my level."

I guess I'm not on your level, then. Brie barely managed to keep the thought to herself and got a few words in as Marty slammed a large piece of steak down his throat.

"So you've dated a lot of women?" Brie asked.

"You see, that's just the thing. I'm not a player. It's not about quantity. It's quality that matters most."

Maybe this is his first date, too? Hmmm. Brie put a forkful of Caesar salad in her mouth to keep herself from asking. He probably wouldn't tell the truth anyway. The salad tasted like the leaves had been washed and were still wet when they were tossed in dressing. It was so bland. Brie wanted to spit it into a napkin, but the thin paper would just make a mess. She bore down and forced herself to chew the watery salad.

"Baby girl." Marty leaned across the table. "You're not like the others. You're quality."

Brie swallowed her mouthful before she was done chewing.

"Guarg!" Brie choked. She grabbed her glass of water and flooded her throat to move the flavorless grass into her stomach.

"Thanks," she managed to say when the leaves finally cleared.

"And look at you." Marty's smile was slick. "So health conscious."

Brie had only ordered soup and salad because everything

else on the menu was beer-battered. *Whoever heard of beer-battered steak?* Marty's meat had a thick coating of golden-brown fried goo encasing it. Like beef wellington gone wrong.

"And even though you work at a gym, you don't waste your life working out," Marty said. "I like that."

"Why are you assuming I don't work out?" *I don't.* But he didn't know that. He was implying she was out of shape. *I am.* But he didn't have to point it out.

Marty put his hands up. "Hey! Don't get all hot-headed on me. I just made an observation. I'm cool with it. Look at me. Some people don't have to work out to look good."

Marty was in no better shape than Brie's father. Possibly worse shape. At least Thorne tried to move around a little.

Brie gave up pretending this was a real date. *That's not what I came for.*

"Your grandfather works out all the time." Brie watched Marty closely for a reaction. "Except I haven't seen him since the New Year's Eve party. How is he?"

"He's chill." Marty shrugged.

"Oh? Did you visit him in his room on Sunday?"

"Nah. He wasn't there."

"How do you know he was chill? No one at the HMCA has seen him in the gym. People are getting worried."

"He called me. It sounded like he was on the road. So he must have driven somewhere or something. He's a grown man. Just like me. He doesn't have to tell anyone what he's doing."

Marty looked completely relaxed. He wasn't worried about his grandpa at all. Either it really wasn't a serious situation, or Marty was such a psychopath he didn't show any remorse about whatever he'd done to his grandfather.

Marty was almost done with dinner. Brie had picked at hers and tried to make it look as eaten as possible. The waitress must have noticed. She came and offered them a dessert menu. "Would you like to try our hops ice cream or our chocolate cake?"

"Chocolate cake sounds good," Brie said.

Marty reached across the table and grasped Brie's hand, even though she held a fork with an uneaten bite of salad speared on its tines.

"We're having dessert at my place." Marty waggled his eyebrows at Brie.

"The icing on the cake is really good," the waitress said. "We mix our Willy Wonka Chocolate Stout beer into it."

Brie stifled a gag. "No thanks."

Brie didn't want dessert at Marty's house either, but her father's snooping made her mad. This was *her* pretend date. She was an adult. If she wanted to go to Marty's house to spy on him, that was her decision to make.

Besides, Barry might be there, and she could solve the mystery of his disappearance. That would really show up Thorne.

Brie wasn't sure how dates worked. This *was* her first one. From what she had gleaned from Hallmark movies and women's magazines, the guy usually paid for the meal. But not always.

When an awkward minute passed with the waitress staring silently at their table, Brie placed her credit card on the waitress's small payment tray. So did Marty, so at least Brie wasn't paying for everything.

"We're splitting the bill," he told the waitress. "Fifty-fifty. I believe in women's equality."

What?!? Brie's awful soup and watery salad had been half the cost of Marty's steak.

She wondered whether Officer Saito was this cheap. *Not that I'll ever find out.*

After the bill was paid, as Brie placed her credit card in her purse, she checked to make sure her pepper spray was still safely within reach.

"Okay," Brie said. "I'm ready."

"Oooooo," Marty crooned. "I like your spice."

After they left the restaurant, Marty drove his tigerish sports car faster than necessary, sliding on the patches of ice left from the previous snowstorm. When he pulled into a convenience store parking lot, Brie imagined Marty living in the brightly lit shop for a moment.

"This baby is about speed, not fuel economy. I just need to feed her a few gallons." Barry patted his jacket pocket. "Have you got a twenty?"

He had paid at the brew pub with a credit card. *Why can't he get gas with it? Is it almost maxed out?* Brie supposed it was another indication of how dull she was, but financial stability was a priority in her life.

Brie pushed her hand carefully into her purse, so Marty's curious eyes wouldn't see the pepper spray. When she turned sixteen, her mother said a woman should always carry emergency cash at all times and handed her a twenty. So far, few situations urgent enough to use her money stash had arisen. She had only had to replace the cash a handful of times over the years. Brie handed Marty a crumpled twenty. *This had better be worth it. For Barry.*

She watched as Marty pumped only eighteen dollars into the car. Brie pursed her lips and frowned. She would demand the change. When he walked inside the convenience store, Brie stifled the urge to scream. She had nothing to actually compare it to, but she hoped this was the worst date ever.

Through the huge glass windows, Brie could see a line at the cash register. This was a prime chance to find out more about Marty Strong. She blamed her obsession with true crime podcasts for making her so paranoid, but the creep meter was on red alert for this guy.

The interior of the sports car was tidy, except for a crumpled fast-food bag on the back floor.

Brie reached for the glove box, feeling guilty. Opening a person's glove box was like digging through a woman's purse, or a stranger's medicine cabinet. It could be dangerous if he had a loaded gun.

She did a quick inventory. A box of condoms – unopened. Packets of ketchup, straws, and plastic-wrapped napkin-spork assemblies.

"What's this?" Brie whispered.

She pulled out a stack of papers and set them on her lap. They were bills from an online car dealership, stamped with the word "overdue" in red ink.

You'd think someone who loved his car so much would be making his payments on time.

Brie glanced up. Marty was next in line at the cash register. *Almost out of time.* She used her cell phone to take pictures of the notices. *Hurry!*

A shadow fell across her. Marty was trotting around the car. She stuffed the overdue car bills back into the glovebox and slammed it shut just as Marty opened the driver's side door.

"What are you doing?" he asked, staring at the phone in her hand.

The camera app was open.

"Uh, taking a selfie," Brie said. "I've never been in a car this fancy."

"You want a photo with me, too." Marty leaned across the console and threw an arm around Brie's shoulders. "To preserve the memory."

Brie snapped a picture. She could delete it later. This date was not something she wanted to preserve for all time. And it wasn't over yet.

"Do you have my change?" she asked.

"Change?"

"I gave you a twenty, and you only put eighteen dollars in the tank."

"I've got something better than two bucks." Marty pulled a lottery ticket from his pocket. "I bought the winning ticket. I'm sure of it."

Brie snapped a photo of the lottery ticket.

"Hey," Marty said. "What's that about?"

"If it does win, that's technically my money."

Marty's expression was sour for all of five seconds. Then he plastered a wolfish grin on his chubby cheeks.

"Maybe I'll win a different jackpot."

24

❋ Thorne ❋

Thorne drove to Marty's neighborhood. He couldn't risk parking in front of the self-proclaimed bear man's house of trucks. *That guy was intense.* Thorne parked Chandos a block away from Marty's house and walked quickly on recently shoveled sidewalks to the front door.

Hidden in plain sight. Act normal, and no one will notice you. It was already dark and cold outside, so Thorne doubted many people would see him. Especially wearing his fedora, trench coat, and sunglasses. He leaned off the front step, attempting to peer through a gap in the picture window curtain. A voice startled Thorne.

"Avert your eyes, Glenda!" an old guy exclaimed. "There's a peeping Tom."

Thorne turned around to see an old couple staring at him from the sidewalk.

"The trench coat," Glenda exclaimed. "He might be a flasher."

The older fellow covered the woman's face with his gloved hand. They crossed to the other side of the street.

My element of surprise is ruined. Thorne punched a finger against the doorbell. Thankfully, it was the old-fashioned kind. No camera reported his presence to Marty Strong. No recording of Thorne's face. Thorne crossed his fingers and waited for Barry to answer Marty's door. He rang the doorbell again. Nothing.

If Barry was in there, he was in trouble. *Or dead.*

Thorne tried the doorknob. Unlocked. Was this some flaw in the Strong family? Never locking doors? Or did it mean someone was home? Marty's dumb orange and black car wasn't in the driveway. He must still be on his date with Brie. Thorne checked Brie's location from the GPS tracker he'd slipped into her pocket. It showed she was moving, but she wasn't nearby. Marty was probably driving her back to her car.

I have time. It's not breaking and entering if there's no breaking going on. Thorne smiled.

He opened the door and braced himself for a scent at least as potent as the interior of his car. The scent of death might even be worse than rotten broccoli. *Maybe.*

Thorne dared to take a breath. It smelled strongly of lemon-scented cleaning products. *Smells better than my place.* The house was cleaner than Thorne's, too. Very little clutter. The carpet looked freshly vacuumed.

I've been too busy to clean. Thorne tried to comfort himself about the potential murderer keeping a nicer home than his own. *Only a psychopath single dude would keep his house this clean.*

Thorne explored the house, looking for any sign Barry had been there. *Or is here.*

Marty had a huge entertainment center with loads of video game equipment. Controllers, VR headsets, and several consoles, some of which dated from before Marty was born. He had lots of sports and shooting games, and several with cute anime-style girls scantily clad on their covers. Thorne saw a case for the 1991 title "Duke Nukem." Thorne had played it as a teenager, though he probably shouldn't have. The game was about a gun-toting, alien-hunting misogynist that wouldn't fly with today's youth. It was a fun game, but Thorne hoped Marty didn't get his ideas about women from it.

At each corner of the black pleather bachelor couch were brand new throw pillows that hadn't been there when Thorne snooped around Monday night. One was still wrapped in plastic. Moving on, the kitchen island had a blender, two margarita glasses, and a mix ready to go. Thorne didn't see any tequila, and he didn't go looking for it.

Not that long ago, the mere knowledge that alcohol was on the premises would have been enough to trigger Thorne's cravings. He had crossed some psychological line, though. The danger of relapsing would always be there, but tonight Thorne felt no desire to drink.

The refrigerator-freezer combo was one of those side-by-side deals. Barry was muscled, but not hugely bulky. Thorne could imagine his body squeezed into the narrow freezer. He braced himself for horror as he pulled open the door. But the only items in the nearly empty freezer were a stack of cheap frozen pizzas and a couple of gallon tubs of Neapolitan ice cream. *Freak. Who eats Neapolitan ice cream?*

Relieved that his friend hadn't been murdered and stashed in a kitchen appliance, Thorne closed the door. *No Barry. Moving on.*

Inside the refrigerator, Thorne didn't find anything the fitness-conscious Barry would eat. No eggs, no protein shakes. Just old carryout boxes and dried-out pizza on a plate, uncovered, and . . . *Whipped cream and fresh strawberries!!!* Thorne slammed the fridge closed in disgust. Marty had ambitious plans for bringing a date home.

Not tonight, buddy. Thorne glowed with pride. Brie wasn't that kind of girl. Although he'd never imagined Brie was a short skirt and garish makeup kind of gal. Did he really know his daughter as well as he thought?

Thorne continued searching. Marty had a lot of expensive things. Money was often the motivation for murder. Seeing Marty's taste for the finer things in life lent credibility to Thorne's suspicion that the guy had offed his grandfather for the insurance money.

In the main bedroom, the plush tiger faux-fur bedspread on the king-sized mattress was covered in new-looking orange and black throw pillows.

What's with all the pillows?

Marty's laptop sat on a nightstand. Thorne took a peek. He rubbed his finger over the scroll pad. No password. The screen lit up and displayed a video, mid-watch.

Across the top were the words "How to fill your castle with princesses." Along the bottom, it said, "Demetrius Foxglove's Master Class in Seduction: Lesson Ten." A very handsome and very thin young black man in a suit was lying on a mountain of throw pillows. Hot women in bikinis were draped all around him. *What kind of a loser needs a class to get a girlfriend?*

He tapped play. Demetrius had a deep voice for a guy who was so skinny.

"Girls love soft things like throw pillows. Right, ladies?"

The girls around him smiled and giggled. They squeezed the pillows with ecstatic expressions on their beautiful faces.

The camera panned to a close-up of Demetrius. "Keep your princess waiting. Be a few minutes late when picking her up for a date. Long enough to make her a bit anxious, but not too long, or you will inspire her anger. My research has determined that twenty minutes is optimal."

Thorne tapped pause. Hot, steaming anger filled him as he realized Marty had kept Brie waiting for exactly twenty minutes. Apparently, the manipulation had worked on his naive young daughter. Thorne restrained the impulse to punch the laptop screen right in Foxglove's face. Instead, he took a picture of the URL. *It might be useful later.* He reassured himself there was nothing he could learn from such silly videos. *It's just for research.*

In the bathroom attached to the main bedroom, Thorne checked the medicine cabinet. No unusual drugs. Only prescription acne medicine. Thorne wrinkled his nose at the ambitious number of condom boxes. Then he smirked when he saw that none of them looked like they had been opened.

A noise startled Thorne. The sound of a muscle car's engine revving sounded very close. Had the date ended already? Thorne silently closed the cabinet and hurried down the hallway.

Outside the front door, he heard muffled voices. One male. One female. Thorne clenched his fists at his sides. That Foxglove guy's tutorial must have worked on innocent little Brie. Thorne glanced around for an exit. The doorknob was turning. It was too late.

He ducked through a door off the hallway. *A full bathroom. Great!* Thorne stepped behind the shower curtain surrounding a bathtub. Plan A: He'd have to climb out the window–

Thorne had made a rookie mistake. He hadn't secured his exit point. The window was the right size for a housecat to climb through. Thorne crouched down and sat in the bathtub.

Plan B. Hide and wait.

25

❋ Barry ❋

In the light cast by the house, Barry could see a dark form hunched behind the trash bins. Barry maintained an outward calm while his heart slammed against his ribs. *Don't frighten Scott and Scarlett.* He and the children were a good twenty yards from whatever was lurking there.

"Is that a bear, Grandpa?" Scott asked. He clutched his half-eaten energy bar in one hand, crinkling the foil wrapper.

These kids insisted on making Barry their grandfather. He didn't bother correcting the boy. *Now is not the time.*

"We need more light," Barry said. "So we can see what it is. I don't have a flashlight, and that darned ninja stole my cell phone."

"The ninja is good," Scarlett said. "She doesn't steal."

She stuck her energy bar into her mouth and held it between her teeth as she pulled her phone from the pocket of her running jacket.

Scarlett flicked on her flashlight app and shone it toward the dark form. With her other hand, she took the energy bar out of her mouth and chewed on a mouthful. Swallowing, she said, "I wish the ninja were here now, to save us."

Save us from what? Barry squinted into the darkness. The figure didn't seem large enough for the bear Scott suggested.

"Maybe it's a really big alley cat."

"We don't have alleys out here in the woods," Scarlett said. "Coyote?"

Scarlett's light reflected off the creature's glowing eyes. The sudden bright light startled the animal nosing around the trash bins. The figure rose behind the bins to a frightening height, placing its front paws on top of one.

Weirdly human-looking fingers gripped the edge of the bin's lid. It growled.

"That's no coyote," Barry said. "Get behind me." He stepped in front of the children.

Scarlett's cell phone light wavered as her little hand shook.

"It *is* a bear!" Scott said.

Now that it was standing, the creature looked much larger. Suddenly, the animal broke in two. Then three. A stack of small bears? The creatures dropped to all fours and emerged from behind the bins. They ambled slowly toward Barry and the kids.

"That's not one animal," Barry said. "There are several." Now that they were separated, they appeared too small to be bears. His brain raced to place the animals in the correct category. Were they carnivores? "What are they?"

One walked at the head of the others, like it was leading them. The ten-year-old girl aimed the light directly at one of the animals' faces. A bandit's mask circled its eyes.

She laughed. "Those are just raccoons. They won't hurt us."

"Are you sure?" Scott asked.

Scarlett shone her light on another masked face. Then another. Even more of them rose out of the darkness. The animals chittered, as though discussing their battle plan amongst themselves.

"They must be mad because Dad and Mom got animal-proof trash bins," Scarlett said. "I'll bet they're hungry."

Barry wasn't sure what a grouping of raccoons was called. *Herd? Flock?* Whatever the correct terminology, Barry thought they looked like a gang of criminals in their masks, their shiny eyes glittering like moist brown buttons. The ringleader was nearly as large as eight-year-old Scott.

"Chitter chitter." The biggest raccoon sniffed the air, then stepped closer to Barry and the kids.

"What do you want?" Barry stood his ground.

The gang ambled forward on all fours, chittering and growling. The leader stood up. The other raccoons followed suit. The whole group stood there for a moment, staring in Scott's direction.

"Why are they looking at me?" Scott whispered. The energy bar wrapper gripped in his hand made another crinkling sound.

Suddenly, the gang of raccoons rushed forward on their hind legs! Their hands reached out toward the three humans like a horde of zombies.

"Run!" Barry yelled. "To the back door!"

The kids sprinted around the side of the house with Barry tight on their heels. But the raccoons swarmed behind them, picking up speed.

Scott and Scarlett's half-eaten energy bar wrappers waved like flags in their hands.

They smell food, Barry realized. *Of course they're chasing us.*

"Kids," Barry barked through ragged breaths, "drop your bars."

"But energy bars aren't good for raccoons!" Scarlett exclaimed, sprinting ahead.

"Raccoons aren't good for small children!" Barry yelled. "Drop them!"

"But that's littering," Scott wailed, panting.

"We'll pick up the trash later!" Barry cried. *If we survive.*

The kids finally obeyed, and the half-eaten bars fluttered to the ground. The raccoons stopped and sniffed at the wrappers as Barry and the kids bolted for the back patio door of the large house.

Almost there. Barry glanced over his shoulder. The

raccoons quickly devoured the snacks, then pawed at the empty wrappers. They locked eyes with Barry, the porch light setting them aglow.

The raccoons doubled down and resumed their chase.

"Get inside," Barry bellowed. "I'll hold them off!"

"Be careful, Grandpa!" Scarlett exclaimed.

"Please don't get rabies," Scott cried. "I don't want a grandpa with rabies."

Scott and Scarlett sped up even faster and raced across the paving stones to the back door. Scarlett tapped on her phone, and the lock clicked open. The kids stumbled through the doorway.

They're safe. But before Barry could follow them, he felt a tug at his running slacks.

Barry turned to face his furry, black-masked doom.

The raccoons clutched at Barry's running slacks with their hands, pulling at him. He detached one set of paws, only to have another raccoon grab him.

"What do you want from me!" Barry cried as he tried to escape them. Then he remembered the third energy bar in his pocket. If he could just toss that bar to them, maybe he could–

But the raccoons were winning this battle. With one sudden united tug, they pulled his pants down around his ankles. Thankfully, his athletic boxer briefs stayed snugly where they belonged.

Barry tried to back away, but his legs were locked at the ankles by his pants. The ring of raccoons had him trapped. He pitched backward, over two of the animals. Barry landed in the dirt onto his firm backside. Several raccoons mobbed him, crawling on his chiseled bare legs. He could feel their claws delicately pawing at his thin windbreaker. On his stomach. His chest.

Are they going to eat me?

"Oh no, you don't!"

Barry wrestled one raccoon off, then another, pushing them aside. He scrambled out of his pants and onto his knees, shaking a raccoon off one of his arms. The other.

I have to be brave, for my grandkids. I mean, for those kids.

With one mighty effort, he stood, freeing himself from his living, clawing, squirming raccoon coat. The animals tore at his pants on the ground, retrieving the energy bar from the pocket and giving all their attention to their prize.

Before Barry could get away from the distracted raccoons, the ringleader of the furry gang darted in front of him.

"Grrrrowl."

The mega-coon stood between Barry and the patio door.

Barry took a step to the left. The raccoon blocked him. He stepped to the right. One of the smaller raccoons waved its hands at him, forcing him to stop.

"Okay, Bandit," Barry said to the big raccoon. "Bring it on." He motioned with his hands, waggling his fingers to encourage the raccoon to step closer.

Bandit lunged, leaping toward Barry's chest and wrapping its arms around his shoulders. The animal's mask circled angry eyes. Its lips curled back from a frightening set of fang-like canines. *Maybe this animal really does have rabies.*

There was no cure for rabies once it took hold. *At least Scott and Scarlett are okay.* Flashes of Barry's life played through his mind. Would his late wife, Mavis, welcome him with open arms from the other side? Would she wonder what happened to his pants?

26

❋ Brie ❋

"Welcome to my castle, Princess." Marty pushed open the front door and extended one arm.

Brie stepped across the threshold cautiously. The small house looked normal enough, at first glance. The true crime podcasts she followed warned the torture chambers were usually hidden.

I'll be fine, as long as I don't go into the basement. Although it didn't look like this older house had one.

It was a nice place for a single guy, though he had obviously cleaned up recently. Vacuum cleaner trails crisscrossed the sand-colored shag carpeting. The faint scent of artificial lemon cleaner and ammonia permeated the whole place. Had he cleaned so rigorously to cover up dealing with Barry's body?

A tremor of fear crawled up Brie's spine. *Why did I come here?* She shivered.

"Cold?" Marty asked.

"No, I, uh, just a little itchy." Brie scratched at one of her hands. Was itchiness a good reason to shiver? *I'm so obvious.*

"Well, if you are chilly, I have something that will warm us up." Marty led Brie to the kitchen. "Tequila!"

"No, thank you," Brie stammered. "I don't drink alcohol."

"Why not?"

Why did people always demand a reason? Worse, why did Brie always feel obligated to provide them with one?

"I'm allergic."

"Really?"

"Yeah." It was a lie, but it usually shut people up quickly. If she told the truth, there would be a never-ending chorus of "just try it" the rest of the evening. Brie had tried alcohol as a kid. Her father always had it lying around. The stuff tasted like poison. But what soured Brie on alcohol the most was watching her father self-destruct under the influence.

Marty looked disappointed for a moment before saying, "I can still make you a virgin margarita."

"That would be nice. Thanks."

Marty salted the rims of two margarita glasses and put ice, mix, and fresh lime juice into a shaker. He poured them both drinks. A recent true crime podcast talked about a man spiking drinks at a bar, and a woman running over a pedestrian as a result. That convoluted investigation and court case had been fascinating, but Brie's takeaway had been to guard her beverages carefully. Brie watched his hands closely to see if he slipped anything into her drink. He didn't. He passed Brie her glass. Now that she had it, she'd keep a close eye on it until it was empty.

"Aren't you going to add tequila to yours?" Brie asked.

"It's not fun to drink alone," Marty said. "Cheers!"

Huh. He was respecting Brie's choices. That was nice.

They clinked their glasses together and sipped on their salty limeades. Brie gagged.

If a mixed drink is this awful without the alcohol, I'm never going to start drinking.

At least she wouldn't have to guard her drink now. No way was she going to take another sip. She'd have to find a discreet way to dispose of it. But at least Marty was trying to make her feel comfortable.

He's not that bad. She could tell he wanted her to have a

good time. He was just really awful at it. *Don't get taken in, Brie.* Marty had barely mentioned Barry all evening. It was like he was avoiding the topic. Shouldn't he be more concerned about where his grandfather was? Brie reached into her purse and closed her hand over the pepper spray for a moment to reassure her own safety. No more wasting time. Brie needed information.

"So you said you heard from your grandfather?" she asked. "When was that?"

"Of course I have," Marty said. "I'm his only grandchild. He called me, um, just the other, er, day." His forehead wrinkled like he was deep in thought.

"Is he really on vacation?" Brie asked.

Marty shook his head. "Let it rest, would you? I didn't think you were the nagging type."

Nagging?!? Brie fought hard to calm her emotions. She wanted to slap Marty's pudgy face and storm out the door. *As if I would ever do anything that violent.* Instead, she took a calming breath. *Easy, Brie. You've come this far.*

"Barry is dedicated to his workouts," she said. "I don't call concern for his well-being nagging. Has he stopped working out because he's injured?" When Marty didn't answer, she added, "You said he wasn't at home when he called you."

"He didn't mention where he was calling from." Marty took a gulp of his salty limeade, then his face puckered. "He told me he went to the HMCA New Year's Eve party. I haven't seen him in person since almost a week before then. He might be mad at me."

"Oh?" A week before New Year's Eve was Christmas. Had they fought on that special day? *How awful!*

"He doesn't like my car," Marty said. "What's not to like about the Gourami? Grandpa thinks it's not the right kind of car to drive in Colorado. You know. On the snow. But, hey, do you want to see something cool?"

Not really. Marty's story left much to be desired. *Where's Barry?* Maybe she'd learn more as the evening went on. She put on a smile she hoped didn't look too fake. "Sure!"

"Follow me." Marty took Brie to the black couch in the living room. It looked almost new, except for the indentation in a cushion that must have been Marty's favorite spot to sit. She tucked her short red skirt under her thighs. Her bare legs broke out in goosebumps against the cold pleather. She reminded herself she wasn't wearing this outfit for comfort. *I'm undercover.* She leaned back against a throw pillow that was wrapped in plastic. It made a squeaky sound. *Why are there so many pillows?*

"Sorry about that!" Marty grabbed the pillow from behind Brie and ripped off the plastic. He shoved it behind her back. It still smelled like plastic. "Do you like anime?"

"I used to watch some." She hadn't kept up with it since she was a teenager.

"Why'd you stop?"

"I don't know. It's not like I don't like it. I just . . . got busy?" Plus, most of the shows Brie watched were geared toward young teens. She hadn't branched into adult anime for fear of graphic content that would make her uncomfortable. *I'm such a prude. Not that that's a bad thing.* "I used to love Naruto."

"Cool! So you like ninjas?"

"Yeah, I guess so." Brie loved the plot of Naruto, but she wasn't sure that made her a fan of ninjas in general.

"Oh man, then you're gonna love this!"

Marty hurried toward the television screen. It dominated most of the wall. Beside it was a set of shelves filled with DVDs. Marty unlocked a cabinet sitting on top of the shelves. He pulled out a rectangular box.

"Is that?" Brie blinked at it a couple of times. "A VHS thingy?"

"They're called video cassette tapes."

"Yeah! That's right. I had a couple when I was a kid." Her mom told her she had worn out a copy of The Little Mermaid when she was a toddler. Brie had a vague memory of opening and closing the big plastic box it came in.

"This isn't just a VHS cassette. It's a treasure." Marty gently placed the worn cardboard VHS box in Brie's hand.

Tommy Tigerclaw's The Art of the Ninja: Part One - The Ninja's Secret. The cover had a shirtless brown guy on it with rippling abs. He looked like he might be mixed, but maybe half Asian and half black, instead of white and black like Brie.

"Tommy Tigerclaw?" Brie asked.

"Have you ever heard of him?"

"No, sorry," Brie said.

"He's an incredible ninja. He made this series of four videos back in the eighties, but he only released fifty copies of them. None of them were copyable. And he never released them digitally. The pirated copies are terrible quality because they're just videos people filmed pointing cameras at TV screens. And even those versions are almost impossible to find. The original VHS tapes are some of the rarest videos on the planet."

"Is this one an original?" Brie asked.

"Yup," Marty said proudly.

"Oh, wow. How did you get this?"

"I actually have all four. I won them, gambling."

"Neat." Brie had no idea what to say. "So, um, do you want to watch one?"

"No way. That wears out the tapes." He said, putting the cassette back into the cabinet and locking it up again.

She couldn't see where he put the key. *Why on earth did he show me that?*

Marty was a gambler. That might explain why he was behind on his car payments. With all the nice stuff in his home, it was hard to believe Marty was pressed for money unless he lost it gambling. *Did Marty do away with Barry to cash in on that life insurance?*

True crime podcasts taught her that criminals could act like normal people. They didn't all show guilt with sweating and nervous behavior. Marty could be a total psychopath. And Barry could be stashed in a crawlspace, or buried outside in the frozen flowerbed.

"Do you like video games?" Marty asked.

"They're fun," Brie said. She was pretty good at a few.

"Want to play?"

"Sure," Brie said. But the drink was still in her hand, and she had to find a polite way to get rid of it. "I need to use the bathroom first."

"Okay. It's over there."

Brie kind of wanted to leave, but she might be able to get more information about Barry. And at worst, she could at least enjoy playing some video games.

She closed the bathroom door and dumped the drink in the toilet. After she flushed and washed her hands, she composed a message to her father. She attached the photos she had taken of the overdue car payment notices and hit send.

Suddenly, she heard a man speaking from behind the shower curtain. "Elementary, my dear Watson!" Was Robert Downey Jr. in Marty's bathtub?

The shower curtain twitched to one side. Brie spun around to see a man's face. Staring at her.

Brie opened her mouth to scream.

27

❋ Barry ❋

I can't show up to Mavis like this! Mauled by a trash panda? She'd laugh at me for the rest of eternity.

Barry tried to calm his mind and think rationally as the crazed raccoon dangled from his shoulders. The raccoon was not frothing at the mouth. Barry was becoming more and more convinced the animal didn't have rabies. It was just one big mean son-of-a–

The raccoon lunged and tried to bite Barry's face. Barry flinched backward. The raccoon only managed to bite air. Barry spun around in a circle with the raccoon draped in front of him like a furry cape, its claws gripping his windbreaker. Barry threw his arm around the raccoon's neck. He wanted to control the animal, not choke it. The beast clawed at his arm, tearing the fabric of Barry's windbreaker. Barry used his considerable strength to turn the raccoon around into a full-Nelson hold.

"Concede!" Barry yelled in his fuzzy ear. "I don't want to hurt you."

The raccoon snarled menacingly. The other raccoons had finished Barry's energy bar and were coming back in a swarm to help their leader.

This is the end.

Suddenly, a metallic clanging shattered the wrestling match.

The sound seemed to stun the animals into statue-like stillness for an instant. Barry unlocked his hold on the startled animal and quickly lowered it to the ground. "Bandit" shook a fist at him and snarled, ready to attack again. But before he could, the Brauny family ran out of the house beating pots with wooden spoons like warriors' drums. They raced out to Barry.

"You're family now, Dad." Garrett's face looked hardened as he stared down the raccoons. "It's our job to protect you!"

Bandit bared his sharp teeth. The rest of the gang of raccoons lined up behind him. One looked like it was cracking its knuckles.

Garrett and Buffy rushed at the animals full-speed, holding their cooking implements like swords and shields. Scott and Scarlett leaped in front of Barry.

"Don't worry Grandpa. We'll save you." Scott looked so brave.

"Sorry we left, but we had to get Mom and Dad. This is a job for our whole family." Scarlett flexed her biceps and gripped her frying pan tightly.

Garrett chased half the raccoons into the forest as Buffy dashed around him like a football player on the playing field driving off the rest. Most of the gang bolted for the trees. Finally, Bandit stood alone, undefeated.

"Come on," Barry told the children. "Now your parents need our help."

Barry, Scott, and Scarlett joined Garrett and Buffy in their position in front of Bandit. The family formed a huddle.

"We've got to work together now," Barry said. Everyone nodded. "We're going to take back this yard once and for all."

They formed a wall between Bandit and the house.

Barry cried, "Let's give it everything we've got!"

Barry and the Braunys let out war cries and sprinted at Bandit.

The raccoon threw his hands in the air and ran for his life into the woods. Bandit vanished into the darkness.

"Are you okay?" Buffy reached out and patted Barry's bald

head. "Do we need to call an ambulance?"

"My jacket is torn." Barry dusted himself off. "But I seem to be none the worse for the wear."

"That's good," Garrett said. "I'd hate to call the Department of Wildlife on our furry neighbors." He waved the spoon at the forest.

Scott and Scarlett wrapped their arms around Barry's waist. It was a much more pleasant situation than being mobbed by raccoons.

"You saved us, Grandpa!" they both cried.

"That must have been terrifying," Buffy said. "I'm sure they were just looking for food. They didn't mean to hurt anyone."

"We recently changed our trash bins to animal-proof ones," Garrett said. "We don't want the wildlife to get in trouble because we don't lock up our trash properly."

The family guided Barry indoors to the kitchen. Buffy insisted on examining Barry for bites or scratches, although he was certain the raccoons had not hurt him.

"The only damage was to my dignity," Barry said, patting his bare legs. He wasn't sure he wanted those pants back after the raccoons had rummaged through them.

"We can't thank you enough for standing between the kids and danger," Buffy said.

"It's a good thing you were here," Garrett said, solemnly. "Our family really needs you."

"Our hero!" Scott yelled.

"Are you ready to sign the contract now?" Buffy asked. She placed the parchment paper and black feather pen on the table beside Barry.

Garrett was right. The family needed a guy like Barry. And, he had to admit, he needed them too.

But Barry's grandson was in a pickle. He only hoped it wasn't too late to save Marty from the mess he'd made.

Barry gently pushed the feather pen away. "I need one more day to decide."

28

❋ Thorne ❋

"Hush!" Thorne said in a husky whisper. "I can explain!" If only he'd remembered to silence his phone, his Sherlock Holmes-themed text tone wouldn't have revealed his presence to Brie.

"Don't bother, Dad. There's no explanation that's going to make this right. I told you not to crash my date! How could you do this?"

Thorne cringed. She was speaking way too loudly.

"Give me a chance, will you? We don't want Marty to find out I'm here."

"Why not?" Brie asked. "I'm sure all Marty's dates bring their mommies and daddies along."

Thorne remembered the whipped cream and strawberries in the fridge. The margarita mix on the counter. The instructions in debauchery on Marty's laptop. His naive young daughter had walked right into an evil spider's web of seduction.

But protecting Brie from falling into Marty's clutches was only part of his mission. "This man could be dangerous!"

"You think I don't know that? You have to stop treating me like a baby," Brie said. "I'm twenty-five years old, Dad. And you weren't around for most of my childhood. Not really present, anyway. It's kind of late to try to be my father now."

He felt like an idiot, seated in the dry bathtub, staring up at his angry kid. Until Brie showed up, Thorne had been reclining in Marty's bathtub, pondering the life choices that had brought him to this point, for too many minutes. He struggled to unfold his stiff legs. Scrambling, almost falling down, he grabbed the shower curtain rod to catch his balance as he stood. How was he going to escape this situation? Without further damaging his already tenuous relationship with his daughter.

"I came here looking for clues to Barry's disappearance," Thorne said. "I didn't think you'd come back to Marty's place."

"Well, I did." Brie crossed her arms over the Turkey Tornado 5K T-shirt.

Thorne could hear Marty's heavy footsteps plodding across the shag carpeting. A fist tapped on the bathroom door.

"Hey, whatcha doin', Brie?" Marty asked. "Did you fall in?"

"Just having a little problem with my zipper," Brie said, glaring at her father.

"Let me know if I can give you a hand with that," Marty said. "Sticky zippers are my specialty."

Thorne could imagine the kid's leering grin. His hands tightened into fists. Unfortunately, one fist was still clamped around the shower curtain rod. The flimsy aluminum rod pulled away from the wall and fell to the linoleum floor with a clatter.

"Dad!" Brie looked furious.

Marty banged on the door. "Brie! What's going on?"

She turned the knob lock tab and jerked open the bathroom door.

"There's an intruder hiding in your bathroom!"

The jig is up. My own daughter's blowing my cover.

"Dude," Marty spoke over trembling lips. "How'd you get in here? Did he hurt you, Brie?"

"No. He's just a creep," Brie said. "My Da – Dan, is spying on us!"

Smooth thinking, Brie. At least she was protecting his identity.

"You can't trust this guy." Thorne jabbed a finger at Marty.

"I don't trust him!" Brie yelled. "That's why I brought this!"

Brie pulled a small pink canister out of her purse.

"Is that the pepper spray I gave you?" Thorne recognized the canister camouflaged as a large pink tube of lipstick. He was touched that she had kept it all this time.

Brie aimed the canister toward Thorne's feet and squeezed the trigger. When a stream of noxiousness flowed, she looked as surprised as Thorne.

"Are you kidding me?" Thorne yelled.

A puff of weaponized pepper filled the bathroom.

29

✳ Barry ✳

After Barry showered and replaced his pants-less outfit with a set of blue cashmere pajamas, he padded his way to his captors' kitchen in soft slippers.

"You look like you could use a cup of chamomile tea." Garrett placed a warm mug in front of Barry and sat across from him at the kitchen table.

Barry took a seat. "Thanks." He took a sip without a second thought. If they were going to poison him, they probably would have already.

Buffy was tucking the kids into bed, so Barry and Garrett were alone together. The last time this happened, Barry had made his escape.

Escape. I'm still technically in captivity. The contract sat nearby. Barry couldn't help glancing at it every few moments. It was so tempting. He loved being these people's prisoner.

"You were amazing out there. I wish I'd seen the whole battle," Garrett said.

"Fighting off errant bands of raccoons is just part of a grandpa's duties," Barry replied. At Garrett's expectant smile, he added, "Not that I'm ready to take on that role quite yet."

"Right," Garrett said, his face falling. "We want you to be the grandpa of this family by your own free will."

Barry laughed. "You can't be serious. I'm not allowed to leave, you confiscated my cell phone, and you're saying I have free will?"

"Well, think of it this way," Garrett said. His considerable muscles flexed as he lifted his hand to rub his chin stubble. "If we were blood-related, you wouldn't get a choice. No one-week trial period. You'd be stuck with us."

"That's completely different, and you know it."

Garrett chuckled. "Maybe it is. But wouldn't it be nice if you could choose your family members?"

That's not how it works. But it sure would make things easier. Barry felt responsible for Marty only because he was his biological grandchild. Barry would never go through all of this for someone he wasn't blood-related to. He was sure he'd see right through false friends who only wanted him around for his money. Though he had heard of that happening with friendships, too.

Where were people supposed to draw the line? *I'm two months behind on my rent. Have things already gone too far?* What if these people were living above their means like Marty? Would they expect Barry to take up the slack for them, too?

"Garrett, mind if I ask what you do for a living?"

"Me and my little brother, Reed, inherited money from our parents when they died in a freak accident. Reed couldn't get over it. He insisted they were murdered . . ." Garrett looked toward the ceiling. "But Reed's always been less rational than me. He used his inheritance to leave the country to look for the supposed killer and find himself spiritually. I used part of my money to start my own small business–" Garrett started just as Buffy walked into the kitchen.

"Don't let this guy fool you," Buffy piped in. "His 'small business' has taken off."

Garrett poured Buffy a fresh cup of tea. She kissed him on the cheek in thanks and sat next to Barry at the kitchen table.

"What is your business?" Barry asked.

"Have you ever heard of fitness vacations?" Buffy asked. "Wellness retreats, stuff like that?"

"Sure," Barry said.

Garrett tapped his smartphone and showed the screen to Barry. There was a photo of a group of muscled people wearing weighted vests climbing a mountain above timberline. Garrett, the leader of the group, was waving at the camera. The handsome, well-built guy was a great advertisement for his own business.

"I take people who want to get in shape on literal fitness journeys."

"That looks like fun," Barry said.

"It is. And after Dwayne Johnson came on one of my excursions–"

"The Rock?"

Garrett showed Barry a video of himself doing pull-ups off the edge of a sheer rock cliff in Madagascar with Dwayne (The Rock) Johnson.

"Now Garrett can't keep up with the demand for his services," Buffy said.

"I imagine not," Barry said.

"Buffy is a sports therapist specializing in motivational reflex stimulation," Garrett said proudly.

Barry had no idea what that meant, but the couple obviously didn't need Barry's meager quantity of money. The nice house in the woods and state-of-the-art home gym weren't splurges for these people. They could definitely afford this stuff.

Barry yawned uncontrollably. The day had been long and challenging. He had a lot to consider, and he needed to be fresh to wrestle with the hard decisions facing him.

"I'm tired. I'm turning in," Barry said.

"Of course. But Barry," Garrett said, "sleep on this idea: I'd love to have you with me during my next excursion. You've already helped me and my family so much. I hate to ask for more help, but there's so much I can learn from you."

"So much that we *all* can learn from you," Buffy added.

Barry felt touched as he walked down the hall to his private suite. The Braunys just wanted Barry for himself. Marty acted like Barry was an ATM. *But you don't choose your family.*

As disappointing as his grandson was, Marty was the last connection to his only son, snatched from life all too soon. Barry felt tears welling. He didn't try to stop them. He sank onto his bed and released the emotions that he'd been fighting during the past insane five days. Abandoning the last blood relative in Barry's life was not an option.

30

❄ Brie ❄

Awkward. Brie instantly regretted pressing the button on the pink canister. She hadn't meant to, but in the heat of the moment, it just sort of happened. The cloud expanded quickly, filling the small bathroom.

Thorne pulled his shirt up over his nose. He grabbed Brie's arm and pulled her toward the open door. Brie hadn't intended to actually hurt her father. She'd aimed at his feet, not his face, but the pressurized spray had plans of its own.

"Cover your face," Thorne told her, his voice muffled by his shirt.

Brie pulled the neck of her Turkey Tornado T-shirt over her nose. But the spray made her eyes sting. The pepper spray canister slipped from her fingers and rolled behind the toilet. She bent down to pick it up, but her eyes were blurry with tears. She groped for where she thought it had landed. But she couldn't find it with her fingers.

"Never mind that," Thorne said. "We need to get out of this tiny room,"

He pushed Brie toward escape, but Marty blocked the doorway.

"Who are you?" Marty asked Brie's father. "And what are you doing in my bathroom? With my date?"

With Thorne's shirt over half his face, and the stupid PI hat pulled low on his forehead, there was a chance Marty might never know the intruder was actually her pathetic, snoopy father.

Thorne didn't answer. He released his grip on Brie's arm and tried to squeeze past Marty in the narrow doorway. They both had large tummies that prevented an easy exit.

"Ugh!" Thorne grunted.

"Oof!" Marty groaned.

Maybe Brie could still salvage this pretend date and find Barry. She grabbed Marty's arm and yanked him into the bathroom with the noxious cloud. She darted out with her father, then slammed the door closed.

"My eyes!" Marty shrieked. He began coughing.

"Huh," Thorne said. "I didn't expect that pepper spray to still be that effective after all these years."

"Help!" Marty pounded on the door. "Let me out! I can't breathe!"

Brie grabbed hold of the doorknob and held on as Marty tried to open it.

"Go, Da – Dan!" she yelled through her T-shirt fabric. "Look for Barry! Hurry!"

"I already did," Thorne said. "He's not here."

Brie's hands strained to keep the bathroom closed.

"Then get out of here!" Brie yelled.

He didn't hesitate. But then, both of Brie's parents were good at abandoning people. When she heard the front door slam closed, Brie released her grip on the bathroom doorknob.

Marty burst out, his arms up and his hands clenched into fists.

"Where is he? Let me at him!"

"The intruder ran away." Brie tugged down the T-shirt from her face.

Marty blinked rapidly, tears streaming down his plump cheeks.

"Wait. That was *you* holding the door closed? Trapping me

inside with that toxic cloud? I could have died!" Marty coughed uncontrollably.

"It wasn't mace or teargas! It was just pepper spray. Are you okay?"

"I've been assaulted in my own home by an intruder." Marty wrapped his arms around himself. "I feel violated."

"No one was hurt," Brie said. "We should play that video game now."

"Are you kidding? I'm calling the police. I need an ambulance." He coughed and tapped 911 on his phone before Brie could stop him.

The call connected, and Marty provided the details to the operator.

He pulled the phone away from his ear and asked Brie, "Did you get a look at his face?"

Brie shook her head. Marty resumed speaking with dispatch.

If Thorne got arrested for breaking and entering, he could lose his PI license. His only means of support. Getting a real job might be good for him. Not another corporate career like he had when she was a kid. Something he didn't have to think about when he came home at the end of the day. *Retail perhaps? Running a curbside hotdog cart? Working at The Celery Maiden with the juice bar hippies?* Even so, Brie couldn't be the one to fink him out.

"Help is on the way," Marty said as he hung up. He glared at Brie. "This whole deal seems pretty strange."

"What do you mean?" Brie asked.

"I heard you call that guy Dan. You knew him. It sounded like he gave you that pepper spray. Was this all a setup?"

"For what?" Brie asked.

"To steal my Tommy Tigerclaw videos?"

"I never even heard of Tommy Tigerclaw before. Why would I–"

Marty raced to the living room and unlocked his video

cabinet. He checked each of the VHS cases. "They're all still here." Marty breathed an audible sigh of relief, then succumbed to a coughing fit.

"I wasn't casing your place, Marty. This is just an ordinary date. I–"

Before Brie could finish speaking, sirens silenced her words. A heavy fist beat on the front door. Marty rushed to open it, and a policeman tumbled through the doorway.

The policeman, followed by a uniformed woman who must be his partner. *Hopefully, Riggs doesn't recognize me. How could he?*

Riggs only saw her in that first stage of her makeover's destruction, with snow-smeared makeup and windblown hair. Since then, Brie had further ruined her new look by attempting to fix the damage, creating a garish mask of makeup and glam rock crazy hair. She was now in the final stages of fashion death. Her eyes felt red and puffy from the cloud of pepper spray. Makeup-colored tears streamed in rivulets down the Turkey Tornado shirt that definitely did not go with the red ruched skirt.

There's no way he can tell who I am.

"Hello, Ms. Bramble." Riggs looked at Brie, raising one eyebrow.

If a person could die of embarrassment, her misery would soon end. Unfortunately, her heart continued to beat as he turned to Marty.

"I'm Officer Saito. And this is Officer Murdock."

A plump middle-aged white woman with blond curls cut into a mom-do stood next to Riggs. She smiled, but she had a look in her eyes that reminded Brie of the Happy Marmot logo. *Deranged.*

"An intruder was in my bathroom." Marty pointed.

Riggs trotted to the closed door. "Is there anyone inside now?"

"No," Marty said. "He ran off. Some guy named Dan. *She* knows him." Marty pointed at Brie. "I was lured into letting her into my home. The two were casing my place for a robbery."

Riggs and his partner stood on either side of the bathroom door. He tapped lightly. No one answered, of course. No one was inside. As he reached for the doorknob, Murdock abruptly raised her right leg. She kicked, forcing it open, splintering the door frame.

"You're wrecking my house!" Marty howled.

"Oops!" Officer Murdock giggled. "I did it again! I swear it was an accident."

"You've got to stop doing that," Riggs said with a groan.

"Whoa," Murdock said. "Pepper spray. Smells like a whole canister's worth. It's making me hungry." She rubbed her tummy and giggled again.

They backed out and pulled the splintered door more or less closed.

"Did the intruder spray you?" Riggs asked.

"No. She did." Marty pointed at Brie. "My supposed date. I feel like such a fool."

"Marty, I'm a victim, too." *A victim of my own meddling father.* "I wasn't aiming for you."

"Are you denying you locked me in the bathroom, trying to kill me with that toxic spray?" Marty yelled.

"Sir, are you accusing this young lady of assaulting you?" Riggs asked.

"Don't be fooled by her innocent looks," Marty said. "She plays herself off as an ordinary chick, but Brie is a dangerous seductress."

"Oh, I'm not fooled." Murdock's blue eyes grew wide. "Girls can be dangerous." She pulled out her handcuffs.

"Do you want to press charges?" Riggs asked Marty.

"You mean like have her arrested?" Marty shook his head. "I just want a restraining order!"

"I'm not a threat, Marty," Brie said. She hoped her light brown complexion and the thick coating of melting makeup hid the blush burning across her cheeks like a raging wildfire.

"We can't give you one," Officer Murdock said. "You have to request a restraining order from a judge in court. Are you sure she didn't assault you?" Murdock held her open handcuffs, eager to spring.

"Like a girl could overpower me?" Marty flexed a doughy bicep. "I'm no weakling! Can you just get her out of here?"

"I'd be happy to leave, but you drove, Marty," Brie said. "We're nowhere close to my car. I left it at the HMCA."

"Take the bus!" Marty yelled, his voice rising to a high pitch. "Walk! I don't care how you go. Just go!"

"We can take you back to your car," Riggs said.

"That would be great," Brie replied. Her humiliation overrode any sense of relief.

"I'd rather take her to jail," Murdock grumbled. "Give me your bag." Officer Murdock held out a hand. Brie gave the older woman her purse. "Gotta check you for weapons."

The only weapon Brie owned was in Marty's bathroom, behind the toilet. *I'd better not mention that. It would make me look even more guilty.*

The ambulance and fire truck arrived. Marty got his vitals checked and insisted on receiving oxygen. He glared at Brie while he hyperventilated into the plastic mask.

As first dates went, Brie was certain hers had been epic. *Epically bad.* How would she tell Lovey and Sam what had happened?

Riggs and his partner escorted Brie out of the house. Officer Murdock opened the back door of the cruiser. Brie tugged at her short red skirt, then folded her legs into the tight back seat behind the sheet of plexiglass protecting the police from dangerous criminals like herself.

"What were you doing in there?" Riggs asked. "That guy is terrified of you."

Thorne ruined everything. Her plan to use the date with Marty as a cover for searching for clues to Barry's disappearance had failed. She needed professional help. From the police. *And maybe a therapist, too, after what Dad pulled.*

"Marty's the one we should all be scared of," Brie said. "He did something to his grandfather."

"Like what?" Riggs's partner, Murdock, asked.

"I don't know," Brie said. "But Barry Strong is missing. He lives at Hummingbird Gardens. He usually works out every day, but he hasn't been to the HMCA gym in nearly a week."

"Why didn't you file a missing person's report?" Murdock asked. "We can't find people if we don't know they're lost."

"I've been at the HMCA a lot lately," Riggs said. "Now I'm wondering if getting my Grandpa George an apartment there was a wise choice. Does this happen a lot at Hummingbird?"

"No. The Gardens are very safe. I would have filed a report, but everyone else insists Barry is on vacation," Brie said. "I don't believe them. Where is Barry Strong?"

"'Where is Barry Strong?' Is this like a conspiracy theory?" Murdock asked with a grin. "Sasquatch. Fake moon landing. Missing senior citizen."

"He really is missing," Brie said. "This is real. He's not on vacation."

"Why do you believe that?" Riggs asked.

"Barry would never miss a workout." Brie blurted out all the information she could think of. "Sure, he called Marty, but he didn't say where he was. And he owes my dad a celery juice. Dad says that Barry isn't the kind of guy to deny him juice."

"Huh," Murdock muttered. "Sounds to me like this guy is just taking a vacation."

"Well," Riggs said to Brie with a dazzling smile, "whatever you do, stay far away from Martin Strong. I don't want to have to arrest you for violating a restraining order if he does get one."

They think I'm crazy. Worse yet, after almost arresting her, Riggs would never ask her out. There would be no more dates in Brie's sad, lonely future. And Barry Strong was still missing.

31

✳ Thorne ✳

While the blonde female officer shoved Brie in the back of the police car, Thorne remained hidden in the bushes, waiting for them to drive away into the dark night. That Riggs character showed Brie no mercy. At least that potential relationship had already nipped itself in the bud. And Marty would never want to see Brie again. Finding Brie a boyfriend Thorne approved of would be his next personal project, now that she'd finally shown interest in dating.

Thank goodness Brie aimed the pepper spray at my feet. Thorne ran back to his car. His daughter must have some love left in her heart for him. She didn't even rat him out to Marty and the cops!

Thorne couldn't come to her rescue without admitting he'd been in Marty's house. Without permission. Basically committing a B&E. Breaking and Entering, but without the breaking part. *I think that's just trespassing.* That didn't sound too good either.

When Thorne reached his sedan, he eased his car door shut and drove as stealthily as possible. He had no idea which precinct Riggs worked, so Thorne had no choice but to tail him to his station. Chandos had no trouble keeping up with the law-abiding police car. Thorne didn't have to use Brie's GPS tracker to find her location this time.

Thorne made a plan: When he arrived at the station, he would come to Brie's rescue by bailing her out of jail. With what money, he wasn't sure. Maybe he could pawn some electronics, like his old VCR.

After tailing them for several blocks, Thorne realized Riggs wasn't headed for a police station. He took Brie to the HMCA. Thorne parked behind a dumpster and observed. Riggs let Brie out of the police car. Thorne saw Brie give Riggs what looked like a tearful "thank you," and then she got into her car.

They must not be arresting her.

Maybe Riggs wasn't as big a jerk as Thorne thought. But Brie still looked devastated. He followed her back to where she lived. The home he used to share with Brie and her mother, Eden.

When he saw the garage door close, Thorne sat and contemplated his next move. The idea of stepping into that house made him want to escape to drink away his troubles . . . No, not with a tumbler of whiskey. Those days were long past. He couldn't wreck his two years of sobriety. Thorne would drown his troubles in a tall glass of salty celery juice. But he would have to face Brie eventually. Dealing with this right now seemed like something a good father would do. *And this is the year I will finally be able to say I'm a good father.*

Thorne stepped up the flagstone walkway to the heavy front door. Eden loved her yard and always wanted Thorne's help working on it. Those flagstones had sat stacked on a wooden pallet in the garage for three years while Thorne kept putting off laying them out. He never did do the work himself. Instead, he put in crazy overtime hours at his corporate job at Warehouse Amalgamated Appliance Apparatuses, and paid a landscaper way too much.

Maybe I didn't overpay. The walkway still looked amazing, ten years later. *But I paid too much.* Thorne's drinking was often his outlet for the stress of all the overtime he worked. Maybe if

Thorne had done a little yardwork instead of worrying about how much money he made, Eden wouldn't have flown off to Tibet.

Thorne rang the camera doorbell and waited. He wondered how much of the interior of the house had changed.

Brie didn't open the door. Instead, a video of her face appeared on a small square on the door frame.

"What do you want?" Brie sounded hoarse. Was it from the pepper spray, or from crying?

"I just came to make sure you were all right," Thorne said, "and to thank you for covering for me."

"Unbelievable." The screen with Brie's face on it went black.

Thorne pulled out his cracked phone, which resembled the current state of his heart, and texted Brie an "I'm sorry" gif with a Photoshopped cat in a pleading position on its knees, clasping its little paws together. The door stayed firmly shut in his face. Thorne trudged back to Chandos and slid behind the steering wheel. He held his ruined phone and stared at it, waiting for a text from Brie. That was when he noticed he had already missed one from her.

He tapped on a stack of photos and zoomed in. Overdue notices for missed payments on Marty's Garfield car. He owed thousands. His Cheesy Brie had done some expert sleuthing of her own and struck gold.

What does this mean? Both Barry and Marty are broke?

Based on Barry's checkbook register, Marty was clearly dependent on Barry's money. This presented two possibilities. Either Marty murdered Barry so he could collect the insurance payout. Or Marty needed his grandfather alive in order to benefit from his continued generosity.

Neither one of these potential solutions explained why Barry was missing. Marty needed a body to collect the insurance or the living man to keep mooching off of him. *Nothing makes sense.*

Thorne felt hopeless. He was no closer to finding Barry, and he had officially failed at two of his three New Year's resolutions. He was still out of shape, and his relationship with his daughter was worse than ever.

Maybe if he could prove he was a good PI to Brie, she would forgive him for his other failings. It was more important than ever that he solve Barry's disappearance.

He drove home with his shattered dream of improving his relationship with his only child weighing heavily on his soul.

32

❋ Barry ❋

When Barry woke Thursday morning, he felt invigorated. After the wild battle last night, he was ready to announce his decision to the Brauny family. Barry was staying. But first, he had unfinished business to complete.

He walked into the kitchen. The scent of fresh bananas, whey powder, and fish filled his nostrils. Garrett, Buffy, Scarlett, and Scott sipped on protein drinks and munched dark green seaweed cakes topped with black sesame seeds.

The contract and pen sat on the kitchen table where they'd been last night. Barry examined them more closely. The parchment looked like ancient rice paper he'd seen in a museum. The pen was a long, shiny raven's feather. The rainbow of colors that gave the illusion of black glinted off the feather like an oil slick in the bright kitchen light.

Suddenly, a fifth face appeared at a seat at the table. Or rather, a mask.

The ninja.

Barry's heart would have skipped a beat if his cardio health weren't so excellent.

"Grandpa!" Scott hopped off his chair and raced to Barry.

"My hero!" Scarlett yelled.

Barry squatted to bring himself to hugging level with the

children. "How are my favorite eight and ten-year-olds this morning?"

They chattered about the raccoon encounter for a minute, until the ninja spoke in her altered-sounding voice.

"Barrington Strong. Your deadline is tomorrow. It is time you made your decision."

"I'm glad you're here, ninja lady," Barry said. "Because I am ready to sign that contract."

The children screamed with joy and raced around the kitchen, while Garrett and Buffy did a little jig and expressed their happiness at a lower volume.

"However," Barry said, "I need to attend to one important personal matter first. And to do that, I need to go to Colorado Springs for a day. Maybe longer."

The ninja pushed the contract across the smooth tabletop. "Sign, and you will be free to come and go as you please."

"I will sign. When I get back. After–"

"After what?" Garrett interrupted.

"What can be so much more important than the happiness of your grandchildren?" the ninja asked.

"I already have a grandson," Barry said. "He's in trouble, and he needs my help. If it's not already too late."

"I'm not in trouble," Scott said. He looked at his parents. "Am I?"

"Not you, dear boy," Barry said. "My *real* grandson."

"Real?" Scott's mouth fell open. Tears welled in his brown eyes. "I *am* your grandson, and you *are* my grandpa! I love you for real! But you don't love me!"

He ran from the kitchen.

"Scarlett, go help your brother," Buffy said. When the girl looked from Barry to the ninja, obviously hoping to hear more of the drama, Buffy added, "Now!"

When Scarlett was out of the room, Barry frowned. "You see what your game has cost?" he asked the ninja and the parents. "The children are confused. They don't understand the difference between your fantasy and reality."

"Family is not always a blood relationship," the ninja said. "It is a rare and wonderful privilege to be adopted into the open hearts of caring people."

"I want a relationship with this family," Barry told the ninja. "The Brauny family is exactly the sort of folks I'd want to be related to, if I could choose. But I had a family. Most are gone now. All I have left is Marty. My grandson by blood, not imagination."

"This isn't a game to us!" Buffy exclaimed. She rushed from the room.

"Dad," Garrett said harshly. "Or should I call you Mr. Strong? You really don't get it, do you?"

"You're in," the ninja said, tapping a gloved finger on the contract. "Or you're out. This family is not a revolving door. Perhaps this will help you decide." The ninja pulled a very un-ninja-like modern cell phone from a nearly invisible pocket on her black outfit. She tapped play and turned it to face Barry. "The money you have given Marty. The sacrifices you have made. This is where it's going."

Barry stared at the small screen. The date stamp indicated two days ago. Flashing lights and pinging, clanging noises poured out. It was unmistakably the interior of a casino Barry had visited years ago in the nearby mountain town of Cripple Creek. A man faced a slot machine, only the back of his balding head visible. He shoveled coins into it, then yanked down on a handle. The colorful wheels spun. A cherry. A cherry. Then a lemon.

The man turned, his scowling face now captured by the ninja's phone camera.

Marty. After he'd promised Barry none of the money he "borrowed" would be used for gambling. All the therapy. All of the gambling support groups. Marty hadn't bought in. He was still committed to his terrible vice.

"You cannot help your grandson," the ninja said. "He is past your ability to save him."

"But he's been threatened," Barry said. "Marty told me something crazy about a thug taking his legs."

If they haven't already. Barry's stomach churned, his imagination going into overdrive as he considered what that might involve. *Are legs like kidneys these days?*

"Marty does not need your money," the ninja said. "Money *you* can ill afford to throw away on *his* addiction. Self-control is a discipline that can only be learned through one's personal experience. Some seeds must be planted at the base of a vessel in order to grow."

"What's that mean?" Garrett asked.

Barry thought he understood. "She's saying he needs to hit rock bottom."

The ninja nodded.

Barry felt a welling despair. Although Barry had suspected his only living relative was taking advantage of his generous nature, the video confirmed his worst fears. Marty had been lying to him.

Barry reached for the feather pen. Marty had betrayed him. The Braunys were Barry's last hope for a loving family.

"Don't bother," Garrett said. He jerked the contract away from Barry, crumpling it into a tight ball. "You crushed the hearts of my wife and children. I'm not letting you hurt them ever again."

33

✳ Thorne ✳

Thorne pulled a pillow over his head. *I wish I could go back to sleep.* All night, he'd been wracked by coughing fits and watery eyes from his exposure to pepper spray.

At five o'clock Thursday morning, he gave up trying to sleep and attacked his messy house. The priorities were the front foyer and the home office, where he saw clients. That is, where he *rarely* saw clients. These were the only two parts of his house that might be viewed by strangers.

The clutter was overwhelming, but Thorne steeled himself to tackle the paper mountains. Labeling folders and alphabetizing took up most of his time. He still had paperwork from his old job that he wasn't ready to let go of. So much of his life had been dedicated to being the Head of Regional Legacy Product Sales at WAAA. Recycling all those files would be like throwing away a part of himself. He shoved most of the papers from his desk into folders, then crammed them into his gray metal filing cabinet.

There were also folders of Brie's accomplishments. The well-check visit summaries from when Eden was pregnant, and from Brie's childhood. Her dental and orthodontic records. Awful pictures she drew for him in elementary school. Grade reports filled with mostly B's and a few C's. All of the parts of his daughter's life he had ignored while they were happening. It was more of a matter of rearranging items than getting rid of stuff. And dealing with the raw emotions this trip down memory lane stirred up.

When his files were in order, he tackled the more obvious clutter. Guests had nowhere to hang their jackets and purses when they visited because the rack near the front door was full of his own vintage trench coat collection. *A coat for every occasion.* Thorne moved the black leather overcoat, the beige raincoat, a camel hair parka, the gray and sage green pinstriped jacket, the chinchilla fur tunic, and a gold and rust tweed cagoule, to his bedroom closet. He only left his favorite tan trench coat and his winter overcoat in brown wool with blue plaid lining, with a chocolate-colored fedora that more or less matched most of his outer garments, on the coatrack. If the winter coat hadn't been buried under all the others, he wouldn't have nearly gotten frostbite when he was surveilling Marty's house.

Thorne dusted the bookcase and polished every horizontal surface. He swept and mopped his hardwood floors. It was noon before Thorne felt his office and foyer were acceptable. He assessed the rest of his house. When he noticed the cobwebbed Christmas tree in the living room corner leftover from his first holiday in his townhouse, his energy level plummeted. *Good enough, for now.*

One last task involved cleaning and sanitizing his office coffee machine. Thorne scrubbed the bookcase top free of sticky old coffee and creamer spills. He found a tray to organize the sugar cubes and mugs. *Perfect.* As a reward for his morning of labor, Thorne brewed a hot cup of rich, dark coffee. He poured it into the hand-painted "cat" mug Brie gave him when she was only six years old. He threw in five sugar cubes, adding a generous splash of cream. *Heaven!*

Sipping the energizing drink, he contemplated Barry's disappearance. Maybe Thorne was going about this all wrong.

Thorne didn't trust Marty, but the way the guy handled the whole situation with Brie, he doubted Marty had the skills or stomach for murdering his own grandfather. The kid couldn't even get a date without a Demetrius Foxglove Master Class teaching him how. There might be Master Classes about getting away with murder, but would that help a soft dude like Marty?

But what if he had help from someone else? Thorne got on his laptop and performed a background check on the woman Brie had told him about. Poppy Prince's record was pristine. There were no mugshots for Thorne to compare the woman to the mystery lady he'd seen Barry dancing with. Although the wig and makeup probably made that a moot point anyway. Poppy's only oddity was her registered support animal.

A danger to herself and others without her cat, eh?

Thorne tried a different track. He performed a search for her cat, Professor Fluffingston. The orange Persian was on every social media platform Thorne had ever heard of, plus a few more. He took ribbons in shows and even had a website for his stud services.

Ewww.

Perusing the cat's online presence, Thorne finally found some pictures of the redhead Brie had described. *Although she seems too young, she could be Barry's dance partner. But where's the motivation for kidnapping him?*

Poppy clearly had a lucrative business centered around her manly cat, plus a full-time day job at Hummingbird Gardens. She probably didn't need ransom money. As for making Barry her love-slave, she seemed to only have eyes for Professor Fluffingston. Killing Barry for love or money was a big leap in assumptions. One of George Saito's zebras. *I'm not in Africa. I need to look for a horse.*

It was probably a dead end, and maybe Barry wasn't the dead part. Thorne's gut was telling him that Barry was still alive.

And that Thorne needed something more than a cup of coffee in his stomach. Thorne walked down the short hallway to the coatrack and reached into the pocket of his tan trench coat.

Down to my last piece of peanut brittle. When he pulled the delectable candy out, another object was stuck to it.

The paper-wrapped celery star! The vegetable was wilted and browned at the edges. Only Barry would leave a celery ninja star and a bodybuilding flyer in Thorne's car. He unfolded and smoothed out the New Year's Revolution flyer. Maybe it was being surrounded by cleanliness and order, or perhaps the caffeine had kicked in, but Thorne suddenly understood the message. *Barry plans to show up at this event. And when he does, I'll be there.*

Solving this case could repair things with Brie, too. He had messed up his daughter's date royally. If she saw her father in action, solving a case in real-time, she'd definitely be impressed. Thorne called Brie and left her a voicemail to meet him at the event. He snapped a picture of the flyer and wilted celery ninja star and texted it to Brie.

Would that be enough? Marty sent her away in a police car after threatening to serve her with a restraining order. Things were pretty bad. A great PI like Poirot or Chandos would pull all the threads together in a dramatic conclusion with all the players present, blowing everyone's mind.

A brilliant idea flashed into his brain. He looked at his photo of the address book page with Marty's contact info. Thorne had given up on his theory that the guy had offed his grandfather. Marty was pretty helpless and stressed out. Maybe that was because he was worried about Barry, too.

Thorne found a satellite view of the bodybuilding competition's location. The perfect plan formed. He composed a message to Marty using an anonymous texting app that may or may not be legal. But did the law really matter when the greater good was involved?

Meet me at the New Year's Revolution Family Bodybuilding Competition on Saturday at 10:00 a.m. But don't come inside! I'll have a surprise for you in the back alley behind the City

Auditorium. Love, Grandpa Barry.

Thorne would keep Brie a good hundred yards away from Marty until he had patched up things between Barry and his grandson. Once he'd reunited the two men, the whole misunderstanding between Marty and Brie would get cleared up in the process.

Everything was going to be all right.

34

❋ Barry ❋

All the worst decisions, hasty words, and wrong turns Barry had made in his life flitted through his mind. *Failure, after failure, after failure.* Garrett was right. Barry had been cruel to the family who only had the ninja kidnap him because they wanted his love.

Barry felt two inches tall as the long list of what-ifs accumulated during his seventy years pressed down on his shoulders like an overly ambitious deadlift gone wrong.

"Thank you for showing me that video," he told the ninja. Barry turned to Garrett. "And now, I'll get out of your lives. Forever." A tear stung his eye, leaking out. Barry caught it with his cheek muscle and tipped it back into his eye. It stung a little. "Take me home," he told the ninja. "I'll even wear that stupid hood."

"A ninja does not accept defeat from a worthy adversary without a fight," the ninja said. "I would not have brought you together if I did not believe this was a heart match."

"They are the perfect family for me," Barry said. "But now I've blown it. Worse than that time I ate an entire deep-dish pizza the night before a bodybuilding championship."

Garrett's eyes opened wide in shock. "You mean, I'm not the only one who did something that stupid?"

"That's not the half of it," Barry said. "I could tell you tales . . ."

"I want you to." Buffy stood in the kitchen doorway. "Barry, I hate the idea of not having you in our lives."

"You . . . you want me to stay?" Barry asked. "After what I said?"

Buffy locked eyes with Garrett. "Maybe this is just a rough patch. One of those things a family has to help each other get through."

Garrett loosened his grip on the wadded up parchment contract. "But Buffy, I don't want your feelings to be hurt. And the children . . ."

"It hurts us more to not have Barry in our lives," Buffy said firmly. She clenched a fist and her brachioradialis muscles popped out impressively, making her forearm resemble the trunk of some great tree. This strong woman was fighting to have Barry in her life. It was time Barry fought for himself.

Barry slapped his hands onto the table. "I promise to be the best darned grandfather these kids have ever had. Not imaginary. Adopted. Permanent. I want to be part of your forever family. Because . . ." Barry said with a sniffle. "You are my only family. I know that now."

"Then we must alter our agreement." The ninja picked up the crumpled contract and flicked her wrist. The paper was completely smooth once again. She scribbled an addition. "This states you must never again allow your blood grandson to take advantage of your generous nature."

"That's easy," Barry said. "His lies have broken me. I no longer want to be an enabler. I'll share my retirement funds with my new family."

"No," Garrett and Buffy said at the same time.

"Your money remains your own," Buffy said. "You're joining a family, not buying a lease on a spare bedroom."

"Although you're free to return to your apartment at Hummingbird Gardens if you choose to live there," the ninja said.

Barry thought about his Spartan apartment. The Gardens was a great place to live, but this home, with the state-of-the-art gym, the cozy bedroom and attached spa, and a kitchen designed with his special diet in mind, was a better fit.

"If you'll have me," Barry said, "I'd like to live here. But I want to keep my membership at the HMCA. For the group classes and socializing with my friends. You all could join, too."

"That might be nice," Buffy said. "The kids could cross-train by taking swimming lessons."

"We've thought of putting a pool in," Garrett said, "but in our Colorado climate, it's really impractical."

"Then it's all decided," the ninja said.

Barry picked up the raven feather pen. Denying his financial help to Marty wouldn't be easy. But it was a step he needed to take. His grandson hadn't cared if Barry lost his gym membership and his apartment. Barry needed to do what was best for Barry.

And my new family.

Gripping the feather pen like a lifeline, Barry hesitated. There was the matter of his PI friend Thorne. He was supposed to be helping the guy tone up his dad bod. He'd even left him a clue, hoping Thorne could rescue him. Of course, he didn't want to be rescued now. But he needed to let Thorne know he was okay.

"One last request. I have something I need to do at the New Year's Revolution Family Bodybuilding Competition tomorrow."

Garrett and Buffy looked uneasy. Did they suspect he was going to spring some fresh drama on them?

"My friend Thorne is a private investigator. I dropped him a clue that I'd be at the competition. I know he'll figure it out and be there tomorrow. He's a good PI." Barry said. Well, adequate PI might be more accurate, but Barry had some faith in the guy.

"What exactly is it that you want?" Buffy asked. "Being a part of this family doesn't mean you can't have your old friends anymore."

"I just need to set things straight with the guy," Barry explained. "And I don't want you all to think I'm bolting again when you see me talking to him. The way that guy dresses . . ." Barry thought of Thorne's Inspector Gadget getup. *He even wears that stuff to the HMCA to work out.* The family might think Barry was turning them in to the FBI for kidnapping. "I promise I won't leave. I want to stay here forever. You can trust me."

"Okay," Garrett said. "We have to start building our trust somehow."

"Just like we build triceps and lats," Buffy said. "It doesn't happen instantly."

Barry signed the contract with a flourish, the long, iridescent feather practically taking flight. "Done!"

Buffy and Garrett squeezed him in a muscly hug.

"Grandpa!"

Scarlett and Scott had apparently been listening from the hallway. They rushed in and joined the group hug. Barry felt delirious with happiness.

Only one thing nagged at him: the fate of his grandson.

35

❋ Brie ❋

Brie had only Thursday to recuperate from her disastrous first date. She made her own broccoli cheddar soup without beer in it. For a treat, she baked herself a boxed confetti cake that she frosted with a tub of whipped cream that she mixed with French vanilla instant pudding mix.

While she noshed, she binge-watched "Naughty Neighbors." The true crime docudrama chronicled cases where neighbors took things too far. There was the Lawn Leper, an extreme athlete who ran in circles all night long on patches of his neighbor's grass, only to make trouble with the HOA and get themselves hired as a landscaper. And the Evil Ice Cream Truck. The truck owner was a vile woman suffering from irritable bowel syndrome. She decided to inflict her experience on her neighbors by including large quantities of carrageenan gum in her homemade ice cream recipes, constipating the entire block. These stories renewed Brie's lack of faith in humanity.

It was back to the grind on Friday.

Since it was Poppy's day off, Brie couldn't spy on her to find out if she was responsible for Barry's disappearance. So Brie had a normal, boring, but busy January workday at the HMCA.

"How was your date?"

Brie looked up from her computer screen to see Lovey Dearheart. The senior woman propped her elbows on the reception counter above Brie's desk. Lovey looked fabulous as usual, despite her attempt at casual fashion. She wore a pink silk designer sweatsuit with pearls. Every wave of her silver hair was fixed into position. Brie was certain not a single hair would move, even while she taught her lively dance class.

"Give us the deets." Sam Slate moved next to Lovey. For someone so skilled at hair and makeup, Sam always looked neutral. Loose jeans and a blue polo shirt covered their shapeless figure. Short gray hair drooped limply atop their pale head. Even their expression was mild and bland.

"It, um, went okay," Brie said hesitantly. She told the two as much about her evening as she could while omitting the part about the pepper spray, the ride in the police car, and her date's request for a restraining order. "I had an interesting time. But I don't think we'll be going out again." *And by that I mean* ever.

"Oh, well," Lovey started, "that's okay, dear. There are plenty of marmots in the mountains. You just have to bring enough granola bars to catch them."

"I'm available to help out again whenever you need me," Sam said without any emotion.

"Thank you so much." Brie gave both of their hands quick squeezes before they walked away. If she never got another date, at least this one was memorable.

Buzz. Brie's phone had been vibrating all day with texts and missed calls from her father. She had ignored every attempt he made to communicate. But the noise was distracting her.

Brie switched it from vibrate to silent and focused on work. She was closing out accounts for members who hadn't used their memberships in five years, and sending termination emails to people who were six months past due on payments. Barrington Strong was only two months behind. One week had passed since he disappeared. He'd never been out of the weight room for so long.

If only her ill-fated date had yielded clues about Barry. It was all for nothing. She felt tears sting her eyes, and took a deep breath to calm herself.

"Excuse me, Miss Bramble," a deep voice brought her back to the present.

When she glanced up, Brie's breath caught in her throat. Forcing herself to breathe steadily, she managed to utter, "Yes, Officer Saito?"

Brie hoped he hadn't come to formally serve her with the restraining order Marty had threatened.

"Just Riggs," he said. "I'm not on duty." So he still wanted her to use his first name. Maybe he didn't hate her. "We match."

Riggs pointed to himself. Instead of his police uniform, he had on the same HMCA T-shirt Brie was wearing. It was the newest design. The Happy Marmot was playing pickleball. Its eyes bulged out of its head, pointing in slightly different directions, making the deranged animal look confused.

"Wow, what a coincidence," Brie said. "I have a dresser full of HMCA shirts. I almost wore the one with the Happy Marmot playing basketball today."

"Grandpa George didn't want his free shirt, so he gave it to me," Riggs explained. He smiled, and then looked more serious. "How are you today?"

Brie didn't know what to say. Nothing scrolling through her mind seemed appropriate. *Relieved you're talking to me like a normal person instead of a criminal you apprehended . . . Tired from crying all that night and half the day yesterday . . . Pretty good overall, except my knees hurt from bumping into the wall in the back of your police car . . .* Brie finally settled on, "Fine. And you?"

Riggs smiled. "I'm well. I'm here to see Grandpa George, but you probably figured that out."

"Yeah," Brie said. *It's not like he came to see me specifically or anything like that.* Even though the policeman could have gone directly to Hummingbird Gardens across the atrium. It was a little out of his way to come to her desk. Her heart filled with false hope. It was probably just part of his job to check on people he'd nearly arrested. A CYA thing to keep her from suing the Colorado Springs Police Department for mental damages.

"Did that missing senior ever show up?" Riggs asked.

So that's why he's here.

"No. You actually believe me now? I thought your partner was going to throw me in jail."

"I'm sorry about Murdock. She's new to the force. Her experiences as a soccer mom have made her a little intense. After we dropped you off, we went back to question Martin. The thing is, Martin wasn't able to tell us where his grandfather is. Mr. Strong may really be missing, and in this winter weather, we can't risk having a senior citizen lost outdoors somewhere."

Brie felt her heart stutter with panic, imagining poor Barry lying in a ditch, frozen.

"We have to find him," Brie said. "Before it's too late!"

"Don't worry, the CSPD is on the job," Riggs said. "Let me know if you see him. Well, take care." He left.

Brie watched him go. She annoyed herself by thinking about him the rest of the afternoon. *If only he weren't so handsome!*

Brie had done a great job ignoring her father's texts and calls all day, but curiosity got the best of her at the end of the workday. On her way home, she listened to her voicemail on speakerphone in her car.

"Brie, it's true I was spying on you at dinner. But I was only at Marty's house to find out what happened to Barry. I know you have a good head on your shoulders. I never dreamed you'd show up there. At his house. On a first date." *Was that condemnation in his voice?* "I'm going to find out what happened to Barry no matter what, and my gut is telling me he'll be at the New Year's Revolution Family Bodybuilding Competition tomorrow. I texted you the address. I want you to come with me. We can solve this case together. Meet me at The Omelette Parlor tomorrow morning so we can make a plan. Breakfast is on me."

Brie wanted to stay mad, but what her father said made sense. What better place to find Barry Strong than a bodybuilding event? She really wanted to know what happened to the missing HMCA client. And she could use a good breakfast. Her stomach still churned from her cake and broccoli soup combo. How could she turn down a free meal? It might make up for what she paid for Marty's dinner the other night.

Brie sent a quick text to Riggs, sharing her father's theory that Barry might show up at the City Auditorium tomorrow. Her dad wouldn't like it, but the police needed to know. She hoped she wasn't wasting the officer's time. *Considering the source of information . . .*

36

✳ Barry ✳

Barry sighed with happiness as he exited the Brauny family's SUV. He recognized a few faces among the crowd walking briskly into the blond brick City Auditorium. Guys he'd gone bicep-to-bicep with on many occasions. But most of the faces were younger. There were fewer and fewer men in his age category as Barry aged upward. Still, he was a lot younger than the building, which had been built in 1923.

Buffy, Scarlett, and Scott hurried through the open front doors. Before Barry could follow, Garrett touched his workout jacket sleeve.

"Hold on. I have something to say." Garrett reached into a side pocket of his gym bag. "The week is up." He handed Barry his cell phone. "Welcome to the family, Dad."

Barry grabbed the device and fired off a quick text to Thorne. He noticed he had missed several messages, but he'd have to check them later. He had important things to say in person.

"I've certainly put *you* through the wringer," Barry said. "And the kids." He paused, almost breathless at the thought. "My grandchildren." Then he tested a word he hadn't used with a living person in many years. "Son."

The grin on Garrett's face said it all. He slung a muscled

arm across Barry's shoulder and led him inside.

In moments, Barry was immersed in preparations for the competition. He was not too late to enter, and quickly filled out the forms at the front desk. The Brauny family had worked tirelessly for this day. But the children sought out Barry's last few words of encouragement and advice.

"Tilt your right heel forward slightly," Barry instructed Scott. The boy inched his small foot forward and frowned in concentration as he tried to get his vastus medialis muscle to pop out. His shiny blue posing trunks were more like bicycle shorts instead of the tiny thongs adult bodybuilders wore. But the judges would still be able to see Scott's muscles clearly through the tight fabric.

"Just a little bit more. There!" Barry clapped.

The kid's inner thigh bulged with the lumps he'd worked so hard to make. The spray tan and oil helped define the rest of Scott's muscles for display.

"What about me, Grandpa?" Scarlett's sparkly red unitard pulled up tightly as she flexed her impressive biceps.

"Elbows backward, straight spine, hips back," Barry told her. She did as instructed. "Perfect!"

"I think they've got this in the bag," Buffy said, tightening the strings holding on her bikini. Then she whispered to Barry, "Look at their competition. They're amateurs."

Of course, they're amateurs. They're children. But he had to admit that Scott and Scarlett were leagues ahead of the other youth. Barry had taught them dozens of poses that had earned Barry trophies in the past. And by bulking up some lesser-known muscles, the kids looked like titans compared to their competition.

"We're as ready as we can be," Garrett told Barry, adjusting his tiny green posing trunks. "Thanks to you." He paused for a beat, then added, "Dad."

Barry's heart nearly melted like massage oil on an overworked quadriceps muscle. It felt good.

An announcement boomed over the gathered crowd. "Fifteen minutes until showtime. Youth competitors, please line up backstage."

There were two age classes before Scott's seven to eight-year-olds. He would be standing around for thirty minutes or more. Barry wished he could wait backstage with the boy, but only one family member was allowed to attend to each child. The tension could be awful, especially for young competitors.

"It's time to go," Buffy told Scott and Scarlett.

"Good luck!" Barry said.

"That goes for you, too," Garrett told Barry.

The kids gave Barry oily hugs.

"I'll be cheering you on from the audience," Barry reassured them. "It will be a long time until my age class comes up."

After the family departed, Barry scanned the audience for Thorne. Had his PI buddy deciphered the clue he left in his car? Surely he'd seen the text Barry had just sent. *Where is the guy?*

Although competitions wired him up, he forced himself to take a seat in the audience. Barry studied his phone, and the barrage of notifications about missed texts and calls. There seemed to be dozens left over the past week.

There was a video attachment in a message from "The Ninja." No phone number displayed when he tapped the contact. And the video was one Barry had already seen: Marty gambling at Cripple Creek. Barry shook his head. He downloaded the file to keep as a reminder if he ever grew soft later.

Barry skipped many voicemails and texts from Marty, playing only the most recent one.

"I got your message to meet you in the alley. I don't know why you sent it anonymously, but whatever, Grandpa. I'll see you at ten o'clock."

Barry held his phone away from his face, giving it a quizzical look as though it could offer an answer. *Message? I didn't send that text to Marty.*

Another possibility thrust itself into his mind. Maybe a bookie or loan shark was pretending to be Barry so they could lure Marty into the alley. *To take the boy's legs.*

37

✳ Thorne ✳

Thorne entered the auditorium with Brie walking nervously by his side.

"I know that was Marty's car in the parking lot," Brie said. "Do you see him?" Thorne watched her head turn on a swivel. "I haven't been served a restraining order yet, but . . . what if–"

"Don't worry about Marty. Barry's here. He texted me," Thorne said. The text didn't offer any explanation for why Barry had been missing. "I'll set things right with Marty. Just leave everything to your dear old dad," he said with pride.

Brie made a snorting noise that must have been a sneeze.

"Gazoontite," Thorne said.

"You mean gesundheit?" Brie asked.

"That's what I said."

Everything was falling into place for Thorne's master plan. He was only missing one player for the final Agatha Christie-style parlor room reveal scene.

"Keep an eye out for Barry Strong," Thorne said.

"Yeah, okay," Brie said. But she still looked nervous.

Thorne scanned their surroundings for his friend. The padded theater seats were nearly full of spectators, while bodybuilders of every age milled around, waiting for their weight class to compete. The heat must have been cranked up.

Possibly because most of the attendees were scantily clad. Thorne regretted wearing his warm, brown trench coat with the blue plaid lining. He tugged at his collar, feeling sweat dampen his neck.

Thorne had never seen so much muscled, oiled, human flesh in one place. The itty-bitty bikinis and skimpy Speedos left nothing to the imagination. That was the point. The New Year's Revolution Family Bodybuilding Competition was about displaying the results of months, and often years, of work in gyms across Colorado.

What caught Thorne off guard were the youth and kids. Not their posing costumes. Those were more modest than their elders. Boys wore longer bicycle shorts, and girls wore unitards. Much more coverage. It was their dedication that startled Thorne.

When he was in grade school and high school, his main interest in life was video games, not working out. He patted a hand absent-mindedly against his paunch. He could have had better hobbies, but that ship had sailed decades ago. *And I guess I could have gotten a to-go box from the Omelette Parlor instead of eating that entire platter-sized stack of pancakes all at once.* But what choice did he have? He had already saturated the entire plate in maple syrup. Better to have the pancakes turn into mush inside his stomach instead of inside a box.

"Do you see Barry yet?" Thorne asked Brie. *I need Barry to get out into the alley where Marty is waiting. No one else in town drives a Garfield-colored car. Marty definitely took the bait.*

"Mr. Strong stands out in the HMCA gym," Brie said. "He's the most muscled guy there, of any age. But here?" Brie put her hands on her hips. "All I see are muscly people."

"Barry left me a flier for this bodybuilding competition," Thorne said. "Along with celery bitten into the shape of a ninja shuriken. You know. A martial arts throwing star."

"I get the flier. But martial arts?"

"It's not on the program." Thorne glanced at the schedule

of events he'd downloaded onto his phone. "Maybe Barry's been learning ninjitsu, and that's why he's been missing. He could be doing a demo?" He looked at Barry's text again. "He's definitely meeting me here."

Brie tugged on Thorne's arm. "Quiet, Dad. The competition is starting."

Multiple toddlers clustered on the stage. Thorne stared, fascinated by the incredibly fit children. Their tiny muscles didn't bulge like the older kids and definitely not like the adults. But they looked more toned than Thorne had ever been in his life.

The situation was getting dire. What if Marty left before Thorne pulled everyone together to make things right? Thorne was about to sneak backstage when Brie jerked on his trench coat sleeve.

"There goes Barry," Brie whispered.

Thorne's eyes followed Brie's gaze. Barry wasn't dressed for competition, or rather, undressed. A nice-looking tracksuit covered his substantial muscles. But Thorne would recognize that shiny bald head anywhere.

Barry!

"Come on!" Thorne said. "Let's find out if he really was on vacation."

Thorne and Brie headed for the senior bodybuilder. Light poured through an exit door as Barry stepped outside.

"Why is he leaving when the competition is just starting?" Brie asked.

"He's going to the alley," Thorne said. *I only texted Marty. I wanted to talk to Barry before he saw his grandson.* Thorne scrambled mentally to recalibrate his plan. If they saw each other first, it wouldn't be as dramatic of a reveal, but Thorne could still piece it all together.

Brie suddenly stood still.

"Hurry up, Brie," Thorne said. "We've got to catch him."

"I can't. Look who's out there."

Marty grasped his grandfather's arm and pulled him into the alley.

38

✳ Barry ✳

Barry let Marty drag him out of the exit door and into a narrow alley. Snow from the last storm had drifted against a tumble of empty cardboard boxes and black trash bags. Flecks of dirt and dried leaves soiled the slushy white.

"You're late." Marty crossed his arms over his tummy.

"Late for what?" Barry asked.

"I don't know. You're the one who told me to be out here at ten o'clock."

"I didn't send you that message," Barry said. "I'm here because *you* texted *me*."

"Maybe you just forgot." Marty pointed at his head. "I know you're getting older and stuff."

Barry frowned. He'd spent most of the past week questioning his own sanity. But at this moment, he was certain he was in his right mind. "Your insults are uncalled for. I don't have time for this nonsense. I'm going back inside."

Barry turned to leave.

"Wait! I can't go into that freakshow!" Marty said. "It's too loud to talk inside, with all those steroid junkies yammering at the same time."

Why did everyone assume all bodybuilders abused steroids?

Barry turned back to face Marty. He wanted to chastise his

grandson for his hateful opinions of the bodybuilding community, but there wasn't time for that sort of correction. Barry needed to get to the point and get back inside to see Scott's competition. Although he couldn't stop himself from making one observation.

"Marty, you would benefit from weightlifting." Barry jabbed a finger at Marty's protruding belly. "Instead of criticizing what you don't understand. I'd be happy to help you get started."

"We've had this conversation before, Grandpa," Marty said. "I'm not interested. Where's the money?" Marty rubbed his hands together expectantly. "They're going to repo my car."

"How can that be? I've been giving you money for months!" Barry exclaimed.

"I told you. I've got some things going on. I owe other people money. This really bad dude is going to take my legs if I don't pay him today."

"That's not my problem, Marty." Barry took a deep breath, then made the most difficult decision he'd made in years. "This sounds like a problem for the Colorado Springs Police Department. I'll help you speak with them and get this all sorted out. But I'm not giving money to thugs. I don't have any more to give. I know you've been gambling again."

"That's a lie!" Marty exclaimed.

"I have proof," Barry pulled out his phone and played the video the ninja shared with him.

Marty blanched, but tried to play it off. "So? Lots of people enjoy going to casinos."

"That's fine for some people on occasion. But you've already been in treatment for your problem. After all you've been through, you're back to blowing your money at Cripple Creek. Or should I say, my money?"

"You can't abandon me, Grandpa. I need you."

"I haven't been helping you. I've been making things worse. Enabling you." Barry squeezed his grandson's arm and looked him in the eyes. "You need to return to professional counseling. And rejoin Gamblers Anonymous. I still have the number–"

"No! I don't need to do that anymore!" Marty pulled his arm away from Barry. He looked frantic. "I don't have a problem! I chose to do this. I just got in over my head again. With a little seed money, I can turn this around."

Another announcement sounded. The five and six-year-olds were getting on stage. *Scott's age group is next.*

"I have to get back in there," Barry said. Scarlett and Scott would be shattered if he didn't watch their performances.

"For what?" Marty asked. "To show off your stupid muscles for the billionth time? Why do you even bother? No matter how buff you are under your clothes, you're just one more little old man to the outside world. Getting closer and closer to falling apart like everyone else your age. You won't live forever. I'm your only legacy that matters."

Barry took a deep breath and said, "You're right about one thing. I won't live forever. Which means I have to make all the rest of my moments matter. That's why I came here today. Not just for myself. I'm going to watch my grandchildren compete." It felt good to say. It felt right.

"But, but," Marty blubbered, "I'm your only grandson."

"Not anymore. I have more than you to think of, to care about now."

Tears welled up in Marty's eyes. "I need the money," he said, pleading. "Just this one last time. Then I'll never ask again."

"No, Marty. The cash cow has been milked dry."

Marty pulled a pink canister out of his pocket.

"What is that?" Barry asked. It looked like a really thick tube of pink lipstick.

"I didn't want to have to do this, Grandpa." Tears streamed down Marty's puffy cheeks. "But I need my car. And the loan shark is gonna take both of my legs! You've given me no choice! We're going to an ATM, and you're giving me that money."

Marty threw his arm around Barry's neck. After battling wild raccoons, Barry was certain he could free himself from his grandson's grip. But Bandit hadn't been in possession of a weapon.

The door to the auditorium flew open. A man burst into the alley.

"Stop!" A voice yelled. A brown trench coat swirled around the man's legs.

"Thorne!" Barry yelled.

"Don't you dare hurt my friend!" Thorne practically growled the words.

Marty held the canister to Barry's face. "Hold it right there, or I'll shoot! Er, spray!"

39

✳ Brie ✳

Brie peeked from the open door to the alleyway and watched in horror. *My pepper spray!* She assumed the police had confiscated it after it fell behind the toilet on the floor at Marty's house. She had pretty much forgotten about it. But now, here it was. Dangerously close to Barry's blue-gray eyes.

Marty's back was to Brie, and her father stood in front of him and Barry. Brie's father was trying to diffuse the situation. She was close enough to hear him babbling.

"Now Marty, calm down. You aren't the only one Barry owes. He promised me a celery juice, and–"

If this was her father's strategy, he was going to speed up Barry getting sprayed, and get a face full for himself. The situation didn't look good.

Brie needed to keep her distance from Marty. After the text she sent Riggs, the police might pop up from behind a corner. Brie should just duck back indoors and let the CSPD handle the rest. *If they show up.* She had given Riggs the information, but would he actually act on it?

Seeing Barry in danger, after days of worrying about him, spurred her into action. She had to do something.

There was a stack of pallets near the doorway, offering a narrow gap beside the yellowish-cream brick wall of the building that might hide her from Marty's sight. Just past the pallets, a little closer to Marty, was a nasty-looking dumpster. She crouched low and inched behind the pallets, sucking in her tummy. *That darn confetti cake. . .* Step, by step, by–

Her father stopped talking and stared at her for a moment. Of course, pallets weren't a full coverage hiding place. A person could see right through the gaps in the boards if they happened to look that way. Brie caught her dad's eye and made a hand motion, trying to get him to keep talking. Thorne shook himself and resumed his banter.

"Grandparents and grandchildren are a lot like snakes and lizards. They are *exactly* the same, except lizards are snakes with arms. So you see–"

Brie sprang behind the dumpster and flopped to the filthy ground. *Gross!* She peeked around the edge. A startled crow flapped its wings, disturbed from its feast in the open dumpster.

"What was that?" Marty turned to look behind him, still keeping the pepper spray aimed at Barry's face.

Brie held her breath. Not only to stay quiet and keep from moving, but because the trash stank.

"It's just a bald eagle," Thorne said. "Anyway, as I was saying–"

An eagle?! Brie's head nearly imploded. *How did the World's Greatest PI mistake a crow for an eagle?*

Of course, Marty looked more closely toward the dumpster, probably trying to catch a glimpse of America's favorite bird. Brie eased further back. Her foot squished into . . . something. *Ewww!*

The bird wasn't the only creature taking advantage of the free - if rotting - buffet of people food. A mouse crawled over the top edge and nimbly walked down the rusty metal side of the dumpster. It was heading right for Brie.

"Eeep!" Brie squeaked. She shooed at it with her hand. It ran out into the alley and straight for Marty.

"Mwaaaa!" Marty screamed in a high-pitched voice. He

hopped from one foot to the other in a mincing way as the mouse raced around his feet in circles.

With Marty focused on the rodent, Brie got bold. This could be her last chance to save Barry. Brie scrambled to her feet and eased around the side of the dumpster. Before she could make her move, a gloved hand covered her mouth, and another trapped Brie's arms behind her back, locking her in place. Brie strained to look at her captor. All she saw was a glimpse of black clothing. The figure wasn't any taller than Brie.

A woman's voice spoke quietly in her ear, sounding oddly artificial. "Wise ninja lesson number one: never risk a restraining order when one is in possession of a shuriken."

Still clamping one hand over Brie's face, the woman reached into a pocket. She flicked a vicious-looking metal ninja star right at Barry's face. Brie tried to scream through the gloved hand covering her mouth. She struggled to free herself, but it was too late.

The star soared straight for Barry.

40

✳ Thorne ✳

Ting! A shiny object flicked into the canister of pepper spray, knocking it out of Marty's hand.

Was that . . .?

A ninja star fell near Thorne's feet as the pink canister Marty had been holding skittered across the alley. The canister looked like the same brand of ancient pepper spray Thorne had given his daughter when she graduated from high school seven years ago. The spray that she'd fired at him in Marty's bathroom. But the shuriken wasn't made of celery this time. Where did it come from?

None of this had been in Thorne's master plan to reunite grandfather and grandson. He had no time to come up with a new strategy or puzzle out what had just happened. He picked up the ninja star and pocketed it in his trench coat. Then, with the immediate threat to Barry neutralized, he dashed forward and grabbed Marty's arm.

"Let go of Barry!" Thorne cried. "You two can still work this out! You'll get his insurance money in due time, but he has to die of natural causes or suicide. Otherwise, nobody gets the money!"

"What are you talking about?" The younger man wrestled, escaping Thorne's grasp, keeping his hold on his grandfather. "I don't want him dead!"

"Enough!" Barry wrenched Marty's arm from around his neck and spun it behind the younger man's back. "Concede."

"Grandpa! You're hurting me," Marty wailed.

"Concede!" Barry yelled.

But Barry must have loosened his grip because Marty twisted out of his grasp.

"No!" Marty cried. He wrapped his arms around his grandfather, locking Barry's arms to his torso. Thorne was about to grab Marty again when the door to the building flew open.

A little boy wearing shiny blue trunks called out, "Grandpa! We're next!" The boy ran into the alley. "Hey! That's my grandpa! Let go!"

"What's going on?" A little girl in a sparkly red unitard peeked through the door. "Oh no!" She sprinted next to the boy.

Both kids threw themselves at Marty. Thorne stood back. The children had bigger biceps than Thorne. They looked like they could hold their own. A dozen more muscly children flowed through the alley door.

"Get the doughboy!" one of the kids yelled.

The children all dogpiled on top of Marty. With their help, Barry dislodged himself from his grandson. He climbed out of the throng and stepped to Thorne's side.

"Blugh!" Marty cried as he fell to the ground. Thorne saw his arm shoot up out of the swarm of kids before slowly sinking under.

"Wait!" Thorne cried. He covered his eyes with one hand and peeked through the gaps in his fingers. "Don't kill him!"

The kids stopped mobbing Marty and sat on him, pinning him in place.

"We're not gonna kill him," a young girl wearing a red unitard said in a sweet voice.

"But we have to do something." The little boy in the blue shorts twisted Marty's arm. "He tried to hurt my grandpa!"

Marty let out a cry of pain. Thorne almost felt sorry for the guy.

Before Thorne could do anything, the blare of a siren wailed, getting closer. Thorne watched as a police cruiser screeched to a halt at the entrance to the alley. Two officers climbed out.

Great. That Riggs guy and his weird partner, Officer Murdock. Just what my day needed.

"What's going on here?" Riggs asked.

"That's Barry Strong!" Brie stepped out of the shadows and pointed. "Arrest Marty! He assaulted his grandfather."

"Where's Martin Strong?" Murdock asked.

"Over here," Marty gurgled out.

"He's under that pile of kids," Thorne said.

"We can let the police handle things from here," the girl in the red unitard said.

The kids stood, revealing the crumpled heap that was Marty. The guy was curled up like a shrimp. A giant, chubby shrimp. Maybe more of a prawn. Thorne's stomach grumbled.

"So, Martin Strong," Officer Murdock said with a giggle, "we meet again. Under different circumstances."

Marty barked. "Help me!"

"We'll help you," Officer Murdock said, with a gleam in her eye. "Right into the back seat of our vehicle."

"Grandpa!" Marty slowly unfurled from his protective position. "I was just kidding around with that pepper spray! I'm the victim here. Those kids are guilty of assault."

"Do you need another ambulance?" Riggs asked. "And what about you, Barry? Brie told me you've been away. Are you all right?"

"Where have you been?" Thorne asked Barry.

"Paradise." Barry had a dreamy expression on his face.

"So you really were on vacation?" Thorne asked, annoyed. "Why didn't you call me? I worried about you, man."

"Grandpa was okay. He was with me and Scarlett!" the boy in the blue shorts exclaimed. "I'm Scott!" The kid put out a spray-tanned hand to shake Thorne's.

"I didn't know you had other grandkids." Thorne winced as Scott crushed his hand.

"He doesn't!" Marty shrieked. "I'm his only grandson! Something weird is going on."

"The only thing weird here is you," Murdock said. "Come along with me."

"You can't let them arrest me, Grandpa," Marty whimpered.

"We only need to talk to you, sir," Riggs said. "To get your side of the story."

"Marty," Barry said. "This is for your own good. Talk to the police. You'll be safe from that punk who's threatening to take your legs. Now is your chance to do the right thing and turn in this criminal."

"What's this about?" Riggs asked, putting on a serious cop-face expression.

Marty slapped his hands to the sides of his face and groaned. "There's nothing to tell the police, Grandpa Barry. I've only been to Cripple Creek a few times. I do most of my gambling legally online."

He must be talking about that video game I saw him playing.

"I have an avatar I make bets with," Marty continued. "My avatar's in trouble if I don't pay up."

"Avatar?" Barry asked. "What's that? Like those blue people in that movie?"

"An avatar is a representation of a real person," Brie said. "It's an animated character you can walk around as in video games."

"Right!" Marty exclaimed. "One of the other players has a shark avatar. He's the loan shark. He's gonna bite off my avatar's legs and my character won't be able to walk around for the next twenty-four in-game hours."

Seriously? Thorne nearly laughed out loud. No wonder the kid couldn't get a date.

"Are you kidding me?" Barry exclaimed. "All this falderol

has been over a cartoon?"

Marty looked sheepish. "But the loan shark did loan me money in real life. The money we play with online is real. That's why I couldn't make my car payments. I had to give the cash to him."

"Well I guess your avatar is just going to have to grow his legs back." Barry snorted with disgust. "I thought your life was in danger."

"But I'm gonna lose my car," Marty whined. "The Gourami FSX is my life!"

Barry turned away and allowed the two children to lead him back toward the auditorium door. The rest of their pint-sized muscle-squad bounced along behind them.

"Wait, sir," Officer Murdock yelled. "Do you want to press charges against this perp?" She rattled her handcuffs, looking ready to spring.

That would have been Thorne's choice, but Barry seemed to think for a moment. He shook his head. "I believe my grandson has learned his lesson."

A tinny voice announced the next age level. "Seven and eight-year-olds. Line up!"

"Hurry, Grandpa!" Scott said. "Or I'll miss my competition."

Barry rushed inside the auditorium, surrounded by muscly children. The door slammed closed.

While Officer Murdock questioned Marty, Riggs grilled Thorne and Brie.

"I thought I warned you to stay away from Martin Strong," Riggs told Brie.

Thorne jumped in, hoping to save his daughter some grief with the zealous cop. "She was helping me, Officer. We found Barry Strong." Thorne pointed to the door Barry had just entered. "He's not missing anymore because of me and Brie."

Riggs didn't seem impressed. "A bodybuilder found at a bodybuilding competition," he muttered.

Brie said, "The ninja saved Barry."

"A ninja?" Riggs rolled his dark-brown eyes. "Where is he?"

"*She*. I don't know!" Brie spoke a mile a minute. "She disappeared before I could ask–"

She told a crazy story about a ninja tossing a throwing star at Marty's hand. Thorne figured Brie must have been inspired by the picture of the celery ninja star he sent her. She must have found this star in the alley. It was weirdly coincidental to find a real shuriken in the alley, after Barry had left Thorne a celery shuriken in his car. Were the two incidents related?

Horses. Not zebras. They were outside the City Auditorium where there could have been a recent martial arts competition. Brie jumped on an opportunity, then let some imaginary person take credit for knocking the pepper spray out of Marty's hand. She just wanted to avoid another run-in with the police.

Elementary, my dear Watson. Thorne knew exactly what had happened.

Because there was no one else in the alley but them.

41

❋ Brie ❋

Riggs acted like Brie was crazy as she described the mysterious, black-hooded woman.

"We'll be on the lookout for this, erm, ninja person," Riggs said with raised eyebrows. He didn't seem like he was taking her seriously.

But the ninja is real.

The serious expression on Riggs's face softened. "Thank you for the tip, Miss Bramble. I'm glad Barry Strong is okay. I'm confident my Grandpa George will be safe at Hummingbird Gardens with people like you watching over him."

A compliment from Riggs? Brie just stood with her mouth open as Riggs and Officer Murdock let everyone go. Including Marty. After Murdock pushed the trigger on the pepper spray and nothing happened, it was given a final burial in the dumpster Brie was intimately acquainted with.

By the time Brie and her dad made it back into the auditorium, the kids who had mobbed Marty were finishing their performances. Brie and Thorne slid into seats next to Barry in the audience.

"My daughter is next," Barry said. "Buffy Brauny. Isn't she lovely?"

There was no Brauny family listed on Barry's HMCA

emergency contact list. Weird that they just suddenly showed up. But she bit back her desire to interrogate him and tried to enjoy the competition.

Barry's mystery daughter made the winning score. Next, his never-before-mentioned son, Garrett Brauny, easily took his category.

The father of the little muscle kids walked off stage to wild applause. Buffy, now wrapped in a thin, silky bathrobe, hugged him. Brie had to admit, the couple looked pretty hot. Definitely no mom or dad bod vibes there.

How did two perfect-looking people like Buffy and Garrett find each other? *What was their first date like?*

She would discuss it with Lovey first, but Brie hoped her "date" with Marty could be erased from counting as her first one. That had been an abysmal failure. Brie wanted a clean slate.

If she ever had the chance again, what kind of guy would she consider going out with? Marty had nearly soured her on the entire dating game. Out in the alley, Officer Saito had looked as amazing as any bodybuilder in his police uniform. He was nice, too. She would definitely date a guy like Riggs.

But not Riggs. Brie was pretty sure any chance of him asking her out had ended. How could a cop date a girl who almost got arrested for assault, and who crept around in dirty alleys imagining ninjas no one else could see?

Not to mention, she stunk like garbage, and her clothes were wrecked.

The emcee announced, "Our final individual competition in the New Year's Revolution Family Bodybuilding Competition is the Senior Men Seventy and above."

Brie blushed at seeing the older gentlemen in their tiny posing trunks. But then, she'd been embarrassed by all the scantily-clad bodies parading around on the auditorium stage. The older men's age might show a little in their faces, with the inevitable crow's feet at their eyes, and laugh lines from long lives. But their bodies glistened with grease, showing every ropey muscle.

Not having any prior experience with watching this type of performance, Brie had no idea which senior man had given the most impressive poses. Barry seemed really into it, giving the audience saucy smiles while he made individual muscles bunch and relax. When the scores were announced a few minutes later, Barry had swept his category.

The two kids who called him "grandpa" rushed onto the stage, their faces beaming. Barry scooped them up in his impressive arms and hugged them.

The stage was cleared, and the crowd anxiously waited for the family totals to be tallied. Barry settled back into a seat between Brie and her father while the Braunys gathered their gym bags and robes.

"My score might have opened the grand prize trophy to my family," Barry said.

"You never mentioned any family except your grandson Marty," Thorne said.

"Well, Thorne," Barry said. "You know how it is."

Thorne grunted in agreement, as if Barry had given an actual explanation.

Brie tapped Barry on his shoulder. "Can you share any more details?"

Brie expected a story about being estranged and suddenly repairing a familial rift. Or perhaps they had lived far away. Even overseas. Colorado Springs was a military town. Lots of young people were stationed here and left during tours of service. When they got old enough to retire, they often returned to the beautiful city. Although Garrett and Buffy didn't look old enough to have spent twenty years in the armed services, their age category of 40-49 placed them in that range.

When Barry didn't respond, Brie prodded further. "Seriously, Barry. Who are these people?"

While Thorne looked out at the crowd, Barry leaned in and whispered to Brie, "They needed a grandparent. I was available.

So they adopted me."

Not the explanation I expected. In fact, Brie had even more questions now.

"Here comes your family," Thorne said.

The kids and their parents walked down the aisle to Barry. He stood, and they pulled him into their muscled arms.

"We need to wait backstage," the mother said. "In case we're up for an award."

"Wait, Barry," Brie said, standing up. She leaned closer to him and whispered, "Did you see that ninja in the alley?"

Barry didn't answer. He winked at Brie, then left with his family.

Adopted. Brie glanced at her father. What a mess her own family was. Mom in the Himalayas at some yoga ashram. Thorne living his joke of a life as a private investigator.

Barry's new family disappeared behind the curtain.

I wish I could be adopted by people this cool.

42

✳ Barry ✳

Barry turned the volume on his hearing aids down as the announcer's voice blared over the speaker system. "And now, introducing the top three finalist families, based on the cumulative average scores for each of their individual competitions. Judges have tallied up the points. Presenting our prize trophies is last year's champion family–"

Scott and Scarlett each held one of Barry's hands as the announcer rattled on. They all shook with nervous energy.

"Taking the bronze cup is . . ."

Barry held his breath.

"The Mescal Family!"

Scott groaned.

"It's okay," Scarlet reassured her brother. "There are two more cups to win."

After the audience quieted down, the bronze cup winners stepped to one side of the stage.

"The silver cup goes to . . ."

Barry felt Scarlett's fingers cross in his hand.

"The Quinlan Family!"

Buffy and Garrett took the children's other hands in theirs, and they all formed a circle.

"Remember, whatever happens today doesn't matter,"

Barry said. "We all had fun, and there's always next year."

The family all nodded, but they still looked nervous.

"And now, the moment you've all been waiting for! The gold cup goes to . . ."

"Hurry up! I can't take the suspense!" Scott whispered.

Barry's heart pounded like he'd been doing sprint intervals. "The Brauny-Strong Family!"

Barry and his new family erupted into cheers. They raced to center stage. Scott took the massive cup and lifted it proudly over his small head. He passed it to Scarlett and the rest of the family. A photographer took pictures of them in classic competition poses for the website. When it was Barry's turn to hold the gold cup, he lifted it high in the air. The Braunys all wrapped around him in a firm, sweaty, oily hug.

"This is the best day ever!" Scott yelled.

"We couldn't have done this without you." Garrett and Buffy squeezed Barry so tightly he could barely breathe. A first for Barry.

Barry had never finished a competition feeling so happy. "This *is* the best day ever!"

Barry looked out in the audience for the strange woman who threw the shuriken in the alley. From the moment she danced into his arms at the HMCA New Year's Eve party, the mysterious ninja had sent his life on a new trajectory. And now it was complete.

He didn't see her, but he smiled at the shadows. Because ninjas always lurk in the shadows.

43

✳ Thorne ✳

The crowd was still cheering when Thorne and Brie walked out of the City Auditorium into the chilly January air. He glanced at his daughter, then wrinkled his nose. No wonder she was having a hard time finding a decent man to date. She really smelled bad. *Thank goodness we drove in separate cars.* Chandos was finally smelling normal again, and Thorne intended to keep him that way.

Foul odors aside, Brie was the heroine today, throwing a shuriken and saving Barry's life. *Or saving him from a dead pepper spray canister.* Nobody knew it was empty. Being sprayed at close range could have killed the old guy. Brie deserved the credit, even if she chose to keep her involvement secret.

Plus, at least part of Thorne's plan had come to fruition. Brie had joined her dad in solving the mystery of the missing senior citizen. He was on his way to healing their relationship.

"We found Barry," Thorne said with pride. "The two of us! He's safe and sound."

"Barry wasn't actually missing," Brie said. "And I've only got more questions now that we found him. This case isn't closed."

"Of course it's closed!" Thorne said. "Everyone's got their

happily ever after."

"I guess so," Brie said. She looked sad. "Barry looks so happy with his new family. I wish . . ."

Her words trailed off, but Thorne guessed at what she meant. Brie wanted her family to be normal. Well, Eden wasn't coming back from Tibet anytime soon, that was certain. Brie was stuck with a single-parent situation, and that parent was Thorne.

"You've got me, Cheesy," Thorne winked.

Brie didn't look any happier. She hugged her puffy coat tightly around her body as she avoided stepping on a crack in the sidewalk.

"Maybe this will make you smile." Thorne pulled the shuriken out of his trench coat pocket. "Here." He tried to hand it to Brie.

Brie pulled her hands back. "Hey! I'm not touching that! It's sharp! And you're ruining the evidence with your fingerprints! I thought you were a PI. You should know better."

"I'm a fine private investigator. I know very well what I'm doing." *And I already know whose fingerprints are on this thingy.*

"I guess it doesn't really matter that you touched it," Brie said. "The ninja had gloves on."

There she goes with that ninja story again. My Brie is so creative.

Thorne watched his daughter's face as they neared their vehicles in the parking lot.

A shout startled Thorne.

"Wait!" a man yelled frantically.

Thorne spun around and saw Marty jogging across the parking lot.

"Is he chasing after us?" Brie asked.

"Maybe he wants to apologize," Thorne said.

"To us?" Brie asked.

"To you. For calling the police on his date," Thorne said. "He should apologize. To a lot of people."

Marty's voice called out, "Stop! My car!"

"I should have known." Thorne shook his head. "He only cares about that Garfield car."

Marty's belly bounced as he breathlessly raced for a tow truck positioned directly in front of the Gourami FSX. The driver shook his head and pulled a lever. The front of the car lifted. With a loud whining noise, the car eased onto the tow truck's flatbed as Marty dropped to his knees and wailed to the winter sky.

"My tiger! Noooo!"

"I guess there really is justice in this world," Brie said with a grin.

Everyone was finishing the day on a happily ever after note.

Thorne had his workout buddy back. His office was clean. And Brie was talking to him. *That old lady's cookies must be working.* He was well on his way to keeping his resolutions. The year was off to a great start.

But lingering questions coiled in Thorne's sensitive PI gut. Why had Barry been so evasive about where he had been? Thorne shook his head. *Quit overthinking it.*

Barry had simply had a New Year's relocation. Another mystery solved. Case closed.

The End

New Year's Resolution Cookies

Yields 2 dozen rum raisin-filled cookies

Note: The pastry dough and filling must be chilled before baking. Feel free to make them both a day or two in advance. Chopping the raisins into bits makes these cookies a hit, even with raisin haters.

Pastry Dough

In a food processor fitted with a cutting blade, combine:

> 2 cups all-purpose flour
>
> 1/4 teaspoon cream of tartar
>
> 8 ounces (1 package) cream cheese, cut into 1-inch slices
>
> 3/4 cup (1 1/2 sticks) unsalted butter, cut into 1-inch slices

Pulse into crumbs. Then blend for about a minute, or until mixture forms a smooth ball of dough.

Transfer dough into an airtight container. Refrigerate for at least an hour, preferably overnight.

Rum Raisin Filling

In a small saucepan combine:

> 6 tablespoons sugar
>
> 1 1/2 teaspoons cornstarch
>
> 1/8 teaspoon cinnamon
>
> 1/8 teaspoon nutmeg
>
> 1/8 teaspoon cardamom
>
> The zest of 1 mandarin orange

Stir well. Set aside.

In a food processor fitted with a cutting blade combine:
    1 cup raisins, packed
    1 peeled mandarin orange (those easy-to-peel
    ones are so tasty)

Pulse until fruit is chopped into small pieces. Add fruit
to saucepan along with:
    1/4 cup water
    1/4 teaspoon vanilla extract
    1/4 teaspoon rum extract (or more vanilla
    instead . . . but they won't be rum raisin
    anymore)

Bring to a boil over medium heat, then reduce
temperature to a simmer. Simmer for 3-5 minutes,
stirring frequently.

When sauce thickens, remove from heat and set aside to
cool. Store in an airtight container and tuck it
somewhere safe from eager tasters in your refrigerator.
Chill for at least 3 hours, and preferably overnight.

Assembly

Preheat oven to 350° F and line a large baking sheet
with parchment paper.

Place chilled dough on a lightly floured surface and
roll to 1/16-inch thickness. That's very very thin! Any
thicker and you might wind up with gummy cookies,
and nobody wants that. Cut an even number of cookies
using a 3-inch star-shaped cookie cutter. Half the stars
will be bottoms, and half will be the tops of the cookies.

For the bottom halves, set dough stars an inch apart on the parchment lined baking sheet. Scoop about 1 teaspoon of the raisin filling into the center of the stars on the baking sheet.

For the tops, brush one side of stars with water. Lay the moistened dough, wet side down over the prepared bottom halves, like little raisin sandwiches.

Gently press around the edges of the sandwiches to seal the dough around the filling. Or make them even fancier by pressing the edges with a fork.

Bake for 15 minutes, or until bottoms and edges turn light brown. Avoid underbaking, or the cookies will not be pleasantly crisp.

Cool on wire rack. Once completely cooled, write Happy New Year with purple icing, or other messages to personalize them. Top with fancy golden sprinkles.

Instructions for use:
Focus on your New Year's resolution while you eat a cookie to ensure your success. Remember, you need to eat one cookie per resolution to maximize the effect.

— The Cookie Lady, Hummingbird Gardens Senior Apartments

Acknowledgements

Thank you Beth Stevens, Jeff Schmoyer, and Deborah Brewer for reading the early manuscript. Each of you provided valuable comments that were critical to improving this strange story.

To the woman we sat next to at the Left Coast Crime conference in Denver, 2025, who told us she wished a ninja would kidnap her and place her in a family in need of a grandparent. And to all of the senior citizens who feel the same way.

We're indebted to the folks in Pikes Peak Writers, Mystery Writers of America, and Sisters in Crime for workshops, conferences, and social events. Writing groups provide opportunities for interaction with other writers and publishing professionals. They push us to leave our writing caves to capture the energy that only happens when you bounce ideas and questions off live audiences.

Visiting and caring for senior citizens, and spending time in a variety of retirement homes, inspired many of our characters. Being exposed to multiple generations enriches our lives. Our real grandparents, and the grandparent-like influences in our lives, shaped this story.

And as always, we thank our families. None of this matters without them.

About the Mother-Daughter Writing Team

Catherine Dilts is the author of twelve novels. Her short stories appear regularly in Alfred Hitchcock's Mystery Magazine. Most of her published works have a cozy mystery flavor. After a career in environmental compliance for a global corporation, Catherine now gets to write fiction full time. Her work experiences inspire her fictional environmental themes.

Catherine has completed two marathons and one ultramarathon. She enjoys spending time in the mountains and out in nature. She shares her life with her wonderful husband, two daughters, three granddaughters, three grandcats, and one granddog. You can find Catherine on her website at www.catherinedilts.com, on Facebook @catherinediltsauthor and on Instagram @diltscathy.

Merida Bass taught mathematics at the college level before pursuing her artistic dreams. When she isn't working on the novels she co-authors with her mother, Merida writes and illustrates children's books, and creates massive pencil and ink artwork measured in feet, not inches. Her YouTube channel features videos of her actively drawing, and her blog follows her training for and participation in extreme endurance events.

Merida, her husband, and three children, love international travel, camping and hiking through America's National Parks, and dressing in homemade costumes for cosplay at anime and science fiction conventions. Merida can be found at www.merida-creates.com, and on YouTube, Instagram, and Facebook with @meridacreates.